MAMA TRIED

Crime Fiction Inspired By
Outlaw Country Music – Vol. 1

MAMA TRIED

Crime Fiction Inspired By
Outlaw Country Music – Vol. 1

EDITED BY
JAMES R. TUCK

Down & Out Books
3959 Van Dyke Rd, Ste. 265
Lutz, FL 33558
www.DownAndOutBooks.com

Cover design by James Tuck

ISBN: 1-943402-31-0
ISBN-13: 978-1-943402-31-1

Dedicated to Willie, Waylon, and the boys.
You all lived lives to be envious of.
Outlaws ride or die to the end.

CONTENTS

CONTENTS

A Word from the Editor
James R. Tuck

I sit and write this on the day of Merle Haggard's death and, dammit, another good one gone.

This anthology you hold began as a random Facebook post by me saying, basically, "Someone should do a crime fiction anthology based on outlaw country songs called *Mama Tried* so I can write a story for it." You see, Intrepid Reader, I grew up on country music. The first twelve or so years of my life I really didn't know there was any other kind of music, so this shit is formative for me. I love it and I love crime fiction and the two marry together really well. Crime Fiction and Country Music have one thing in common: Outlaws. Sometimes it's hardened criminals: murders, thieves, and convicts. Sometimes it's just a poor fool driven to the edge by hard times, hard drinking, or a hard lover. The songs and the stories evoke the same noir feeling.

So I hit *post,* thought nothing else about it, and went back about my business. I come back to Facebook to find that the status has seen some action. Serious action. I had a list of completely badass writers saying that they would put a story in that anthology if it existed.

Serious. Badass. Writers.

The amount of interest generated made me decide that this project had to become a real thing so I cleared my schedule and began working on it. Bouchercon 2015 happened and Eric at Down & Out Books caught me and said he really wanted to work together soon. I had *Mama Tried* almost ready for launch and Down & Out was a perfect home for it. Eric said yes and boom, bang, pow; the work began in earnest.

Writers were contacted, stories arranged, and then it was a matter of waiting.

Then the stories began coming in.

And, holy hell, were they *awesome*.

I have been a part of many anthologies, both as a contributor and editor, and this one is something special. You have a group of great stories by some incredible authors that will put the same smile on your face as it did mine when I got them.

Enjoy this anthology and raise a glass to the singers and writers who made this shit happen.

Whiskey River
Charles R. Rutledge

All Wade Griffin wanted was a cup of coffee. A late night ride, on his way back to Wellman, Georgia, from Chattanooga, had left him tired and annoyed. He had tracked down a runaway teenager and let the parents know where the kid was, then hung around until the parents arrived to make sure the boy didn't rabbit. Mom and Dad had taken their sweet time about showing up. Griffin probably should have just gotten a hotel room and stayed the night, but he was tired of Tennessee and tired of people in general.

Thankfully the Waffle House next to a truck stop on the state border was mostly deserted. No giggling groups of teenagers. No drunks waxing philosophic through a haze of alcohol and regret. Just Willie on the jukebox and a lone truck driver a couple of tables over, paging through a bass fishing magazine.

Then the woman walked in.

Tall. Built. Wearing snug jeans and a top that managed to show both generous cleavage and a danger-ous amount of tanned midriff. A trucker's wet dream and the trucker was definitely smitten, his fishing maga-zine forgotten.

Griffin was careful not to make eye contact. If the woman was looking for company, he wasn't interested. He needn't have worried. She made a beeline for the trucker's table, and slid into the booth across from the guy without waiting to be asked.

Something was amiss. The woman was way too clean and way too attractive to be a truck stop whore. Also, her clothes were a little skimpy for the weather. What did she want with bass boy? Griffin noted that he was thinking like a private detective and nobody was paying him. Hell, maybe bass boy knew the woman. Not Griffin's problem in any case.

Griffin turned his attention back to his third cup of coffee and what was left of a slice of chocolate pie. He thought about calling his girlfriend, Charon, but she was likely asleep by now. He glanced at the windows. Outside a drizzling rain was falling, making the world beyond the glass indistinct, an impressionistic painting on black velvet.

Griffin heard the sound of an eighteen wheeler firing up. There had only been the one truck in the parking lot and no other vehicles had arrived since Griffin had been at the restaurant. He looked over at the other table and saw that the driver was still talking to the woman. She had her arms crossed on the table and was leaning forward so that her cleavage strained for freedom. Bass boy was enthralled.

And someone was stealing his truck. Griffin stood up and started toward the table.

"Sit back down, big guy," the woman said, raising a shiny silver snub nose .38 just above the level of the table.

Griffin sat down.

Bass boy's eyes goggled. He said, "Hey now."

"Shhh, honey," the woman said. "Let's just sit here

quietly for a few minutes. You can keep staring at my tits if it makes you happy."

Griffin had his .357 in a shoulder holster inside his jacket. He had little doubt that he could reach it now that he was out of the direct line of fire, but he didn't think shooting up the interior of the Waffle House was a good idea. Too many civilians.

The woman lowered the .38 below the table again. The restaurant staff was oblivious to the little drama in their midst. After about five minutes the woman slid out of the booth. She kept the gun down by one leg. She said, "Don't try to follow me out. I'm a pretty good shot."

The woman walked quickly to the door, her high heels clicking on the tile. Griffin stood up the second she was out the door and headed for the parking lot.

"Hey, wait!" bass boy called. "She said she'd shoot us if we followed."

Griffin drew the .357 as he reached the door. "She's welcome to try."

The woman had parked close and she was closing the door on a red Honda as Griffin stepped into the parking lot. The Honda slid out of the parking space and burned rubber toward the exit. Much for the same reason he hadn't drawn his gun inside the Waffle House, Griffin didn't try to shoot the car's tires. Too many variables. He also didn't consider a stolen truck that wasn't his worth killing someone over.

Instead he hurried to his pickup truck and climbed in. As he turned the ignition, bass boy came running toward him. Griffin rolled the window down.

"Are you going after her?" bass boy said.

"Yeah, thought I might."

"Shouldn't we call the cops?"

"Feel free. By the time they get here she'll be long gone."

"I'm coming too then."

"Might not be a good idea."

"I'm an ex-con, man. I lose this cargo and it's my ass. I'll never get another job."

Griffin nodded, "All right. Get in."

Bass boy went around to the passenger side and got in. After thirty seconds or so had passed, he said, "Aren't you going after her?"

Griffin said, "I'm giving her a little space. If she realizes we're following her, she might try to lead us away from her whoever took your truck."

"What if you lose her?"

"I won't lose her. I've done this before."

"You a cop?"

"Private."

"Like Thomas Magnum."

"Exactly like that, yeah."

"You sure you shouldn't go after her?"

Griffin said, "You got a name?"

"Clay Travis."

"Clay, if you don't shut up I'm going to throw you out of this truck."

Clay shut up. Griffin gave it a little more time, then pulled out. He had seen the direction the woman was going and he headed that way. She hadn't gotten on to the interstate, but instead had taken a two-lane road.

There wasn't much traffic and it didn't take long for Griffin to catch up. He had noted that she had a rear brake light out and it made it easy to spot the car. There were two more cars between Griffin and the woman and he let them stay there. Hopefully she hadn't noticed his truck in the parking lot. He didn't think it likely.

Clay said, "I know you told me to shut up, mister, but why are you doing this? This ain't your problem and she has a gun."

Truthfully Griffin hadn't thought much about it. He had a tendency to act and then think about it later. Part of it was that he had been a cop for a lot of years and he still tended to think that way. Bad guys run. You chase them. Part of it was just that he enjoyed the action. Griffin's business cards read private detective, but his real work was as a mercenary. Or had been until recently. He was trying to settle down some. So far it wasn't working.

And the last bit, he suspected, was that he just didn't like anyone pointing a gun at him. That made it personal. Griffin didn't respond well to threats. You point a gun at him and you were going too sure as hell regret it. What he finally said was, "What were you hauling?"

"Believe it or not," Clay said, "about eighty thousand dollars' worth of designer whiskey."

"That's a lot of whiskey."

"Not as much as you think. Stuff's like twenty years old. People will pay a mint for it on the black market from what I hear. Some of it can bring like a grand a bottle."

That explained the precision of the heist. This wasn't a nickel and dime truck theft. The woman and her compatriot or compatriots had known what they were stealing. The woman had been sent in as a distraction while the other thieves broke into the truck. If there had been a few more trucks in the parking lot, Griffin knew that he probably wouldn't have noticed the big rig starting up. The crooks had just been unlucky.

It also made it likely that the hijackers had someone on the inside. They had known the truck's route and stops the driver was likely to make, or maybe they had been following him.

Griffin saw the single brake light and then the Honda pulled off onto a side road. This was the hard part. There had been traffic to hide behind so far, but no one else took the side road. As Griffin made the turn he spotted an old sign that said read *Dead End.* He pulled the truck onto the side of the road and turned off the headlights.

Ahead he could see the lights of the Honda through the trees. They didn't go far before stopping. Griffin said, "This must be where they stashed your truck. Pretty smart. Get it off the road quickly."

"What do we do now?"

"You stay here. I'm going in on foot."

"Why can't I go with you?"

"The woman had a gun, as you noted. I'm sure her friends do too. Still want to go?"

Clay said, "No. I still think we should call the cops."

"I agree. Call and give them our location."

The smart thing to do would just be to sit there and wait for the local law. But there was still the matter of the babe with the gun. Griffin got out of the truck. The drizzling rain was still falling and the cloud cover made the night as dark as a witch's hate. That allowed Griffin to see a faint light through the trees. He headed toward that, moving as carefully as he could. The road, which apparently was more of a driveway, was cracked and full of potholes.

After he had gone several hundred yards, Griffin could see the light seeping out of the edges of a big door. He could just make out the outline of what looked to be an old barn. A great place to hide an eighteen wheeler for a short time. These crooks really *were* prepared.

This close, the light from inside made the ground visible enough that Griffin was able to move silently up to the door, or doors, as it turned out. Griffin put one eye to the crack of the double doors. The truck was inside all right. Someone had backed it in and detached the trailer from the cab. Griffin didn't see any sign of the original cab, it may have been tucked away around the barn, but there was another one parked, idling and ready to be hooked up. A fresh license plate, the new cab, and maybe a little more camouflage, and the rig would be ready to travel.

Griffin could see two men inside and the woman with the .38. She was leaning against a crate, smoking, and watching the two guys hurrying around the truck. No doubt they were in a hurry to be on their way before the cops had time to mobilize. What to do? He had the drop on them. If he went in with gun drawn he could tell them all to get on the floor and wait for the police.

Griffin had been so preoccupied looking inside that he didn't hear the sound of a car engine until the headlights silhouetted him against the doors. A second later a car door slammed and someone started shooting. Griffin dodged to one side, out of the headlight beams and into the dark. He crouched low and scrambled toward the woods beyond the barn. A few stray bullets whizzed by, but Griffin knew the shooter couldn't see him.

Then the barn doors swung open and the area was flooded with light. Griffin had reached the edge of the woods and put a big oak between himself and the shooter. Now he could see that the car was an old Camaro. The woman, the two guys from the barn, and the new arrival were milling about. Griffin could hear them talking, but he was too far away to understand what they were saying.

New guy went back to the Camaro and opened the passenger side door. He reached inside and dragged Clay Travis out into the spill of light. Clay fell to hands and knees and stayed there.

"Okay, big guy!" the woman called. "Eric tells me you came here with my trucker friend. Come out into the light or Eric's going to pop a couple of caps through your pal's head."

Griffin considered his options. From his position in the darkness he could see them but they couldn't see him. He could probably shoot Eric before he could kill Clay, but the woman was armed and the other two guys probably were as well. Eric had already demonstrated willingness to shoot to kill. Stepping into the light wasn't an option.

"I'm not kidding here," the woman said. It dawned upon Griffin that she was the leader of this crew. "I'm going to count to three and then, bang!"

Griffin shot Eric in the head. The .357 hollow point didn't leave much but Eric's lower jaw. Clay started crawling away as Griffin lined up on the woman. But she and the other two men started firing in the direction of

Griffin's muzzle flash and he had to duck for cover.

"Oh God. Oh Jesus," Clay said as he continued to crawl away. The woman fired two shots his way, but neither struck.

Griffin moved away from his original position and fired twice toward the woman and her friends to give Clay a chance to get clear. The two men crouched behind the Camaro but the woman ran into the barn. Griffin angled to his left, staying well away from the light. He wondered if Clay had managed to alert the cops before Eric had found him.

Griffin's flanking move put him where he could see the two guys behind the Camaro. In the light, they were sitting ducks. He yelled, "Drop the guns!"

They didn't, of course. Both turned toward the sound of Griffin's voice with weapons raised. He shot the first man before either could get off a shot, and the second as the man fired. The second man's shot went wide. That just left the woman. Griffin didn't see any sign of her.

Then the headlights of the idling cab came on. The cab lurched forward through the doors of the barn. It hit the side of the Camaro, knocking the car out of the way. The driver's side wheels rolled over one of the fallen gunmen. If the .357 hadn't killed him, he was sure as hell dead now.

Griffin popped open the cylinder of the big Smith & Wesson and dumped the brass. He slapped a speed loader in and flipped the cylinder closed. The cab was barreling his way. Decision time again. The window or the tires? The woman wasn't an immediate threat so shooting her wasn't necessary. He tried not to kill anyone he didn't have to.

Griffin put three hollow points into the driver's side front tire. The tire exploded and the truck spun sideways and slammed into a tree. It didn't catch fire like in the movies. Griffin started forward, gun pointed down, but ready. He heard the unmistakable sound of a shotgun round being chambered and threw himself on the ground as the shotgun boomed.

Jesus, this bitch was serious!

Thanking whatever gods look after fools and mercenaries that the woman's shotgun wasn't an automatic, Griffin sat up and fired three times into the side window of the cab. He was already popping another speed loader into the .357 as he rolled to his feet and angled out of the line of fire. Then he moved up to the truck door and flattened against the side of the cab. He listened for a moment, but heard nothing.

Griffin grabbed the door handle, pulled the door open, and fired twice into the cab. He needn't have bothered. The woman rolled out of the cab with a quarter of her pretty skull gone. Griffin took the shotgun anyway.

Now he finally heard the sounds of sirens. Whether Clay had gotten through or someone had heard all the gunfire and called the cops didn't really matter. Griffin walked back to the barn and put the .357 on the ground. He didn't want the cops to shoot him when they rolled in. He wouldn't have Sheriff Carl Price to clean up his mess this time. This was going to be a long night.

Clay Travis came creeping into the light. He said, "Jesus. Are they all dead?"

"Looks like it," Griffin said.

"You okay?"

"Dandy."

Clay said, "Jeez, but you killed a lot of people."

"Clay?" said Griffin.

"Yeah, man."

"Shut the fuck up."

L.A. Freeway
J.L. Abramo

I was sitting at the bar in the Power House on Highland Avenue in Hollywood staring at my empty beer bottle.

I had been thinking a lot about getting away from Los Angeles before my chances were less than slim—and before Susanna got tired of waiting.

I must have been thinking out loud because the first thing Jimmy Stills said when he pulled up a stool beside me was, "I found your ticket out."

Jimmy started in about a big score, a valuable coin collection, throwing in catch phrases like *easy pickings* and *falling off a log.*

I didn't know anything about Jimmy's experience with logs—but had seen him fall off a bar stool once or twice.

"What do you know about coins?" I asked.

"I ran into Billy Mullins."

"With your pickup truck I hope."

"Twenty rare gold coins, you could fit them in a Cracker Jack box, worth over a million. Mullins knows how to get at them and he has a buyer lined up. He needs help."

"What for? He and his psychopath brother need a hand finding an empty snack box?"

"Roy is out of the picture, back east on some other

gig. Billy just wants to talk with you. He'll be here tonight at ten."

"I'll think about it," I said.

I threw a twenty down for old man Clancy behind the bar and headed for the door.

Out on the avenue I stood awhile.

Watching the losers and the lost go by.

I needed to hear from Susanna, again, about how desperately she wanted to say goodbye to all this concrete.

Susanna was doing her devil's advocate thing.

"You said you would never work with Mullins again."

"I said I wouldn't be in the same room with Roy Mullins. The man is a head case. Billy is fairly harmless. He's also dumb as a box of rocks, so this may be nothing—but I see no harm in hearing what he has to say."

"And if it's *something*?"

"Then we can decide."

"Together."

"Together. And if it's *really* something, we can pack up all the dishes."

"I guess it won't hurt to hear what he has on his mind," Susanna said, "but I want to know every detail."

I walked into the Power House at ten.

I looked around the room, taking in all the players.

The cast of characters hadn't changed much.

I walked up to the bar.

Clancy was pouring shots for Tommy Conlon and Kevin Doyle.

"Have you seen Jimmy Stills?" I asked.

"He said they needed somewhere private, I said they could use the office. He's with Billy Mullins."

"I know."

"If you're smart, you'll go the other way."

Clancy thought I reminded him of a son he had lost to gambling and alcohol. He tried to look out for me.

"It's my night to be stupid. Pour me a Jameson. Make it a double."

I carried my drink back to the office where Billy surprised me with an impressive presentation.

"The nineteen-thirty-one Saint-Gaudens double eagle. A twenty-dollar face-value coin—weighing a little more than an ounce. The gold value is just over a grand. Market value, mint condition, seventy-five grand. There are twenty of them."

I quickly did the math. One and a half million.

"I have a buyer. Our end is seven hundred fifty thousand," Mullins added.

"Who's going to give us fifty cents on the dollar?"

"The owner. Philip Simon. He scores the insurance settlement and then gets to keep his precious coins. He will be out of town with plenty of witnesses when we hit his place."

"So, why do you need us?"

"Jimmy will stay outside—keep an eye out and the engine running."

"And me?"

"You get us past the security system. It needs to look like a legitimate break-in. Simon can't give us the disarm code, but he gave me everything else you need to know about the system set up. With your talents it will be a walk in the park," Mullins said, handing me the alarm system schematics.

It appeared both Billy and Jimmy had brushed up on their metaphors for the occasion.

I gave the specs a quick look over and had to agree— it would be like taking candy from a baby.

"What's the split?"

"A hundred fifty thousand for Jimmy—you and I split the rest equally. When Simon returns to Los Angeles, we'll all meet him for the exchange."

"How did Simon find you—in the yellow pages?"

"He's a lawyer. He helped me and Roy out of jam a year ago."

"No offense," I said, although I couldn't care less if I broke his heart. "If I see Roy anywhere near us I'm gone."

"My brother is in Jersey cooking up some action with Johnny Roselli. He won't be back for at least a month."

"I'll have to think about it."

"Think fast. Simon leaves town on Friday and we go in Saturday night."

My old man was an Indiana farmer and the son of an Indiana farmer and when he lost the family farm he moved us down to Texas where he would work on a farm because it was all he knew how to do. And dream.

He mostly dreamed of California. He talked about the sunshine and the palm trees, the convertible sports cars and mansions, and the freeways paved with gold.

He idolized James Dean, the Indiana farm boy who went to Hollywood and became immortal.

I remember my father coming into my room one night when I was eight years old. He woke me. We sat and looked at the pictures in a book. Los Angeles, the City of Angels. Dad promised that someday he would take my mother and me to the Pacific Ocean. He died a week later.

After his death I was in and out of trouble, in and out of schools, in and out of reformatories, breaking in and stealing out of people's homes, and finally in and out of Huntsville State Penitentiary where I learned a trade that would help me get past alarm systems in other people's homes.

When my mother passed away, and I was going through her things, I came across the book my father had brought into my room years before.

I decided to live out his dream. The only thing in my life that would be difficult for me to leave behind was Susanna. Luckily she believed in me and signed on for the move to California.

But luck ran out and it didn't take long to discover the Los Angeles of my father's dreams was only real in picture books.

I walked into the apartment just before midnight.

It was as unappealing as when I left.

I could hear Skinny Dennis playing his electric bass guitar next door.

Susanna was waiting up for me.

I ran it down for her.

"Three hundred thousand dollars," she said.

"Yes."

"In three days?"

"Yes."

"Do you trust Billy Mullins?"

"About as far as I can throw him—but if push comes to shove I can throw him pretty far."

"So?"

"So, Columbus took a chance."

If you have a mind to, you can always come up with rationalizations for criminal behavior. A popular excuse is the allusion of a *victimless crime.* I was about to help someone rob himself to rip-off an insurance company. No foul.

I bought it.

The heart of the matter? I came to Los Angeles with nothing and I was determined not to leave with nothing.

At eleven on Saturday night I was standing out on Vine Street when the late model Infiniti pulled up to the curb with Jimmy behind the wheel and Billy Mullins in back.

"Nice ride," I said, settling in beside Stills.

"Borrowed it off a dealership lot in Van Nuys," Jimmy said.

"How long before someone discovers it's missing?"

"Long enough," Mullins said. "Let's move."

The house was in Manhattan Beach—a hop and a skip from the sand and surf.

It was a modest sized home surrounded by all of the trees and shrubbery necessary for privacy.

It took me less than ten minutes to disable the alarms and another few seconds to get us in through the back door.

The gold pieces were exactly where their owner had said they would be. They sat out in the open on a large desk in the study in a twelve-inch by ten-inch glass-topped mahogany case. Four rows of five coins. Ten displayed Liberty and ten displayed the double eagle on the reverse side.

Billy Mullins placed the box into a plastic grocery bag.

We left the house and walked casually to where Jimmy Stills waited in the car. I was a few steps ahead of Billy and I hopped into the back seat.

Jimmy stopped the Infiniti to let me out on Vine. As I turned to move off, Billy called me back to the passenger side window.

"I let you know the where and when for the exchange. Don't forget to bring this," he said, handing me the grocery bag without ceremony.

And Jimmy quickly pulled away.

The bag and its contents weighed less than five pounds.

I carried it into the apartment.

Susanna was asleep on the sofa. I gently laid the bag down on an end table and went to the kitchen to pour a whiskey.

When I came back into the front room, Susanna was sitting up with the display case resting on her lap.

"What do you see?" I asked.

Susanna looked up into my eyes.

"A piece of land back home, room to grow food, raise horses, breathe. A chance to get off of this L.A. Freeway."

"I'll drink to that."

Susanna looked back down at the gold coins.

"They are really beautiful," she said.

I heard from Jimmy Stills on Monday. The exchange would take place at Philip Simon's office in Glendale. It was a converted warehouse. A number of retail shops and professional businesses.

Doctors. Architects. Lawyers.

The building would be shut down and deserted by nine.

Jimmy would pick me up at eleven.

At ten-thirty, Susanna took a last look at the gold coins.

"I'd love to keep one."

"I could probably buy you one for seventy-five thousand dollars."

She placed the case into the plastic grocery bag and handed it to me.

"Watch your back," she said.

"I thought *you* had my back."

She gave me a hard punch to the chest.

"What was that for?"

"A reminder to dress appropriately," she said, and she left the apartment.

* * *

Just before eleven I walked out onto Vine to wait for Stills. He pulled up in his pickup a few minutes later and I climbed in beside him.

As we approached the freeway entrance, Susanna's words echoed in my head.

Get off of this L.A. Freeway.

L.A. Freeway is not found on any map. It is not a single route into or out of Los Angeles. L.A. Freeway is a term sometimes used to describe the maze of intercomnected roadways stretching out from the city like the legs of a spider.

Hollywood, Ventura, Santa Ana, Century, Santa Monica, Long Beach.

It's a web—ensnaring the California dreamer like a spider traps a fly.

We exited the leg called the Golden State Freeway at Hyperion Boulevard and crossed the L.A. River into Glendale. As we approached the building I had one hope.

Get off the L.A. Freeway without being killed or caught.

When we walked into the office they were waiting.

Philip Simon. Billy Mullins standing beside him.

An open attaché case on the desk filled with cash.

I took a few stepped toward the desk.

Suddenly Billy had a gun to Simon's temple. He pulled the trigger. The man was dead before he hit the deck.

Then two shots from somewhere behind me and Jimmy Stills went down.

I turned—the plastic grocery bag with its treasure still in my hand.

I recognized Roy Mullins a moment before he shot me.

My last thought before my head crashed to the floor was *Susanna, don't you cry for me.*

When I opened my eyes I was in my own bed. Susanna was sitting in a chair watching me.

"What time is it?"

"Morning. You've been in and out all night. How is your head?"

"Feels like it was bounced across a hardwood floor," I said, as I managed to sit up.

"Jimmy is dead. You took three shots to the chest. The vest saved your life."

"The best present you ever gave me. It was Roy Mullins."

"I know. We heard the gunshots and saw Billy and Roy running out just before we ran in."

"We?"

"I brought Clancy along for support. You were out cold. He's a strong old timer. I could never have carried you out of there alone."

As if on cue Clancy walked into the room holding a brown paper bag.

"Coffee and donuts," he said.

"Nice."

"The police received an anonymous tip and caught up with the Mullins boys. Billy and Roy tried to shoot it out. They were both killed."

"Thanks for your help."

"No worries. I need to run."

"I thought you didn't open the bar until ten."

"I have to get to Sunday Mass first," Clancy said, and he was gone.

"Well," Susanna said.

"Well?"

"I guess we're here for a while."

"Do me a favor."

"Sure."

"You know the tin box I keep on the mantle?"

"The one you think you're hiding your cigarettes in?"

"That's the one. Please bring it in here."

"Pretty heavy for a pack of Camel straights," she said when she handled me the tin.

I pulled off the lid and spilled the contents onto my lap.

Ten 1931 Saint-Gaudens double eagle gold coins.

"How much are they worth?"

"At thirty cents on the dollar—twenty to twenty-five grand. Apiece."

"Less than I was hoping for," Susanna said, "but it will work."

Skinny Dennis helped us load the car.

Later, we drank a farewell to the apartment—standing in the front room with whiskey in paper cups.

"I'm going to gas up the car," Susanna said. "I'll hit the horn three times when I get back."

She gave Dennis a hug.

"We'll be looking out for your hit record," she said.

When she left, I offered Dennis another drink.

"I have to bounce. Band rehearsal. I'm going to miss you guys."

"You and old man Clancy are about all *I'm* going to miss. I hope your dreams come true."

We shook hands and he headed for the door.

"And, Dennis," I said, as he was moving out into the hallway.

"Yes?"

"Say goodbye to the landlord for me."

A few minutes later I heard Susanna's signal.

I stepped out of the apartment and closed the door behind me.

I reached into my pocket, pulled out the key, and left it in the door lock.

Branded Man
Mel Odom

I avoided Flatt's Hardware Store because I couldn't stand Mrs. Flatt's grimace of distaste when she saw me coming through the door. Like I was some mess she'd stepped in. Dressed prim and proper and finer than most of the women in town, Mrs. Flatt had a way of looking down her nose that was as sharp as a hay hook and cut just as deep. In her sixties, she still wore her hair in a beehive and dyed it so black that the color sometimes soaked into her scalp. Gray hair wasn't gonna sneak up on her.

I didn't look at her as the bell over the door jangled behind me. I just headed to the brackets and hangers Clint said he needed for the kitchen cabinet remodel we were working on. He'd also texted me a picture of the doorknobs Mrs. Robinson had decided on.

In all the years I'd come there, not much had changed. Aisles filled with tools, plumbing and electrical parts, transformers and circuit breakers, pipes, screws, bolts, nails and three models of toilets stood in rank and file in the neat rows. Along the top on the west wall, boxes held Currier & Ives glassware that would fill the display windows out front the day after Thanksgiving and be back in their boxes the day after Christmas. A couple of red plastic sleds stood beside a barrel that contained leaf rakes and snow shovels. The smell of oil and varnish and pine lingered in the air.

The silence in the hardware store when it was just Mrs. Flatt and me was so quiet you could hear grass grow. I felt bad when my boot heels clomped against the varnished hardwood floor.

She never talked to me while I was picking up things for Clint Harjo and Associates Custom Remodeling. Clint was my boss; I was the associates. It was a small outfit, but it kept groceries on the table and I was learning a trade while keeping a roof over Momma's head.

Clint knew I didn't like going into the hardware store, and he knew why. Everybody in Three Jacks, Oklahoma, knew my story. Or thought they did, anyway.

They didn't know the real story. I kept that one hid at the time for good reason that turned out to be no reason later. Life has a lot of twists and turns you don't see coming.

My last name carried a lot of baggage even before I'd added to it. My daddy was a hard drinking, hard whoring man who spent Friday nights in the bars picking up loose women and Saturday nights in the pits fighting chickens. Even at thirteen and near man-sized, I couldn't go to the bars or to the whores, but I could handle his roosters for him during the cockfights.

Scars from gaffs and Mexican slasher knives from handling those roosters still cover my hands. It always hurt like hell at the time, but Daddy used to tell people I could take steel better than any gamecock he'd ever raised. I had to be fast and do it right, because Daddy whooped me when he thought I'd mishandled a rooster and got it killed, losing him his money.

Daddy was gone before my fourteenth birthday. He got into a drunken argument with another chicken fighter named Pete Haskell and ended up shooting Haskell stone dead. Daddy lit out that night and nobody's seen or heard from him since.

That had left me and Momma at home, and times got hard. Momma talked about me going to college and making something of myself, but we both knew that wasn't gonna happen. We had no money, and my grades weren't good enough for scholarships. I was gonna find a job, probably in Latham's junkyard where I'd been working part-time since Daddy left.

Mr. Latham called it "part-time" but I was clocking over fifty hours a week on less than minimum wage and getting "bargain prices" on parts I needed to keep my Chevy Nova running. Those "bargain prices" were only there because Mr. Latham wanted to make sure I could get to work, and he got a lot of my wages back on account of that car being a POS.

Still, me and Momma was making it. Till I went to jail on a meth bust for six years a month before I graduated high school. Mr. Latham repossessed my car from Momma, saying as how I hadn't paid for all the parts. Which wasn't true, but I wasn't surprised he did it either. Everybody in Three Jacks was having a hard time making ends meet.

Mr. and Mrs. Flatt blamed me for their grandson getting into trouble. Hell, me and Ralph Flatt had never been friends. I'd always been too "other side of the tracks" for him. Ralph got a fire engine red Camaro for his sixteenth birthday. He'd had it made in the shade. He hadn't had to get involved with Tinker Davis's meth operation, but he had because he was all set to make money. After growing up so easy, Ralph figured adulthood should come easy too.

When the trial happened and their grandson went away to prison, the Flatts had needed someone to blame. Since everybody knew Tinker was into drugs even before he'd gotten kicked out of high school five years before, they didn't think he could have sucked Ralph into the meth operation. They blamed me because I was the only other high school guy arrested that night.

Ralph got a better lawyer than I did. He spent a year and a day in prison, then got out. Two years later, bikers at a truck stop killed him during a drug buy. Even though I'd been in prison at the time, still having to fight just to survive, the Flatts blamed me for Ralph dying too. According to them, I'd put him on that path.

I did my whole bit, stacked the whole six-year sentence minute by minute, so I wouldn't have to report to a parole officer. I also learned how to do laundry and weld, the last coming in handy sometimes working for Clint.

There was a lot of animosity in the Flatts and the rest of the town. There always is in folks who don't have much except bragging rights over the others around them. Since I'd been to prison, pretty much everybody had that over me. I only came back for Momma.

Clint had apologized for sending me to the hardware store that morning, but Mrs. Robinson was being difficult and he didn't want to leave her alone because she might start thinking of hiring someone else. Clint and I needed that job. We needed every job.

The bell over the door jangled and I glanced up out of habit. Six years in prison will make anyone skittish.

I didn't recognize the three hardcases who walked in through the door, but I knew them for what they were at a glance.

Trouble, and plenty of it.

Standing at least six feet four, the biggest man had dirty blond hair down to his shoulders, and a red beard down to his chest that squirrels could have made a winter home in. He wore an OU sweatshirt that stretched tight across his shoulders and even tighter across his belly. He looked around, nervous, and I knew he was looking to see who else was in the store.

The smallest man snuffled through his nose and had watery, bloodshot eyes, telling anyone who knew about such things that he was a meth junkie. He was mostly bald on top and the fringe of dark hair cut short at the sides of his head hung past his shoulders in back. His jeans and belt were too big for him. So were the boots. He wore a sleeveless denim jacket over a ribbed wife-beater that had gone gray from age. Full-sleeve tattoos ran from his wrists to his biceps, all of them biker-oriented. He glanced at me for a minute, then looked away, but his hand dropped to the folding knife sheathed on his belt.

"Good morning," Mrs. Flatt said sweetly as the third man walked up to the counter. "May I help you with something?"

"Why, yes, ma'am. My name is Darrel Clement." The third man grinned broadly, showing wide, white teeth. He oozed charm like a used car salesman. Clean and neat, wearing pressed jeans, sand-colored Nocona ostrich-skin boots, a starched snap-front Western shirt and his dark hair gelled back from his face, the man looked like he had money. His sports coat fit right and looked good, but it didn't completely conceal the hard lines of the pistol tucked in the back of his waistband. "I'm doing some repairs on a house I just bought, just moved into Hiram, you see. My wife is insisting on some upgrades. Bless her heart, I just couldn't turn her down. Ain't that right, boys?" He glanced over his shoulder.

The two men with Clement nodded like bobbleheads.

Hiram was a town over, twenty-three highway miles away.

"A good wife wants to make a house into a home," Mrs. Flatt said.

Clement slapped the counter with his hand and smiled even bigger. "Why, yes, ma'am, mine is a good one, and she surely does. She's bound and determined, and she told me she wanted the best I could get. Since I moved in, I heard that Flatt's Hardware Store is *the* place you want to come if you want to get good materials at a fair price."

Unless you wanted to drive seventy miles to reach a Home Depot or Lowe's Home Improvement store, that was true. The Flatts didn't mind making a profit.

"We handle quality merchandise," Mrs. Flatt said.

"That's what I want to hear," Clement said like he'd just hit the lottery. He pointed at the *AS FOR ME AND MY HOUSE, WE WILL SERVE THE LORD* sign hanging in the front window. "And I purely do like doing business with God-fearing Christians."

Mrs. Flatt smiled. "There's nothing like the Good News."

"No, ma'am, there is not. God bless."

My gut was crawling, and I figured I knew what was coming. I didn't want to be any part of it. I stuffed what I'd found into a basket and walked to the front counter.

Mrs. Flatt didn't speak to me. She just reached into the basket, took out the items and rang them up. I paid her in cash even though Clint had told me to use his account. I used the money in my front pocket, moved from my wallet while I'd been in the back and totaled up the cost, because you didn't open your wallet with three guys like those at the counter standing around. All of them, even Clement, watched me count out the cash.

I took my three dollars and thirteen cents in change and sacked up my own purchases. Mrs. Flatt never provided any kind of service.

"Well, sir," Clement said, looking into my box, "that is a *lot* of cabinet knobs."

I nodded, polite and quick, making like I was shy to talk, not that I was avoiding talking with him. I'd met a lot of guys like Clement in prison. Guys who were narcissistic and took on slights without warning.

"Make sure you put them on the outside of the cabinet doors," Clement said, and he laughed at his own joke. "Makes it easy to get to them." He hooked a thumb over his shoulder at the big man. "I'm still working with Virgil here on that. Ain't that right, Ronnie?"

The little man nodded and smiled, showing ugly, brown-stained teeth. "That's right."

Virgil frowned and folded his arms across his chest. Evidently he didn't like being the butt of the joke, but he didn't protest.

I just nodded, took my box, and left.

Behind me, Clement said, "I've got a big list of things I need, ma'am. Do you have anyone here who can help Virgil and Ronnie get them?"

"My husband's out back. I'll go and get him."

"I don't mean to put you to any trouble. Do you have anyone else?"

"Not this morning. Let me fetch my mister and I'll be right back. Between your men and him, I'm sure we'll be able to take care of you."

Outside, some of the crawling sensation left my gut and my chest didn't feel so tight, but I knew things inside the store were gonna go bad. If they'd just been there for the contents of the register, Clement would have already had that pistol out in Mrs. Flatt's face.

I set the box in the back of the Dodge pickup I was restoring and worked on taking a deep breath. What happened inside that store wasn't my problem. I told myself that again and again. I told myself that no good deed went unpunished. That's what the business with the meth dealers taught me.

I even managed to open the door and pull myself behind the steering wheel. But I glanced over at the only other car in the small parking lot under the red, white and blue triangular flags flapping from lines tied between the building and the lampposts.

The dark blue Chrysler 300 looked like it was fresh off the showroom floor. A fine rime of red dust coated the sides, and it had Texas tags on the front. Oklahoma is one of the few states that only have rear tags. I figured that Chrysler had a story to tell.

If Mrs. Flatt just looked out the window and spotted the car, she'd realize those men hadn't come there with any intention of driving off with materials. She'd know she was in trouble.

But she was too interested in making money.

That was one thing the Flatts had always done: make money. Herschel Flatt had grown up a farmer's son, and he still held onto the fears caused by the Depression his daddy and granddaddy had gone through. He'd kept the farm, rented the land out, and become an agriculture teacher, finding a way to turn that farmer's knowledge into another paycheck. And in his evenings he'd opened the hardware shop, running it with his son until he'd died of a heart attack a few years after Ralph had been born.

The story went that Ralph's mom had never been any good and had run off the first chance she got. The story also went that Mrs. Flatt had never cared for her and had chased her off.

I took a breath and watched as Clement and his two thugs followed Mrs. Flatt to the rear of the store. The Flatts were judgmental people, and maybe prone to disparaging others, but they didn't deserve what was about to happen to them either. Clement and his men hadn't bothered hiding their faces because they didn't intend leaving anyone behind who could testify.

I knew I was lucky to get out the first time. I even started the engine and shifted into reverse. Then I thought about the kind of men I'd been locked up with, the stories I'd been told by murderers and rapists who had told me tales to scare me, and sometimes because all that evil couldn't stay bottled up in a man. It had to come out.

But when men like them were through paying penance, if ever, they went back to the violence that was the only thing they knew.

I squeezed my eyes shut and told myself to leave. Except I knew Clement and his boys were there for the money the Flatts were supposed to have hidden in the hardware shop. They lived in the second floor of the hardware store. They owned a house, had raised their son and grandson in it, but they rented it out after Ralph got himself killed and Mr. Flatt added that second floor. It was one more way of making money.

And all that money they made was supposed to be in a safe in that store.

In the past, people had broken into the hardware store and tried to find it. No one ever did. Personally, I thought it was stupid to trust that kind of cash in a safe instead of in a bank, but Mr. Flatt didn't trust banks all that much. There were also rumors that the Flatts took money under the table and off the books, and that they had to hide it so the IRS wouldn't know about it.

I didn't know and wouldn't have guessed, but I was certain both of them were about to get dead this morning.

I glanced out at the street that ran in front of the store, hoping someone else would come by. No one did.

Still, I wasn't going in there. No good deed ever went unpunished. I'd learned that first hand seven years ago when Bounce had called me in the middle of the night. Bounce had been my best friend all through high school. His daddy was almost as bad as mine, so Bounce and me commiserated together, got drunk on cheap beer the first time together, and even lost our virginity to the same girl. I didn't know that till later.

At the time, she was supposed to be my girl, but she didn't feel that way, I guess. Bounce slipped right in, and I didn't know till she left me for some guy she met on the Internet. He told me she hadn't been faithful to me because he'd slept with her too before she'd dumped me. He just hadn't wanted to say anything while we were dating.

Even that hadn't come between us. Like he'd said, she'd been the one to cheat on me, not him. It made sense in a way. That's the kind of friends you make when you're a kid and don't think you'll ever have any better.

When Bounce was little, his daddy had nicknamed him Bounce on account of he couldn't sit still. He was always dreaming up stuff, thinking about things, questioning everybody about anything. The teachers said he was ADHD, hyper, but I'd always known him as my friend, the guy who was always there when I needed him to help me bandage my hands after a night at the cockfights. And when Daddy worked me over on a losing night, which was often.

That was why, the night Bounce was with Ralph and Tinker and the other guys at the meth lab had called, I'd gone to get him. Bounce had gotten the heebie-jeebies that night. He said somebody had been stealing from Tinker and Tinker was pissed, and there was a big deal coming up with some out of town guys from Tulsa. Nobody except Tinker knew them. Bounce had been working on the fringes of the group, never taking drugs himself, not like Ralph did, just picking up some pocket money now and again.

That night, Bounce had ridden with Tinker, but he'd wanted to get out of there. He'd called me, and I'd gone to get him. I'd had to park the Nova and walk a mile through the brush to get to the meet site, which was out in the boonies. I'd been surprised Bounce had gotten a cell signal.

I got there and let Bounce know I was around, and we slipped off from the others and started back for my car. Only, as it turned out, Tinker wasn't meeting with dealers from Tulsa. He'd tripped over a group of under-cover cops. They arrested Tinker and Ralph and the others.

Bounce and I ran for the car, but I wrenched my ankle on a tree root and went down. I told Bounce to go on, not thinking he'd do it, but he ran without hesitation. I still almost made it, and I would have escaped if Bounce hadn't driven off as soon as he climbed in the car. I watched the Nova's red taillights vanish in the darkness just as one of those cops tackled me.

During the trial, I didn't squeal on Bounce. Neither did Tinker or Ralph or the others. None of them told anybody I was innocent, either. On the advice of their attorneys, they said nothing. My attorney told me he couldn't do much for me, what with me there and no good reason to give for it.

While I was in prison, Bounce had come to see me when he could, and he'd put some money on the books for me when he had it. He was always hurting for money too because the job he got didn't pay enough. We both agreed that if he tried to tell anyone what actually happened, they'd just lock him up too.

I stared at Flatt's Hardware Store and felt miserable. Desperately, I pulled my cell phone out of my shirt pocket and dialed.

"Sheriff's Office," Carol Butters answered. I'd gone to school with her and hadn't talked to her since then, but I still knew that twang.

"Is Marion working today?" I asked. I figured he'd be the only one who would believe me. This was Tuesday, and if I remembered right, he was supposed to be on. He patrolled Three Jacks and a couple other nearby towns.

"We don't give out that kind of information." The crisp voice turned a little haughty. Pure Carol Butters.

I gave her my name. "Flatt's Hardware Store is getting robbed. Tell Marion to get here as quick as he can. There are three robbers. Tell him I'm here and to try not to shoot me." I hung up before she could say anything, and I hoped help was on close to hand.

Cursing my own stupidity, I turned the phone's ringer off and slid it into my jeans pocket. I pulled my ball cap down snug and walked back to the hardware store. My heart raced ninety-to-nothing. I caught the bell in my hand before it could ring and slipped it off the hook.

I checked the round mirrors mounted in the back corners of the hardware store and spotted Clement and his buddies gathered around the Flatts at the back of the store where an EMPLOYEES ONLY stockroom was.

I laid the bell on a stack of PVC pipes, then picked up a piece of two-by-four scrap lumber from a round bin there. My hands were big and callused, and my fingers wrapped the three-foot piece of timber just fine.

"I *said* open that safe, old man!" Clement's voice no

longer dripped honey. It was hoarse and full of threat. "'Cause if you don't, I'm gonna put a bullet in this old sow's head!"

Mrs. Flatt squalled in fear.

Easing to the end of the aisle, I peered at the group. Clement and the Flatts were out of sight in the stockroom. The big guy, Virgil, stood with his hands in his pockets while him and Ronnie watched the door like they suspected Clement would try to sneak past them with whatever he found.

"All right, all right!" Mr. Flatt's gravelly voice carried fear in it, something I'd never heard from him. "Just give me a minute."

"We're in the chips, amigo." Virgil took a hand out of his pocket and clapped Ronnie on the shoulder with it.

"I wonder how much they got?" Ronnie stuck his head inside the stockroom. "People say they're sitting on a bundle."

I knew I should have stepped in and took a swing, but I was scared. Anything I did might cause the death of the Flatts, and me too.

"You stupid son of a bitch!" Clement swore. Then the basso thunder of a pistol shot rocketed through the store and filled my ears with cotton.

Mrs. Flatt screamed.

And I knew any further hesitation on my part would get us all killed. I stepped out into the aisle and swung that two-by-four like I was Big Papi trying to drive one over the Green Monster. The two-by-four slammed into Virgil's head with a meaty *whock!* and bounced it off the wall beside him. He went down like his legs had turned into spaghetti.

Virgil didn't make a sound as he hit the floor, so either Ronnie heard the wood hitting bone or he caught a glimpse of the big man falling. Yelping, his voice barely audible above the ringing in my ears, Ronnie grabbed the knife from his hip and flicked it open, then drove the blade at me.

I blocked the knife thrust with the two-by-four and drew it back about six inches, then put my weight behind it and slammed it into Ronnie's face. His brown teeth splintered and his lips turned to crimson pulp. He tried to yell, but only bloody bubbles erupted from his mouth.

When you have a guy on the ropes and the stakes could be your life, you don't let up. I learned that the hard way in prison. Brimming with adrenaline, I stepped forward, gripped the two-by-four two feet apart in front of me, and hammered Ronnie's knife hand with one end. Then I rammed that end into Ronnie's forehead. As he fell, I kicked the dropped knife away, shooting it across the hardwood floor.

Breathing hard, I fetched up against the wall and waited a minute, wondering what Clement would do.

"You better show yourself!" Clement shouted. "Show yourself *right* damn now or I'm gonna shoot this old man again!"

I cursed and looked around. I didn't have a gun, but when it came to making mayhem, there were worse places than a hardware store to end up caught in. It's a weapon-rich environment. I reached up for the circular saw blades hanging on the wall behind me and took down a heavy one designed for concrete mason work.

"Do you hear me?" Clement demanded.

After freeing the saw blade from the wrapping, I held it between my thumb and forefinger and peeked around the doorway.

Blood soaked Mr. Flatt's shirt over his stomach as he lay on the ground. The years hadn't changed him much. He wore a steel-gray flattop, and a shirt and slacks that looked like he'd bought them off a rack from J. C. Penney.

He looked out of it, but his chest was moving. On her knees beside him, Mrs. Flatt pressed her hands against his wound and sobbed uncontrollably. On the wall behind them, under a fake set of shelves, a wall safe almost big enough for a man to crawl into stood open. Bundles of cash sat stacked inside, and gold coins glinted beside them.

The rumors were true.

Still holding his weapon aimed at Mr. Flatt, Clement looked at me. The pistol shook in his hand and nervous fire shone in his eyes. "Is there anybody with you?"

"No," I said, knowing that one word drove what happened next.

Clement fired again, but the bullet struck the concrete floor beside Mr. Flatt's head. By that time I was moving, taking a step to the side and turning sideways, whipping the circular saw blade to my side. I threw it like a Frisbee, flinging it at Clement's chest as he raised the pistol.

The disc flew high, cutting across Clement's forehead over his left eyebrow and unleashing a torrent of crimson. Head wounds bled a lot. He screamed and panicked, because blood scared a man when it got in his eyes. He didn't know how badly he was hurt.

He fired again, but I took another step to the side and rushed at him. I caught his gun wrist in my hand and twisted, feeling bones grate against each other, and something popped. Clement screamed again, but by then I knotted my fingers in his hair and banged his head against the concrete wall until his eyes rolled up in his head.

I left him where he fell, gathered up his 9mm and the .38 revolver I assumed Mr. Flatt had kept tucked away in his safe. Then I knelt beside Mr. Flatt and looked at Mrs. Flatt as I took her hands in mine.

"Let me see, Mrs. Flatt. Please."

Crying, shaking, she took her hands back. I looked at the wound, down low and to the side. It bled, but it didn't pump. The bullet had missed arteries. An exit wound, bigger than the entrance, was in his back. I felt for his pulse and it felt strong, steady.

"It's okay," I told her. "The bullet went through and it doesn't look like anything vital was hit. He'll be fine once the paramedics get here. I called the sheriff's office from my truck before I came back in. Let's just patch him up as best as we can."

She nodded and I took my shirt off. We tore the sleeves off and made makeshift bandages to press against Mr. Flatt's wounds. The hole at the back was already slowing, clotting up.

Deputy Marion Bridger shoved his head in through the door, following the pistol in his hands. He had always been heavy, even back in grade school when neither of us was eating right, and the bulletproof vest he wore under his gray uniform blouse made him look even bigger. He wore his hair short and his mustache was thin and neatly clipped.

He looked at me and called my name as if he couldn't believe it. "You leave these two guys out here?"

I nodded. "They were working with this guy." I pointed a bloody finger at Clement.

Still holding his pistol in both hands, Marion eased over to get a better look in the safe. He whistled. "Lordy, but that's a lot of money. How much you figure is in there?"

I shook my head and kept the pressure on Mr. Flatt's wounds.

Marion rifled through the stacks of cash. "Just looking at it, I'd say there's gotta be two or three million dollars in here. Man, these people got more money than they know what to do with." He looked at me, then down at Mr. Flatt. "Is he gonna die?"

"No. I'll be glad when the paramedics get here, though."

"They're on their way. A few minutes out." Marion stood and looked at me. "That's a hell of a lot of money, buddy."

I didn't like the way he said that, but I didn't say anything.

"If you think about it, this here is an opportunity."

I looked at him then, liking the way his mind worked even less.

"Me and you, we've never had nothing. Always had to hustle for everything we got. And nobody knows how much money is in that safe. We could take most of it, leave a little behind. Then tell it like we stopped the robbery too late."

I looked at that shine in his eyes, recognizing it for the greed that it was. He'd always had his daddy's eyes. "The Flatts know how much money is in there."

He grinned. "Maybe they didn't survive the robbery."

"Bounce, you can't—"

His eyes hardened. "Nobody calls me that anymore. Not even you. Now you get right with me, or you didn't survive this either."

Going for broke, I hurled myself at him, but my left foot slipped in Mr. Flatt's blood and I went down hard. Bounce kicked me in the side of the head and I saw his face again that night he'd left me holding the bag to be arrested. Senses spinning, I tried to get up.

Bounce pointed his pistol at me. "I'm sorry, man. I am. Especially after you came for me that night when Tinker and the others got arrested by the cops. But guys like us, we gotta look out for ourselves. That money, it can change my life. Get me outta this town. Like we always wanted to do. I know you understand that."

I did understand it. I wanted out too, but my momma had lived all her life here and she wasn't gonna go anywhere. She'd been living in a rundown garage apartment when I'd gotten out of prison, but I'd worked us into a two-bedroom house that I was planning on buying. It wasn't much, but I'd gotten it the right way. I was proud of that.

I focused on Bounce, trying to put the two images I had of him into one finished piece. "I can't let you hurt these people."

He grinned, but he looked sad too. "You won't. I'll kill you first."

A shot rang out as I pushed myself forward and

grabbed hold of him. I wondered where the bullet had hit me, but I didn't feel any pain other than what throbbed in my skull. Bounce went down like wet cement and laid there. His gun fell to his side and slid from his limp fingers.

His mouth opened and blood spilled out. Then his eyes flattened, the pupils blossoming into black pools that eclipsed the irises. More blood poured from the back of his head.

Against the wall by her husband, Mrs. Flatt still held the .38 in both hands, aiming at me.

Slowly, I spread my hands out and raised them above my shoulders. For a minute, I thought she was going to shoot me too.

Then Mr. Flatt called for her. She dropped the pistol and turned to him. "Help me," she said. "Help me keep him alive."

I went over to her and put pressure on Mr. Flatt's wounds again. The blood was clotting on its own. I thought he'd be fine, but I kept my hands on him all the same because I knew she took comfort in me doing that.

She looked at me with tear-filled eyes, then patted my face with a trembling hand. "I had you wrong. A lot of us had you wrong."

I didn't say anything. I didn't know what to say.

"Thank you," she said.

"Yes, ma'am," I said. Still maintaining pressure on Mr. Flatt's belly wound, I put an arm around her and offered comfort, and she leaned into me while we listened to the shrill of the arriving paramedics.

Pardon Me
(I've Got Somebody to Kill)
Eric Beetner

Bob Earl was a weaselly-faced son of a bitch with a slight wobble in his step thanks to the cottonmouth that hitched a ride on his calf and shot two fangs worth of venom so deep he had to be cut off with a Buck knife taking most of Bob's leg muscle with it to prevent the poison reaching his heart.

Bob Earl came into the Tin Star bearing bad news and he knew just where to go to do the telling. The far back booth was where Donny Lytle could be found most nights holding court with the men who would bend over backwards to do what he said or keeping company with a lady who would shed her Wranglers and bend any way he asked.

It was a redhead that night, but when Donny saw Bob Earl peg-legging it across the barroom like a man on the run from a swarm of hornets, he knew his date was over.

Donny took another swig of beer as he waited for the gimp to finish his trek. He sat back in his chair, legs spread wide and his denim shirt unbuttoned to mid chest. The redhead was sucking an ice cube out of her Jack and Coke and getting horny off Donny's Burt Reynolds charm and mustache.

"Pardon me, darlin'," he said to his date before Bob Earl had even cut a swath halfway through the sawdust on the dance floor. Bob Earl reached the table and stopped to both catch his breath and let his eyes adjust to the light, or lack thereof, off in that corner. He brought with him the musky smell of a man who'd been sweating for a good long time and hadn't showered in an even longer stretch. A date killer, that's what the stench was. The redhead sank deeper into the shadow and sipped at her Jack and Coke until the ice rattled.

"What is it, Bob?"

Bob shook his head as if the news he had to tell would hurt coming out. He sucked a few extra breaths while he set himself for spilling the beans. "It's Jimmy," he said. "They got him."

"Cops?"

Bob Earl nodded, wet strands of his hair clung to his forehead like earthworms flattened on the pavement after a rain. Donny slammed his beer to the table, foam volcanoed up the neck and soaked his right hand. Froth clung to his mustache.

"When?"

"Tonight. They ambushed him. They was waitin'."

The redhead perked up. "They arrested Jimmy?"

Donny didn't look at her. "Time for you to go, darlin'."

She stayed put. Donny leaned closer to Bob Earl. "You think someone snitched?"

"I don't see no other way. They had three cars waitin'. The whole load is gone. They knew he was comin'."

Donny stared a steel rod through the floor. He thought back over anyone who could have put the finger on Jimmy, his kid brother. Jimmy who joined Donny's operation at his own insistence. Jimmy who had been the good kid, the chance, the exception. And Donny had let him in and now got him caught.

He wasn't worried about himself. He took precautions. Nothing would lead back to him. But for a transgression like this, someone was going to pay.

The trial took no time. A tip which led to the bust. More product the county had recovered in one shot since Johnny Cash was still alive. Ten to fifteen was the number the judge handed down, parole in five if he was good.

Donny had to hear about it over the phone. Being in the courthouse was bad business and it would have been too tough for him. He would have broken down crying, or more likely started busting up the place, breaking chairs being a big stress reliever in Donny's world.

He hung up the phone saying, "I know you'll excuse me if I say goodnight, but I've got someone to kill."

In the short few weeks since Jimmy's bust Donny had narrowed down the list of suspects to three. He thought about killing all three to be safe, but he knew that was only his anger thinking for him. Worse than thinking with your prick.

He had his most likely candidate and he knew when he was done with him, Donny would know the truth.

Burly Wilcox knew the time and place. Knew where Jimmy would be even if he himself was twenty miles away balls deep in an underage girl who shut her eyes and took the pain all for a pull on the pipe as reward. Burly Wilcox made bad decisions.

Twice in and out of jail, once on the receiving end of a broken nose from a pissed off dad who didn't like his daughter being pounded by an ex-con and recreational drug user, and three times the reason Donny had to get involved and smooth the waters when deals didn't go as planned.

He once talked one customer out of taking Burly's thumb as payment for damages after a delivery made it to him three days late. Burly claimed car trouble. Almost got him fired and kicked out of the opposable thumb club, but Donny cut a deal and got promises from Burly it wouldn't happen again.

Jimmy living in a cell would be harder for Burly to talk his way out of.

Donny knocked on the door with the barrel of his gun. He brought his razor and wanted to use it if he found Burly was his guy, but that was pleasure and the gun was business.

"Hey, Donny. What's up?" Burly answered the door in his underwear, hair askew, red road map lines across his cheek where the pillow creases left indents.

Donny pushed past him before Burly had a chance to clear the crust from his eyes. "Need to talk to you." Burly watched the gun go past as Donny slid by him.

"Sure...sure, Don. What about?" Burly rolled a blood-shot eye around the front step to see if Donny had come alone before closing the door.

A good five years had gone since Donny did any

muscle work of his own to speak of. His reputation hadn't dimmed the slightest during his hiatus. The embellishments of hindsight had raised his terror level, if anything. Burly knew what an armed Donny Lytle in his home meant, and it was bad.

"Jimmy went down."

"Yeah. I heard." Burly scratched his balls, then thought better of it. Respect and all. He lived with the itch like a tick was burrowing beneath his sack.

"Someone tipped."

"No shit?"

"No shit." Donny watched for a sign, a tell. He held the gun in front of him, hands crossed below his belt and the gun looking like he had his dick out and was pissing all over Burly's already piss-stained floor.

Burly folded under the pressure and broke Donny's gaze. He pawed through the mess on his coffee table until he found a pack of smokes, the box crushed but one bent cig remaining. Lighters were easier to find. The low table held no fewer than three.

Donny watched as Burly lit up and blew nervous smoke at the ceiling. He would no longer meet his eyes. The room stank of sweat and unwashed dishes in the sink, the chemical tang of smoked drugs clung to the fibers of every surface.

Burly was an excellent candidate. Already in trouble with the law. His third strike coming up. Donny thought: say he's busted again. He can pull out this chip—tell them when and where the deal is going down. He gets a free pass and Jimmy get a bus ride and an orange jumpsuit, then a cellmate and a fast lesson in the importance of lubrication.

Plus now Burly's body language. His anxious smoking, his twitchy body. Red flags. Spinning sirens. Neon signs.

Burly really needed to scratch his balls. He really needed to hit a rail of powder. He really needed a cup of coffee. Mostly the itch south of his sack, though. A thin sweat broke out on his lip. His feet wouldn't stay still. He felt like a third grader who needs to pee but can't interrupt the pledge of allegiance.

Donny's hands unclasped. The gun hung loose now.

"Why'd you do it, Burly?"

The cigarette paused halfway to his mouth. "Do what?"

"My fucking brother, man."

"Wait...wait, you think I sang?"

"Tell me why." Donny raised the gun. Burly's naked torso concaved as if a few inches further away would make the difference between life and death. "Who had it over you? What deal did you cut? Make me understand."

"I didn't rat on Jimmy, or anybody else. Jesus fuck, Donny. I would never."

"What was the deal? Stay out of jail? Jimmy took your place, is that it?"

"Listen to what the fuck I'm saying, Donny. I didn't do it. I didn't do shit." The itch in his crotch had gone away. All senses were on hold while his adrenalin pumped furiously, his breathing constricted, his skin went cold and the pale blond hairs stood out like a field of electricity had run through the room.

"You couldn't be a fucking man and do your time. *Your* time, Burly. Now Jimmy has to do it?"

"Donny, you got it wrong. I didn't—"

First shot went in between two ribs. Missed the heart. White bone poked out through the hole. Exit wound sprayed blood. Burly dropped his cigarette leaving a thin column of smoke rising in front of him. The second shot cut the smoke into swirls as Burly's chest sprouted a second bloom of red, this time over the heart.

Burly's mouth hung open. He took a short stagger step backward, stepped on his cigarette ash and felt it singe his skin.

Donny rushed him, teeth clenched and angry spit splashing out. "That was your time to do, Burly." Donny put out a hand to stop Burly from falling to the ground. He held his skinny body up as color drained from the traitor's face. Donny noticed Burly's eyes were no longer bloodshot as his heart stopped pumping.

"Bet you wished you'd taken the time in joint now, huh? Better than time in a hole in the ground."

He placed the gun on Burly's chest, wedged between the two of them. His eyes were wide, his eyelids straining open until they were sore. He squeezed the trigger a third time. Felt the heat of the blast against his own skin, but left the gun there and took the burn.

Donny eased Burly down to the floor, let him drop the last foot. When he hit, he didn't move.

Donny stood, looked at his hand. The hand he'd held up Burly with was smeared with blood from the exit wounds. His shirt was stained too, from their embrace. Burly dead—it didn't help everything, but Donny felt better. Like scratching an itch you've been desperate to get at.

* * *

He arrived home, the place he used to share with his younger brother. Jimmy came to live with him when he started working for Don. Two years of community college hadn't equated to a job for Jimmy. His options were the street, Mom's basement or beg Donny for a job and a room.

Donny peeled off his shirt and draped it over the arm chair in the living room, careful to keep the bloody side turned out so it wouldn't stain his furniture. The bright red smears had soaked into the cotton and the dark grey of the shirt turned the blood black and shapeless.

The burn on his chest was red and swollen, black in the center from the muzzle flash. It would heal, but he went to the bathroom to swab it with antiseptic and tape it over with gauze.

While he worked, he heard the door open. For a second he forgot where he left the gun. The kitchen counter, he remembered. Down a hallway and fifteen feet from where he stood. Bad move.

"Donny?" came a familiar voice. His mother. A woman who never let on if she knew about Donny's work or not, but she'd let it be known that she didn't approve when Jimmy went to work for Don. And she sat front row at every day of Jimmy's trial.

"What are you doing here, Mom?" Donny came down the hall, anxious to cover the gun. He found her running a finger over the dark stains on his shirt. She checked her finger. Away from the fibers of the shirt, the red returned, highlighting the whorls of her print. She looked up and saw her shirtless son with a red welt marking his chest.

"Donny, what's going on?"

"Nothing, Mom. It's nothing."

"It's not nothing." She looked at his wound then motioned back to the shirt. "This is not your blood." She looked over his shoulder at the gun resting on the kitchen counter.

"What are you doing here, Mom?"

She nodded her head down to the empty bags in her hands. "I'm here to clean out some of Jimmy's things. He wanted some stuff. A few books. He's allowed, you know. Or you would if you ever went to see him."

"I'm helping Jimmy in my own way."

"Jesus, Donny, is that was this is?"

Donny stepped forward and swept the shirt off the back of the chair. "Don't worry about it."

"What did you do?"

"I said don't worry about it."

"Donny, I swear to God almighty. I asked you to look out for him. I don't want to believe what I hear about you. What some people in the neighborhood say. But, Jesus, Donny…"

"Whatever I did, I did it for Jimmy. He's in fucking prison, Mom."

"You think I don't know that?"

"Yeah, well, the guy who should've been there instead just got his sentence."

Donny grabbed the gun off the counter and hid it under the balled up shirt in his hands. She'd already seen it, he knew, but somehow it was better to keep it out of sight.

She dropped her bags. They fell to the ground with the sound of wings on dying birds. Brown paper and soft canvas piled at her feet, rooting her to the spot.

"Tell me what you did."

Donny cringed at the choked sound in her voice. She shouldn't be here. Shouldn't see this. Shouldn't know.

But she was and she did.

"Mom, just leave. Please. It's all over. It's taken care of."

"What is?"

Donny squeezed the shirt between his hands until it bled onto his palms.

His mother swallowed back her tears. "What's taken care of, Donny?"

"The one who sent Jimmy to prison. The one who took your baby boy away. Now, didn't I do good? Do you want a fuck like that running free while Jimmy stews in a cell?"

Tears ran down her face, dropping heavy from tired eyes. "That's not your blood," she said again. "It wasn't your blood to take."

"He was a rat," Donny said. "He set Jimmy up. He called the cops."

"No, he didn't," she said.

"Mom, no disrespect, but you don't know what the fuck you're talking about. This is my business now." Donny coiled to explode. "You're right. Everything you ever said about me was right. All the stories, it's all true. And I don't care what the fuck you think about me because I know I'd rather be the kind of guy who puts things right after my brother gets royally fucked over, than some wimp who sits back and does nothing."

After his time in Burly's apartment, he didn't think he had any rage left in him but it turned out he'd kept enough in reserve. Now he was tired. A weight pushed down on his shoulders.

His mother stood firm, tears streaking her face and following the deep contours carved by worry. "He didn't call the cops...because I did."

Donny felt his chest tighten. "What?"

"I called them, Donny. I didn't want your brother working for you. I talked to him about it several times before he moved in here. I told him what you were. And I knew I couldn't reach out to you and ask you to let him go." She wiped her face dry. "I'd rather he be behind bars and learn his lesson than to stay with you and end up dead, or worse...turn out like you."

Donny thought of his vow—to kill whoever sent Jimmy to prison. His rage returned again, burned at the edges by betrayal. His heart felt squeezed, an angry black fist pulling on it.

"Tell me you're lying, Mom."

She shook her head no.

His hands gripped into fists. Locked in them was the gun. She hadn't moved. She stood watching her son and knowing how he felt to learn someone who was trusted had broken that trust. She knew the pain of feeling the bond of family torn like a tendon connecting you to someone else.

"I did it, Donny. And he's better off. He only made one mistake and that was trusting you. He can come back from that. But you...nobody can save you now."

Donny raised the gun.

In the time between his finger on the trigger and the bullet leaving the barrel, Donny already started to scream. "No."

The sound of his regret was swallowed by the explosion in the chamber. He couldn't believe what he'd done as he watched his mother's body jerk backward with the impact. Her thin shoulders, her slightly stooped frame—it all turned and collapsed as if someone had severed all the connections between her bones at once.

Her eyes closed as she fell. Her body gave way to the act of dying. A spot of blood grew on the front of her sweater and as she fell away Donny could see the dark stains left behind by the exit wound.

He ran forward, dropping the gun and rushing to her with his wadded up shirt pressed hard against her chest as he tried to slow the blood from coming. Her eyes stayed closed. She wouldn't look at him.

He spoke to her, pleaded for forgiveness, for her strength to fight the pain and go on. They would work it out, he'd pay for his mistakes, he promised. But she was limp in his arms.

His shirt soaked more blood until he couldn't tell what was Burly's and what was hers. Fitting, he thought. Blood is blood once it's been spilled. Doesn't matter who it belongs to. It's only the blood that binds us while it flows through veins and passes down, from mother to son, that matters in this world.

Everything else is only a stain.

Seven Spanish Angels
Riley Miller

One Week Ago

This will be my last criminal performance.

She gets in touch first, a one-line email that pings my business account. *I'm gonna need to see some of those references,* she writes. A simple signature line too: *Melody.* No introduction. No explanation. I'm drawn to the mystery, the woman who resists that instinctive female impulse to over-explain.

After forwarding the requested documents, my follow-up questions are simple. I ask about her situation. Which of my services interest her. My tone is terse. Businesslike. Still, there's a lot riding on her answers. Around them, I will build my character. Around them, I will create my script. That familiar excitement zings through my gut at low voltage, a hint of things to come. I only get this feeling when I'm about to land a new part.

That night I get my answer. *My husband's loaded,* she writes. *But I don't want to be with him anymore.*

She's a legitimate client. She's given me just enough, but no more. The vague ones, the careful ones—they're the ones who employ me.

I write up her invoice for Package 2: The Kidnapper. After I'm done, I allow my mind to wander.

It's a habit I've had since the beginning: picturing my clients, wondering if they are pretty. I pull out a short stack of photos. Not everyone had let me take one—after all, it's a dangerous game we play. Still, there's something about a visually inspiring leading lady—a muse—that adds zest to my craft.

There's no way to know about Melody yet. I haven't even heard her voice. But still, I picture her as a blonde. Tall, with long feathery hair and an athletic body.

Three Days Ago

My gun's next to the sink—handle facing me, barrel towards the water-stained wall. Having it close by keeps me in character.

Next to it, mustaches in three shades of brown wait to be chosen, like puppies in a pet store window. They crowd the bottles of dye and liquid adhesive. On the other side of the counter, a trucker hat proclaiming *Jesus Saves* balances on top of my Stetson. Next to them lay my blusher and eyelashes set—but that's just in case I get a Package 4: Sister Act. Package 4 is rare.

First: a shave. Then, I try on a brown newsboy. One glance in the mirror—faded in the way only a low-rent apartment mirror gets—tells me it's too hipster for this gig. Maybe I could wear it backwards for a badass vibe? I try it, then toss it back into the pile.

I have a gray wig halfway settled when my phone dings. It's Melody. The message reads: *One hour. Tom Horn's.*

Her bar choice inspires me and I extricate the Stetson from the pile. The missing piece clicks into place and I'm not looking at myself in the mirror anymore—I'm lookin' at my character.

I'm all yours, darlin' I type back.

Along my jaw, I paint on a five o'clock shadow, covering the smoothness I can't seem to grow out of. Afterward, a young Jack Palance stares back at me, and I tip my hat at my reflection, wide blue eyes shining with confidence.

I don't know if Tom Horn's is more famous for its beer or its burgers. One thing's for sure: it's red meat all the way, as expected from a bar named after a famous outlaw. I once saw someone order a veggie burger here, and the server laughed so hard she turned red.

Still. For the promised land—one flowing with liquor and cheeseburgers—there's never enough women. Dudes can be five thick at the bar, and only a few women dot the crowd. More often, the few who come in here hover near the back of the room.

Not so tonight.

A woman sits at one end of the bar. Even the back of her head is shapely—hair wavy and blonde, curving down her bare back, smooth as a sand snake. I'm drawn to her without being sure it's Melody. Still, a cowboy can hope. She's perched on the edge of the bar stool, leaning forward, finishing her drink. Nonchalant. Cool. Casual.

I channel *outlaw.* Strolling forward, I rest my arm on the bar, angling my body so it blocks the rest of the room. I say, "Ma'am?" elongating the middle syllable while my gaze travels over her bosom, telling myself that I'm staying in character.

She taps her empty glass. "I'll take a gin and tonic. Extra lime. If'n you're buyin."

Gin and Tonic. Our code words. She's my girl, and

my heart squeezes out a few extra pumps in appreciation. I adjust my pants so the large belt buckle catches the light. "Jenson. Pleasure to make your acquaintance."

We've already got the bartender's eyes—not because he ain't busy, but because Melody's one to attract attention, especially in a place like this.

I ease into my southern dialect. See, I'm what they call a method actor, and if I'm John Wayne, she's every bit a blonde Maureen O'Hara. A younger me couldn't have landed a babe like her, but now? The older, smoother me knows all the right lines.

If only my high school girlfriend could see me now. She thought I was goofy. Hell, I'd show her goofy.

Craigslist brought Melody and me together.

Here's the thing about being a criminal. At least, what I've figured out in the couple of years I've been at it. Referrals work best, making both my client and me more secure in our business relationship. Besides, I prefer designing my own gigs. But when my creativity's low and money's run out, I run an ad seeking a partner in crime.

It's short. Simple. Bizarre enough that most people think it's a joke. Kids are the main ones to respond.

But some know an opportunity when they see it. Like Melody. She's smart, and standing this close to her, I think she might be my favorite leading lady yet. She leans extra close as we talk, and her fingers on my arm are warm, inviting.

After a few drinks, she says, "We should probably finish planning at your place. Too many curious ears."

The tiny voice in my head that says, *You're goofy,* is

silenced by her red lips and her fingers trailing over my arm.

Thirteen Minutes Later

Melody wanders around the kitchenette while I pop open another beer. Her eyes are heavy, intense. There's something about her that seems familiar to me. Kind of cheesy, but she's like coming home.

"So this is how criminals live?" she asks, eyes wide.

Although it gives me a little thrill that she thinks of me as an outlaw, I consider correcting her. *I'm an actor, baby.* I'll tell her eventually.

I come up behind her while she opens my fridge to grab a beer for herself. As she's closing the door, she pauses in front of her chrome reflection.

She looks at me over her shoulder while combing her long hair out with her fingers. Gorgeous and low maintenance too? I've hit the jackpot with this girl.

"Can I keep you?" I ask, losing my drawl for a moment. I don't remember the last time I felt this way with a woman. They all seem like girls compared to her.

She saunters closer and curls her fingers into my hair. It feels good, her fingers stroking one of the only real things about me. My clothes? My 'stache? My accent? All part of the act. My hair though. It's one hundred percent Pert Plus real.

She kisses me—it's long and hot. "Baby, you can keep me as long as you want." Something in the way she says it reminds me of honeysuckle moonshine—sweet and hot and raw.

After that, all I can think about is taking her like a

shot—fast and deliberate, but she leads me on quite a chase as she wanders around my apartment, opening my drawers and boxes, like she's trying to look inside me.

Yesterday

Lately, all I can think about is getting Melody in my bed and keeping her there. Still, I manage to be professsional long enough to hammer out a plan that allows us to make money and for me to use my acting skills.

Phase one happens today. Tomorrow's payday.

We have lunch at my house, sandwiches and Sprite. As she sips her soda, her gaze flits around my apartment, landing on my bed, my nightstand. I want to ask her what she's gonna do after, how she's going to leave her husband. How she's going to break the news to him.

"I'd be happy to throw in a Package 5 for you. On the house." At her frown, I add, "That's the Gatsby package. Boyfriend from the past enters life to make a scene, givin' you a plausible reason to leave."

"One package at a time," she says, and I'm not sure if she's making a pun or if I just have a one-track mind.

Either way, I grin. "You're making me want a cold shower. Or, we could finish what we started last night."

This time, both of our eyes drift to the bed, but I know what she's going to say before she says it. Nothing had changed in the last twelve hours. "I'm not okay with that, Jenson. Not before I leave my husband. It just wouldn't be right."

She leans her head on my shoulder and the warmth of her skin on my own feels like a jolt of electricity.

I savor the feel of her then scan our plan again,

images and descriptions tacked up on my wall in a grid. I like storyboards, just like the movies.

An old tune comes into my head and I start humming. "Seven Spanish Angels." I've always loved that song, sensed a camaraderie with Willie Nelson and Ray Charles. Those two sure can put themselves into another man's shoes—or boots, for that matter.

And make money doing it.

Like old Ray, I love me a good tragedy—a fiction one, that is. I'd planned a happy ending for me and Melody, though—a happy ending, every night if I have anything to do with it.

My mind wanders to the money I've got stashed in a pillowcase under the mattress. Package 7 had been popular this year; although Package 3 is the bigger moneymaker. Soon enough, I'd be on my way with a nice pile of cash. New York City. Broadway. Roles where I can do more than mustache twirling.

Earlier this year, I'd done a solo gig. I called it "Flea Bitten." I'd scoped out a wealthy single woman in my apartment complex, disguised myself as a member of our landscaping company, and asked to use her bathroom. While inside, I planted fleas in her bed. She'd left in the middle of the night, leaving the empty suite and the cover of darkness to my sticky fingers.

The next day—about a thousand dollars in stolen goods richer—I saw her. Her face a swollen mess, and she kept her eyes down as her sister helped her move out. Her sister had railed loudly about the bugs and the theft, but the woman was silent, itchy and beaten. I decided there would be no more fleas. Also, it was time to ease my way out of the business, and up to New York.

Besides, the curtain has to close before it opens again. That's true in life and it's true on the stage. I imagine Melody coming with me, sitting in the front row while I headline at New Amsterdam Theater. On her feet, clapping, her red lips curled into a "Bravo!"

I excuse myself to touch up my costume in the bathroom and to change into my black jeans and cowboy boots. I survey my appearance before adding a hat. When this is over, I might grow myself a real mustache

I pose in the doorway. "I look dangerous. *The Cowboy Kidnapper*, that's what the papers will call me."

She laughs a little, but I can tell that there's something she's not saying.

As the afternoon sun starts to set, it's time to enact the plan. It's always my favorite part of Package 2— well, other than getting a bag full of money. Tomorrow, we've only got a one-person audience, but today I'll have a parking lot full.

There's this grocery store on the outskirts of town. It's got two cameras on the parking lot, and is understaffed on Thursday afternoons.

She's inside when I arrive, and I pull my big van in twenty-three feet away from the front-facing camera and wait. It's a rental, and I've put some rodeo decals on it and covered the license plate in mud. From their angle, the cops could see the van, but not its passengers.

While I'm waiting, stage fright gets to me a little. An elderly woman crosses with her cart, behind a couple and a toddler. Would they be part of my audience? An

SUV pulls up, beat blaring, and a big guy gets out. Would he enjoy the show?

My side mirror's set up so that when she leaves the store with a small bag, I see her. The couple's gone, but the elderly woman still moves steadily in the direction of her car. A younger woman in a suit walks briskly by. I wish there were more people outside to see the show, but I'll take what I can get. That's part of it—what sells the kidnapping. Eye witnesses.

Melody looks every bit as beautiful as she had this morning, and my breathing speeds up. I stroke the handle of my unloaded gun and remind myself who I am. *Jenson. Badass.*

When she gets to her car—a ripe little Ferrari—she bends over to put her bag inside. I step out of the car, careful to keep my hat lowered, my face angled thirty degrees away from the camera.

No one stops. The old lady has finally made it to her car and she's loading her trunk one bag at a time. The big dude and businesswoman are nowhere in sight. I hold up a finger, motioning for Melody to move more slowly. Right on time, a convertible full of teenage girls pulls across from us. It looks like they've just gotten out of school, and they pile out of the car, all estrogen and LOLs.

I love teenage girls. They make the perfect witnesses—more emotion than sense. Again, the word *goofy* travels through my head, but I remind myself that I'm The Cowboy Kidnapper. Nothing goofy here.

I wait for Melody to get into position, right behind the car's trunk. Moving behind her, smooth like a criminal, I take a deep breath. One of the teenagers watches me. She's younger than the others, thirteen or fourteen, and her eyes widen when she sees me—tall, dashing and dangerous. Next time, I make a mental note to smoke a cigarette. That would be a nice touch.

I frown at the girl to so she knows I'm menacing before grabbing hold of Melody, carefully keeping my face away from the camera.

Her scream is gorgeous. I want to praise her, tell her what an amazing damsel in distress she is, but instead I say, "Quiet, missy. You're comin' with me."

I cover her mouth with my hand, but she still manages to squeak out a "Help!"

Our timing is perfect. After I dump Melody in the back, I start yelling. "I got ya now, and there will be no escape." I brandish the gun so that the girls can get a good view and bang on the back door with a flourish.

After hopping into the driver's seat, I speed away. We're only a block away when she starts giggling from the back. "Did you see that girl's face? That was amazing." She laughs some more while shimmying between the two front seats to sit beside me. Her hair has fallen a little bit over her face.

"Get back!" I hiss. "Can't have anyone spotting us together, talkin' like old friends."

"You seem to like scaring young girls. Do you?" She props her feet up on the dashboard. The jeans that had looked so respectable from a distance are distracting up close. "Besides, if they are close enough to see that, then you got a lot more problems than them wantin' to know our relationship."

She's right. A siren blooms its mating call in the distance, and soon another answers, and another until all I hear are sirens. I pull into the shaded car wash and take off the decals.

My car's parked behind the shop. After throwing my hat and whiskers in the trunk, we head back to my apartment.

On the way, she leans over and rubs her fingers through my hair. The car swerves into the next lane.

"Damn it, Melody."

From the corner of my eye, I can see her smile creeping up the side of her face, a twisted amusement that tells me she's all-too-aware of her charms.

It does nothing to lessen her allure, but I gulp and manage to get back on track.

If I can keep steady for the next day, then I'll have all the time in the world to explore everything Melody's offering.

Once we get to my apartment, I know we've made it. I've got my police radio hooked up, and Melody listens to see if they are on to us, but apparently witnesses didn't notice which way we'd gone and it would take some time to pull up the parking lot cameras.

They are looking for a man about six-four with a handlebar mustache and a ten-gallon hat. I meet my own eyes in the rearview mirror.

And preen.

It'll be a long night hunkering down in my apartment, but I don't mind. She's the best company I could ask for. For some reason, I can't get that song out of my head— the one with the young, tragic lovers. I find "Seven Spanish Angels" online and play it.

She whispers, "I've always loved this song."

Her lips are so close that I have to taste them. I lean

into her and she leans into me, and we lose ourselves in the adrenaline of our afternoon. She licks her lips and pulls away. She sounds a little breathless. "Jenson."

The name sounds so sweet in her mouth, and I lean down to kiss her again. She pulls back. "Wait. Sugar, tell me more about you. Where you're from. What you're about." It sounds like a prayer.

"Sure, angel." I take a breath, ready to tell her about growing up on the fifth floor of a Dallas apartment building. My mom worked retail, and the bus used to drop me off at her store so I wouldn't be home alone. Looking into Melody's eyes, so blue and expectant, I knew I couldn't tell her that. I'm a method actor, damnit. Billy Cochran's past would stay private for a while longer.

"Jenson's my real name, believe it or not. I grew up wranglin' cattle. Pa used to keep me home from school to help out on the ranch—weren't no hand could break a horse fast as I could." I allow myself a sheepish smile. "Even when I was a kid, always had an eye for the ladies."

She cups my face with one hand and rubs my upper lip with the other. It's bare now that I've torn off the whiskers. She doesn't think I'm goofy. I can tell. Still. There's a question in her eyes—a hesitancy that I haven't seen before. Then, it's gone. There's a hardness, a decision made. For some reason, that makes me nervous. I plop down on the bed and pull her down with me. "This is how you wrangle cattle, baby."

She giggles and pushes me away.

* * *

Today

I found a deserted dude ranch half an hour away, and Melody and I are parked in the barn where we have the perfect view of the dirt road entrance. I'd put up a sign in front of the real ranch name: Valley of the Gun, straight out of our favorite song. Melody can't stop laughing. It's perfect.

Her husband shows up right on time. He gets out of the car with bag in hand, just how I'd instructed. It looks full, too. Like it actually has the right amount of cash in it. He's tall enough, and plays his part well, striding up to the drop off point by the big lonely tree. His suit's crumpled and tie askew. I wonder if he's been wearing it since yesterday.

I would have played it a different way. Maybe gone heroic. Maybe brought a gun, waved it around, all, "Come at me, Cowboy Kidnapper."

Melody's looking in his direction, but her eyes are lower, more intent on the state of her fingernails, than that of her husband. I grab one of her hands and squeeze. It feels perfect—delicate without being lazy.

I almost miss her husband start pacing, staring at his watch.

"Uh-oh. He better not have called the cops."

She rolls her eyes. "I told you. He doesn't have the imagination. He'll do what you said."

I like that. How she thinks he doesn't have imagination. She's compared the two of us—business-man and artist—and found him lacking. Rubbing my re-applied mustache, I give her hand a squeeze. "Almost there," I say.

Her eyes sparkle. She's looking at his bag too, and seeing possibilities.

We're halfway to New York in my mind. Between this and the stash I'd been working on, I'll be set for years, with the funds to support my fledgling career and my best girl.

"Alright, get ready," I say. The plan is simple. I get the money, and he gets her. She goes home with him and meets me next week, once she's had the chance to get her life in order. She gets her half. I talk her into running away with me.

She slides out of the car and waits. I grab her hands, roughly. I have to be Jenson through and through now. I push her towards the barn opening, gun trained on her. "I do the talking. Remember that."

She doesn't answer and I twist her so that I can see the look on her face. It's terrified until our eyes meet. She winks. "Got it, sugar," she whispers.

I keep her ahead of me. As we round the side of the barn, her husband comes into sight.

When he sees us, he drops the bag on the ground in front of him, and puts his hands in the air. "It's all here, just like you said. It's all here."

I nod. "Good. Now, don't do anything stupid." I'd always wanted to say that.

He stares at Melody, frowning. For a moment, I think he looks more confused than scared. "Sweetheart, are you okay?"

She nods, but I cut them off. "Shut up. Both of you."

I wave the gun at Melody. "Go get that bag of cash and bring it to me."

The air is still and the heat bears down, baking us. I

keep the gun trained on her as she obeys me. She won't meet her husband's eyes. She won't meet mine either, come to think of it. I have this feeling of imbalance—like I'm about to fall off my horse. I grip the gun tighter. She's walking back towards me now, bag in her hand.

My eyes wander over the horizon, then back to Melody. "Alright, open the bag. Let me see."

She does, and it's all there—beautiful stacks of green twenties.

I adjust my hat and stroke my mustache. "Now. Walk back towards your husband slowly. One wrong move and you're done." The husband's still looking at Melody, eyes scrunched in bewilderment. Can he tell she's my partner?

She licks her lips and meets my eyes, then his. "I rewrote the script," she says as she puts a pair of wide sunglasses on. Now her husband and I have matching looks of confusion as she pulls out a slim canister of something—then another from her other pocket. She sprays some in her husband's face, and he falls to his knees, clutching his eyes.

"First time I've seen you cry," she says, careful to stay away from him. "They told me I'd need extra strength."

I surge forward. "What did you—"

She faces me. "That there was your last speaking part, sweetheart. You think you're the only one with a plan around here?"

When she leans close, I freeze. I'm having a hard time keeping up. Improv's never been my best thing. When she sprays me, I realize what's in the can. Pepper spray. I'm crying and choking, all at once. My eyes burn, and I collapse into the dirt, too. My lungs seize, and my eyes explode, but something in me knows that the show must go on.

All I can do is crawl after her as she disappears back into the barn, but she throws something else my way—it looks like a bomb. When it explodes, I think I might die until I realize that her Phase 2 is some kind of smoke bomb. I'm crying and crawling and mumbling until she reappears out of the smoke.

She rolls her eyes. Her voice is mocking as she says, "Father please forgive me. I can't make it without my man." I'm so disoriented that it takes me a few moments to recognize what she has in her hand. It's my pillow-case, the one with my Broadway fund. "Your car seems to have gotten a flat," she adds, and I realize that her accent had been fake too. We'd been playing each other, but she'd been playing to win.

"You bitch," I gasp. Coughing hurts. Talking hurts. "Water—" I manage.

She looks down at me and starts pulling something out of her hair. Then another. Then another. She scatters the bobby pins across the ground like discarded grenade pins. It seems to go on and on until finally, she pulls her hair off in one swift motion. A wig falls in front of me, and I use it to rub the chemicals out of my face, my eyes. No wonder her husband had been confused when he saw her.

A dark curtain of hair has fallen down around her face, sleek around her shoulders. She leans down, blinking, and when she meets my eyes this time, she's removed contacts to reveal brown eyes.

I blink again, smoke and tears clouding my vision. I recognize her now, my leading lady, the girl who had felt like home. She's the sister of my onetime neighbor in apartment 3B—victim of my Flea-Bitten solo act.

I'm about to call after her, ask her how long I'd been marked, beg to know how she identified me. But pillowcase in one hand and ransom bag in the other, she sidesteps her coughing husband and drives off in his car. I know what I did to her sister, but I wonder what he did wrong. The car's engine echoes like thunder and freedom.

But the freedom's not mine.

Jolene
Grant Jerkins

It was quiet in the bedroom. Mary Louise felt like she might cry. They had only been in bed for ten minutes and she knew it took Kent at least fifteen minutes to fall asleep.

So they both lay there, awake, in the dark.

She needed to say something to him. To clear the air. She had known about his infidelity for over a week now and finally made up her mind to get it out in the open.

Maybe infidelity wasn't the right word for it, but it was close enough.

All during dinner—taco salad—Mary Louise wanted to bring it up. And after the dishes were done, sitting on the couch watching *Wheel of Fortune* together, she almost said something. But didn't. Couldn't. She wanted to ask him about his cheating, but it was just too disturbing, too embarrassing. After the last puzzle was solved (CURIOSITY KILLED THE CAT BURGLAR), Kent went downstairs to the basement and worked on his model railroad. He had a whole little locomotive fantasy world constructed down there—mountains and valleys and Swiss villages and trestles and tunnels. Mary Louise stayed on the couch by herself and watched hour-long dramas about crime scene investigation.

Now, lying here beside him, she could smell vestiges of taco seasoning on his breath, as his exhalations evened out and deepened in the prelude to sleep.

"Kent?"

His breath caught in his throat, and he said, "Huh?"

She paused, quite dramatically, then said, "I just...I need to ask you something."

"What?"

"Do you still love me?"

She heard him sigh. Mary Louise knew that sigh well. She believed that all wives were familiar with that sigh. It was a sigh of resignation and exasperation. It was a sigh that said, *for Christ's sake, are you kidding me with this crap?* But she was surprised when his hand found her hand under the covers, squeezed it, and said, "Of course I do, honey."

"If there was somebody else, would you tell me?"

"There's nobody else. When would I have the time? Or the energy?"

"Kent, all I've ever wanted is for you to be happy. That's all I've ever wanted. And if I'm not what makes you happy, I just want you to—"

"Mary, I'm not cheating on you. I swear."

"I just want you to tell me. We'll work it out."

"There's nobody. I swear. I don't know what else to say."

"If there ever is, just tell me. Don't cheat on me. Don't humiliate me that way."

"You're the only thing in my life. I swear to God."

But that was a lie, and Mary Louise knew it. So she closed her eyes and let the hot tears flow in silence. And she thought, *Jolene. Jolene. Jolene. Jolene.* Over and over and over. Like a spell. An incantation. She pictured

Jolene as she sent thoughts out to her, as though her rival were capable of hearing and responding.

Jolene, I'm begging of you, please don't take my man.

The week before, she'd gone down to the model train room. To clean. Kent didn't like her to clean down there. He was afraid she would break something or throw out some little piece worth keeping. But surfaces collected dust, and she didn't think a feather duster was going to destroy anything.

That particular day she had been a little bored. Kent had left the train out on the tracks. Usually he put it up. So Mary Louise flipped the power switch and heard the transformer hum to life. She nudged the switch forward just a little, and the locomotive moved ahead with hesitation. She pushed the switch a little more, and soon the nine-car train was making its way leisurely around the track. It went under a mountain, hooked a mailbag in a little town. It climbed to where Kent had set tracks high up along the walls with painted scenery. There was a cut-out near the ceiling, at the top edge of the drywall, painted to look like the bricked arch entrance to a tunnel. The HO scale train disappeared into the darkness behind the wall for a few seconds, and then reappeared from another cut-out.

It took about ninety seconds for the train to complete one circuit. She increased the speed, and it did it again, in just under a minute.

Really, it was pretty boring. Once she saw it complete the track, the novelty evaporated. There had been some small thrill in running it alone for the first time, but even that buzz had quickly dissipated. How on earth could a hobby like this keep anyone entertained for hours on end? My God, Kent spent entire weekends down here.

Mary Louise decided to try and see if she could get the train to complete the track in under forty-five seconds. That might be fun.

She had the thing flying pretty soon. She could smell the transformer heating up from pushing it so hard. She had it going so fast, that it derailed one time. She carefully picked the cars up, found no damage, aligned the grooved metal wheels back on the track, and decided to try one last time for the speed record.

The thing screamed down the track. Dangerous. Like an action movie. She imagined the train carrying a deadly virus or a nuclear bomb. If it derailed, it would mean the end of humanity. At this speed, every curve in the track was a potential disaster. She slowed it for the downhill mountain underpass, then barreled it through the little village, picking up considerable speed. It was the uphill climb to those elevated tracks near the ceiling that slowed her down, so she gave it full throttle. The transformer was hot to the touch and giving off the odor of burnt plastic. She was going to ease it back down once it got to the top but didn't time it right, and just as the train disappeared behind the drywall cut-out, she heard it jump the track and fall in the dark space behind the wall.

This was bad. In addition to the end of all humanity, if Kent found out Mary Louise had not only been playing with his train set, but had crashed it, he would be beyond upset.

The man was very particular about his model trains.

She carried a wooden bar stool over to the wall, climbed up, stuck her head through the tunnel opening and peered down into the empty space behind the drywall. It was too dark to see anything.

She went upstairs and found a little LED flashlight in the drawer under the microwave. While she was up there, she grabbed a pair of grill tongs from the utensil drawer, too, figuring she might be able to fish the train cars out from behind that wall.

Once Mary Louise was up on the stool, she stuck her head back through the cut-out. The opening was just barely wide enough for her fit her arm through, too. She clicked on the flashlight. And screamed.

She bumped the back of her head on the drywall, jerking away from the horror she saw back there. The shock and fear had caused her to recoil. She twisted and tumbled from the stool, landing face down on the repurposed ping pong table that supported the sprawling Alpine village.

She had seen a body behind the wall. A corpse.

Mary Louise lay on the table—miniature fir trees poking her stomach and breasts—and cried. She sobbed. She was married to a monster. A serial killer, maybe. She imagined herself doing the correct thing in this situation. She imagined herself getting up and calling 9-1-1 to report what she had found. Let the authorities sort it all out.

Fuck Kent.

That murdering motherfucker.

Then she remembered the cold snap last winter when she had been home alone because Kent was in Las Vegas at a human resources seminar. By herself in bed that night, she heard banging and cracking and called the police to report someone breaking in. A home invasion. Two deputies showed up and cleared the house. They explained that there was no sign of forced entry, and that the sounds were caused by the house contracting in the extreme cold. It was their third such call that night. They had been nice enough about it, but Mary Louise saw the two men exchange a wink and a grin on their way out.

She'd felt like a damn fool.

Maybe she should make sure. Before she called the police. Wouldn't there be a smell? If there was a body back there? It would stink, wouldn't it? She should look one last time. So she could be for-sure. So she wouldn't make a fool of herself. Again.

Flashlight in hand, Mary Louise climbed back up the stool and peered into the recess. It was a body, alright. No doubt about it. A woman's body. But there was something odd about it. For one thing, the body was sitting up. At a little table. With tea cups set out. Tea for two. The woman had auburn hair. Her arms were resting on the tiny table. And there was just something about it that was so familiar. And then it came to Mary Louise that she had set her dolls up like that when she was a little girl, and what she was looking at was not a dead body at all, but a doll. A life size play-pretty.

Kent must have set this up as a practical joke to pull on his buddies. Except that didn't make sense, because Kent didn't ever have friends over. Not down here, anyway. He was particular about people being around his trains.

Mary Louise took the barbecue tongs, reached down,

and prodded the doll. It slumped over and fell to the floor—on top of the derailed train.

How on earth was she going to get down there and get those cars? It wasn't possible. She pulled her head out of the wall and looked around the room, trying to come up with an idea. Maybe she could hook the train out with a fishing pole. Or make something out of coat hangers. She scanned the room. From up on the stool, Mary Louise could see on top of the supply case that rested against the wall just to the left of the tunnel cut-out. The shelves were loaded with supplies like pails of plaster of Paris and extra track and transformers and things like that. Cans of spray paint—green for foliage, white for snow, brown for rocks. From where she stood on the stool, she could see that the top of the shelving unit was covered in thick dust, and even as she reminded herself to run a feather duster up there, she noted that there was a clean spot along the corner. A clean spot in the shape of three fingers and a thumb. As though somebody put their hand up there regularly.

Mary Louse climbed down from the stool and reached up to that spot on the shelf. She used her hip for leverage and gave it a good push. The whole unit moved easily. It seemed to float over the carpeted floor like it was on casters.

There was a door behind it. Just a plain plywood rectangle with a little hook-and-eye latch. It shouldn't have bothered her, this little plain door.

But it did.

Mary opened the door. A long narrow area back there ran the entire length of the wall. Narrow, yes, but roomy enough. Back behind the doll and the little card table, there was a single-size mattress on the floor.

It had clean sheets on it.

She pulled the doll out into the main room. It was heavy, but not as heavy as a real person. Maybe seventy pounds. Dressed casual in blue jeans and a T-shirt.

She was beautiful. The doll. The doll was beautiful. Out in the light, the auburn hair was like flame. The latex skin made Mary think of pink-tinged ivory. The eyes were brilliant emeralds, piercing, drawing Mary Louise in. She couldn't look away. The doll was beautiful.

If she hadn't seen the mattress, Mary Louise's next thought would never have entered her mind. It was too bizarre. It was beyond her comprehension. She could believe Kent was infatuated with the doll, that he was some kind of closet sissy enthralled by huge dolls. But the idea that he kept this doll in order to have sexual relations with it? Not possible. But she had to know. So Mary Louise undressed the doll.

It wasn't a cheap blow-up novelty toy with a circular open mouth like she had seen in comedy movies. It was just like a real person. A replica. Another woman.

It had full, perfectly formed breasts. And down below, what appeared to be a functioning, anatomically correct vagina. Most disturbing, Mary Louise noted that the pink flushed skin tone around the lips was flaking. Worn away. Kent had been getting plenty of use out of it.

That sick son of a bitch.

When she lifted the doll's leg to put the jeans back on, Mary Louise saw that there was a word embossed on the sole of the foot. JOLENE. And under that, a model number.

She searched the little secret room some more and found an envelope. It held a receipt.

Silicone Fantasy Doll.

Model: Jolene.

Weight 30 Kg.

Hair: Auburn

Eyes: Emerald Green

7" Mouth Cavity

Real Human Hair

The total price made her stomach ache. Mary Louise had been doing the dishes by hand for over a year, because Kent said they couldn't afford to replace the broken dishwasher. She put the invoice down after reading there was an option to purchase extra faces for the doll, and that it came with inserts for "hygiene and easy clean-up."

It took her the rest of the afternoon to put the train room (and the sex doll room) back to rights. She had to replace three fir trees that she'd crushed when she landed on the table. But she thought everything would pass inspection.

Then Mary Louise went upstairs, took a Xanax, and lay down on the couch.

What was she going to do? What was she going to do about Kent? About that doll?

Jolene.

She finally got up the nerve to ask Kent if he was cheating on her, but he lied and swore he wasn't. In the end, she decided to do nothing. Not to confront Kent any further. Not yet. She wanted to come to terms with this herself before she dared peer into her husband's sick mind.

Mary Louise stewed on it. Came to view the doll as a rival. Competition. Thought about buying green contacts and dyeing her hair red.

During the day, she couldn't rest knowing that thing was down there. In her house. Under her roof. She decided she wanted to look at it again. So she went downstairs and pulled Jolene out of the dark. Mary Louise noticed that the sheet on the mattress back there was a different color now. He'd changed it.

She carried Jolene upstairs and sat her on the couch.

"Want a Coke?" She asked it. "Slice of pie, maybe? How about an EPT pregnancy test?"

Mary Louise fixed herself a cup of hazelnut coffee and turned on the TV. From the loveseat, she sipped her coffee and watched *The View*. Jolene sat across from her, on the couch, looking toward a plastic ficus tree. Mary Louise got up and tilted the doll's head so that it was watching the television.

After a while, Mary Louise said, "I know you're screwing him."

Jolene neither confirmed nor denied the accusation, and a little later, Mary Louise took Jolene back downstairs and finished up her housework.

She got in the habit of bringing Jolene upstairs every day and putting her back downstairs before Kent got home. She knew it was a weird thing to do, but she liked having the doll visible. Where she could keep an eye on it. Not hidden away.

Not an unseen threat.

Mary Louise would sit and watch television with

Jolene. She would do her housework and drift in and out of the living room. Talking to the doll about anything that popped into her mind.

"*Did you ever see that movie, Harper Valley PTA? With Barbara Eden? That was based on a song. Do you remember that song called 'Ode to Billy Joe?' What do you think they were throwing off that bridge?*"

"*We were best friends. Talked all the time. Cut-up with each other. Laughed. We haven't laughed together in years.*"

"*He's a stranger to us now. Our only son. A stranger. Maybe you blame the drugs. Maybe he was just born like that. I don't know. Maybe we did something that broke him inside. The way we brought him up. I just don't know.*"

"*No, I was a teacher's aide for a long time. Taught deaf children. I still remember a lot of the signs. If you want, I can show you some. Look, this is 'water.' Three fingers like a W. Tap 'em against your chin. See? This one means 'bathroom.' And this is 'friend.' Like this. Let me see your hands. Hook your fingers together. That's it. Friend.*"

"*And he looks me right in the eye, and he says, 'Actually, I do still want sex. Just not from you.'*"

"*And now I'm just a housewife. That's the right word for it, too. I'm married to this house.*"

"*I prayed about it. That's all you can do.*"

"*We were just teenagers. He put an anonymous love letter in my parent's mailbox. My daddy opened it.*"

"*It was atypical. Precancerous. So I was okay. Thank God.*"

"*Mr. Elway, the principal, wanted to have an affair with me. He made it plain.*"

"*Love is an illusion for young people. That's what I've decided.*"

At some point, and without her realizing that a line had been crossed, Jolene began responding to Mary Louise. She wasn't crazy. She understood that Jolene wasn't really speaking, that it was her own voice she was hearing. But if someone had snuck up to the living room window to spy, they would have seen Mary Louise talking to a life-size doll, hands gesticulating—wishing for one of the cigarettes they hadn't held in over a decade. And in the silence that followed, the peeping Tom would have seen Mary Louise cock her head to the side, listening to a high-pitched feminine voice that only she could hear.

It took them a long time to work up to the one thing that they each really wanted to know. *What was he like? What was Kent like when he was alone you?* And so they told each other. Voices hesitant at first. It was uncomfortable. But the truth was gotten at. And they each made peace with it.

And with that peace, Mary Louise felt no humiliation when she acknowledged that Jolene had bested her. She pleaded with her not to take her man. Jolene could have her choice of men, but Mary Louise could never love again. She begged, knowing that her happiness depended on whatever Jolene decided to do. She put it in Jolene's hands. That was all she could do.

As Mary Louise was taking Jolene downstairs before Kent got home, she paused before opening the secret door, and asked Jolene if Kent had ever taken the time to show her his train set, or did he just throw her on the mattress and pump on her. The train was most important thing in his life, after all. It trumped both his women. So she decided to take a minute and show it to her before she put her up for the day.

She pointed out the river pass, the woodland scenes, the coal loader, the functional crossing gates. All of it.

She got the locomotive moving, too. The throttle on the transformer went from zero (stop) to one hundred (full.) By the time she got it up to eighty, the transformer was getting warm. Mary Louise knew she was showing off for Jolene, and pushed it up to ninety. The train shook and shimmied and rocketed down the track. The power pack got hot to the touch, and gave off an ozone odor. The train was whipping along the tracks like death on steel wheels.

Mary Louise pushed the throttle up to ninety-five, cutting her eyes to Jolene and giggling. It was at that moment that two things happened simultaneously. They were both things Mary Louise should have foreseen. First, the train derailed. And then the low rumbling of the electric garage door opener could be heard—even downstairs.

The train was half on and half off the track. Wrecked. It needed to be righted. Jolene was sitting in a cane-back chair, staring mutely at the calamity. She needed to be put away. And the garage door was already closing.

When Kent came inside the house, he would look for Mary Louise. Often, if he'd had a bad day, he grabbed a Coke from the fridge and headed straight for the basement.

There simply wasn't time to put Jolene away and fix

the train both. So she left everything as it was and ran upstairs to intercept Kent.

Running out of the basement like that would damn their already ruined lives.

But even if Mary Louise had noticed that the derailment left the metal train wheels touching both the center rail and the outside rail, she would have thought nothing of it. She would not have known that it could cause a short circuit in the electricity that ran through the track and powered the locomotive's engine. And she certainly had no way of knowing that this short circuit would draw excessive current from the maxed-out transformer, or that the circuit breaker built into the transformer was faulty, that it would fail.

Upstairs, Mary Louise threw her arms around Kent, told him she loved him, and said she wanted to go out for dinner. Golden Corral. Kent said no, he was tired. But Mary Louise pouted and cajoled and produced a few tears until he finally relented. He didn't want a repeat of the *are you cheating on me?* discussion.

Over dinner, Mary Louise decided that there was nothing to do but to let Kent find out that she knew everything. Let him walk downstairs when they got home and see for himself that his secret was out. That she knew about Jolene. She found peace in this. It was time. And there was a possibility that the shared knowledge could bring them closer together. That there could be a healing. And with this hope in mind, she tried to talk to her husband. Just little things. To reconnect with him. To be authentic. To be his friend.

"Did you know this means water?"

"Do you remember when I had that mole removed?"

"I was thinking about calling Ben. See how he is."

"Remember when my daddy read that letter you sent me?"

"Maybe I can give you a massage tonight?"

"Kent, Kent, you never listen to me. What are thinking about?"

"I'm sorry. I just want to get home. I have an idea for a new route."

And Mary Louise thought, *fine*. They would go home. And he would see Jolene sitting out in the open, gazing at the train disaster. Like a lone survivor. And then Kent would know.

They didn't talk on the drive back. With the windows rolled up, the inside of the car a silent vacuum. And when they turned onto their street and saw the red staccato lights of the fire trucks, Mary Louise remembered the transformer. How hot it got. The ozone smell.

Their home was fully ablaze. They got out of the car and ran to it. The firefighters kept them back. The heat was an enormous wall.

Mary Louise imagined Jolene, the flames licking her silicone skin, the ivory flesh blistering and popping and charring. The real-human-hair singing. The eyes of emerald green going dark. All of Jolene reduced to a liquid pool, bubbling blackly away to nothingness.

Kent was telling her something, his voice rising over the chant of the flames, but Mary Louise was having trouble understanding. She thought he might have said something about his trains. But she couldn't hear him. What she heard was Jolene's feminine high-pitched cries, reedy and sharp with pain and terror. Calling out to Mary Louise in a voice that broke her heart. A voice that was all the more haunting because it was her own.

Kent was shouting now, trying to get Mary Louise's attention. She focused on him and heard, "...fingers. What are you doing?"

She looked down and saw that she had thrust her arms out in front of herself, holding them stiff and rigid in a way that made her think about zombies in old-time monster movies, but she had her forefingers hooked together, forming a symbol, like something religious. And she said, "Friend. It means friend."

Mary Louise looked up at her husband, searching his face for acceptance—or at least understanding—but what she saw was the red light from the emergency beacons and the yellow flickering of the flames had colored Kent's face in way that made him look like a villager. A tribesman. And she understood that she and Kent were—in this exact moment—as close as they would ever be. Homeless primitives stripped of all artifice. Their primordial selves. Things might be better for a little while, but she knew in her heart that from this moment forward, they would begin filling their lives again. A new house would be secured, complete with carpeted man cave. Mary Louise's Xanax prescription would get refilled—the dosage likely increased. Maybe Kent wouldn't feel like starting from scratch with his model railroad hobby. But something else would take its place.

And maybe her husband would have need of her one cold night.

But before long, something else would take her place.

I'm the Only Hell
My Mama Ever Raised
Eryk Pruitt

The woman caught Donnie Ray off guard. She never so much as said her name, nor offered her hand to shake. No sooner had she laid eyes on him than she stomped across the asphalt in front of his momma's house and threw wild a finger to his face.

"You can't park there." She pointed to his eighteen wheeler. It took the length of the yard where the Stringers used to live. Where she lived now. "If you park in front of my mailbox, then my mail won't get delivered."

"Ma'am..." Donnie Ray didn't like how his voice creaked out of his throat. He couldn't remember the last time he'd spoken to someone else. "Something tells me I'm not going to be long, so..."

Rather than finish what he was saying, he cut her a look from beneath the brim of his Stetson. Normally, that shut folks up. This woman, however, would not be deterred by something so simple as a pair of cold, road-weary eyes.

"That's what the man said who drove that pickup right there." She pointed to his Uncle Ollie's rusty red Chevy, which had been parked beneath the willow tree in Momma's yard. "And the man driving that blue car, and the family in that station wagon."

He knew some of the cars parked in the front yard, some he didn't.

"And I don't know for certain," she said, "but I'm pretty sure you can't drive that thing down a residential street. Maybe I ought to call somebody and find out."

Donnie Ray pulled his Stetson off his head and held it at the waist. He'd stopped to change after taking his brother's call. He was many things, sure, but a man who would stand at his momma's deathbed wearing dirty work clothes was not one of them.

"Ma'am, maybe you heard my momma's sick in there." He felt his back teeth grind. "Has been for a while."

"I hate to hear it, but—"

"I can't tell you much except I'm told she's not long." Donnie Ray could see Darrell, his brother, watching them from the front screen door. He looked older..."They wouldn't have called me if she weren't pretty far gone."

The woman had more to say, but something told her to keep it to herself. It sure wasn't Donnie Ray, which didn't make a lick of sense to him. Out there—in the real world—folks gave him a wide berth. Or, most did. The ones that didn't cut him one had good cause not to, whether given or taken, which gave him good pause when dealing with the little housewife.

"Ma'am, if you don't mind..."

"I'm real sorry to hear about your mom. Mine passed, oh, about eight, nine years now. Cancer. It was real horrible, especially at the end."

Donnie Ray squinted.

"When finally she went, it was almost a relief," said

the woman. "Now, I don't mean to sound like an ogre, but she was in so much pain. We'd done all we could do, so it was all over but the shouting. And there was plenty shouting, with all of her affairs to look after. Nearly drove our family apart, it got so bad."

Donnie Ray promised he'd punch himself if he offered her the slightest of condolences.

She did not need them: "I hate to see that happen to a family." She leaned forward about an inch. "You all have discussed her affairs, haven't you?"

He knew she imagined the place with a fresh sod and green grass. Without Momma's flowers she grew out of coffee cans or clawfoots or TV sets...out of an old toilet or old barbecue grill or old what-have-you. Maybe a fresh coat of paint and a few new boards across the house or, hell, maybe with the place burned to the ground.

"She's got people handling that," Donnie Ray said. His fingernails dug into the brim of that Stetson. "Me, I'm just here to see my momma off. So, if you will kindly excuse me..."

He shouldered past her.

"You got an hour," the woman called after him. "Then I call the city about that truck."

The screen door slapped shut behind Darrell as he stepped onto the porch to greet his brother. Darrell was a big old boy and his good clothes liked to tug open at the seams. He drank from a can of beer and sucked on a plug of chaw. He side-eyed the neighbor woman, then spit tobacco into the brown grass between two of Momma's coffee-can marigolds.

"That woman ain't nothing but mean," Darrell said.

"I can't believe some of the things she gets away with saying to Momma."

Donnie Ray looked his brother up and down, from his tennis shoes to the fish hook in the bill of his seed store hat.

"Me neither," was all he could say.

Momma wanted to know who else was out there, standing in her living room.

"Oh everybody, I reckon." Donnie Ray held his Stetson at his belt. He kept a tidy distance between he and his momma.

"Is Tommy out there?"

Donnie Ray lowered his head. "Tommy died three years back, Momma."

His momma laughing is what got him to look up. She'd lost nearly everything to her except for that grin. She laughed so hard, she fell to a fit of coughing.

"I know he's dead," she said with a wink. "I'm just funning with you."

Donnie Ray did his best to smile. "They're all out there, Momma. Uncle Dave, Barbara...Uncle Branch..."

"Those kids?"

"They're out there."

Momma rolled her eyes.

"You don't like Branch's kids?"

She spoke slow all her life, so folks wouldn't miss anything. She spoke slower now. "Let me put it this way," she said. "If those ones are the future of this family, it's a good thing I'm headed for the door. I couldn't stand to watch it."

The skin tightened around Donnie Ray's lips.

"It's the morphine, son."

Donnie Ray nodded.

"I've never took so much as a drink my whole life," she said. "The only wine I ever drank was at church and I always felt like I'd need help back to my pew after. This morphine has me wishing I could go back and do things different."

"Oh? Like what?"

"For one thing, I wouldn't have waited to now to take morphine."

It was Donnie Ray's turn to laugh.

"I wouldn't have wasted so much time trying to get your sister into a college." His momma looked to the wall. "A lot of good that did me."

"Her husband takes good care of her."

"I reckon so."

Donnie Ray took a knee alongside the bed. He felt thirteen years old again. It was the same bed she'd shared with his daddy. He could remember standing in that very spot on Christmas mornings, begging them both to wake up so he could open presents. He could remember hiding beneath it when he played games with his big brother and sister. Or how his head had caught the edge of the frame one day when he and Darrell were rough-housing, and needed six stitches. The bed seemed smaller now, as did his mother inside of it.

"Want to know what else I would do different?"

He did. More than anything.

She licked her lips with a pale, purple tongue.

"Do you remember the night your daddy died?" she asked him.

"I never forgot it," said Donnie Ray. Were he the kind of guy to expound on things, he'd have told her he spent more than his fair share of time remembering it. How if he had three wishes, he'd go back to that sticky summer to wait behind the feed store where his daddy worked. He'd wait to catch those bastards that stuck him and left him to bleed out. He'd make them pay.

"I tried so hard to be a good woman," said Momma. "The way I was raised...They'd look down on us, much like I reckon they do now. Your grandfather was a rough-and-tumble sort and my mother, she...I worked so hard to make sure we didn't turn out like that. That's what everybody expected."

It took all he had for Donnie Ray to reach other that blanket and take his mother's bony wrist. There was very little warmth to her.

"But when I saw your father that night..."

Again, she fell to coughing. She'd worked herself up something fierce and Donnie Ray wondered if this was it.

"Momma, settle down. I'll run fetch Aunt—"

"You'll do no such thing," she said. "You'll sit right there and let me finish my story."

Donnie Ray returned to his knees. "Yes, ma'am."

"I'd had my suspicions." She looked to the ceiling. "I'd seen the way he smiled at her in church. I'd catch him whispering into the telephone late at night. Or taking the dog for extra-long walks."

"Momma—"

"And I knew when all of a sudden he was coming home an hour later from work..."

Donnie Ray thought his chest would explode. His jaw hung on a loose hinge.

"When I pulled into the parking lot," said his momma, "I found them parked in his pickup truck. She had her face in his lap and I don't reckon I could stand the look on his face. His stupid, stupid face."

His momma opened her mouth wide and made a face like a fish on the riverbank, sucking air. It took more than a moment for Donnie Ray to realize she was mocking his father's orgasm.

"I didn't realize I was holding a steak knife until I'd already stuck him with it."

She let that sit a bit before she started up again.

"I got him a couple more times for good measure. That woman didn't know what was going on, she kept working his crank. Maybe she thought he bucked and hollered because she was that good, I don't know. I guess she got to wondering why all this blood was washing down over her, because she looked up to see me sticking him with the dinner knife and she wasted no time climbing out of that pickup."

Donnie's grip tightened around his mother's wrist. For years, he'd imagined the faces of the men who had killed his father. He'd seen them every time he'd gotten into a bar fight, or needed to defend himself from another inmate in the Yard. One night, he'd taken so many pills, he'd seen them in a girl he'd picked up at a truck stop and taken down an old service road.

Now, all he could think of was the sad look on his momma's face.

"Why are you telling me this, Momma?"

"I told you there was things I would have done different."

"You don't need to worry about that now," he said. "None of that matters."

"But it does, son."

Donnie Ray waited for her to catch her breath.

"I ain't sorry I killed him," she said.

"Yes, ma'am."

"I'm more sorry I didn't kill her."

Donnie Ray looked into his mother's eyes. The lights were on, sure, but not for much longer. She drew herself upright.

"For months, I sat by that window in the living room. You know what they'd say about me?"

"That you were waiting for Daddy."

She nodded. "They said I'd lost my mind."

Donnie Ray remembered. She'd sit by the window, rub her fretting cloth between thumb and forefinger, and study the horizon. Once a kid in school said something about it and they'd had to peel Donnie Ray off him. Kid ate through a straw, but didn't talk shit about his momma any more.

"I wasn't waiting for your daddy," she said. "I was waiting for the police. I thought any day that woman would break down and tell her husband what happened and soon they'd come to fetch me."

Donnie Ray dropped his head into his hands. He'd withstood some torture in his time, but nothing like his mother's deathbed.

"But that woman never broke down. She never told her husband, and they never came to arrest me. After a while, I started to wonder what kind of woman couldn't be bothered by what happened, and what your father saw in her."

She shuddered and fell quiet. Donnie Ray held his breath. He would have held it longer, had she not started up again.

"It got to where it was all I thought about, and here I lay." She looked her boy dead in the eye. "I want not to think about it ever again."

"There, there." He pat her wrist. "It's okay, Momma."

"It's not okay," she said. "Not in the slightest. I can't lay here dying knowing she still draws air. It will eat at me all the way to heaven."

"For all you know, she's long gone, Momma. How do you even know she is still alive?"

His momma pulled a scrap of paper from beneath her blanket. It had been written with a shaky hand.

"This is her name and where she lives," said his momma. "And where you'll find her tonight."

Her arm felt warmer, and Donnie Ray had no idea if it was because his own blood had run cold.

"I can't ask your brother," she said. "He's a big old boy, sure, but he's sweet and simple."

"No...Momma—"

"Him and your sister...But you...You've carried with you a darkness I ain't seen in my other ones."

Donnie Ray wiped his face with a flat, sweaty palm.

"More than Darrell, more than Barbara..." It took all she had to manage the rest of her words. "You can see me to the door in peace."

He exhaled, and felt no further cause to stand.

I'M THE ONLY HELL MY MAMA EVER RAISED

* * *

When finally Donnie Ray's momma passed, it took nearly a week. One by one, the cars disappeared from the front lawn. They relocated across town to Bynum's where the old man running the place agreed to set her into the ground next to their daddy.

They did it on a sunny day.

She'd asked for a simple box, but her family thought different. Barbara got her husband to throw in some extra money to send her out real fine. She wanted no fuss, but they reckoned her in no position to negotiate.

There, by the graveside, Donnie Ray knelt at the box for longer than he should have. He said his goodbyes, and not for the first time that week. When he rose to his feet, he found his brother Darrell and their Uncle Branch waiting for him.

Donnie Ray said, "Boys..."

"We got a couple matters to discuss," said Uncle Branch.

Donnie Ray wore a brand new pair of slacks. He stuffed his fists into them.

"Momma left us the house," said Darrell. "All her things."

"Way that neighborhood's going," said Uncle Branch, "that ought to net a pretty penny."

"I don't want none of it," said Donnie Ray. "I've done fine on my own thus far."

"Now, Donnie Ray..." If Darrell had more to say, he kept it to himself. Instead, he turned to Uncle Branch for the words.

102

"It's probably best if you sat down with us and took a look at a few things."

Donnie Ray looked back at his momma's coffin. Over the hill waited two Mexican boys with shovels. They smoked cigarettes and waited for their day to end.

Uncle Branch said, "Last thing we need is for you to get down the road and change your mind."

"I won't."

"Because getting you on down the road is real important to us." Uncle Branch, feeling his oats. "Last thing we want to do is get in your way of it."

"I'm on my way."

On the way out, Donnie Ray touched the box they'd put her in. He thought back to when he was a kid. The last time his daddy signed him up for Little League. How he'd struck out to end the game and every kid made sport of him. How it was the only time he'd seen his daddy cry. And he thought back as well to the look on his momma's face after Donnie Ray'd shown the other fellas exactly what he could do with a baseball bat.

He'd thought about that look on her face his entire life.

He thought about it then at that fine box his brother and sister put her into, and reckoned they'd have plenty far to go in order to catch up to him.

Donnie Ray wasn't halfway back to his big rig when up came Darrell. He'd finally mustered the gumption, but kept a distance of ten, fifteen yards.

"Donnie Ray..." he called. "It ain't like you was there for her anyway."

Donnie Ray chewed on it some.

"Maybe," he said. He decided he'd stop by that neighbor lady's on the way out of town. It wouldn't take him longer than ten minutes. "But I'm here for her now."

God's Gonna Cut You Down
Jay Requard

The burner vibrated, the blue light of its outer screen shredding the darkness as John opened his eyes and rolled over. He grabbed the phone with a desperate speed, flipping open the clamshell before he even checked the number.

"Thresher?" called the monotone voice when he placed the receiver to his ear. Distinct with its Slavic accent—probably Ukrainian—it breathed thickly through the speaker. The caller was probably fatter than most, a common trait among the Russian gangs.

"Speaking," John whispered.

"Thirty now, wired the moment we hang up if you wish. Another thirty when you're done."

John arched an eyebrow. That was a lot of money for one person. "Are they hot?"

"No idea. He's at the Gold's on Capital."

He checked the time on the burner's screen. 12:00 AM. He brought the phone back to his ear. "Is the car on the way?"

"Outside your door."

Hanging up, John swung his legs over the side of the bed and put both feet on the cold floor, the concrete's chill caused by the lackluster heating of the old warehouse. Walking to an armoire set against the red brick wall, he clicked on the tower lamp beside it before he opened both doors. Jeans, thick socks, a white T-shirt and his old army boots—the same ones he had issued to him at Bragg before Korengal—and finally, a small box locked with a seven-digit custom combination.

9:2:2:9:7:2:5.

Cast in black steel, the Sig 228 gleamed as it lay dark in its foam square, a devil's brand for the devil's man. He loaded a thirteen round clip, all traces of fear and hopelessness fleeing when he heard it click into the grip. Days in dusty hills and misted valleys disappeared into the depths of memory as he pulled back the slide, loading the only bullet he planned to use. Sticking it in a small gym bag with a few clothes and a suppressor, he threw on an old red canvas coat that had belonged to his dad, the last thing the old man had bought before leaving 'Nam and coming home.

John hadn't brought anything back from Afghanistan, save the damnation he carried.

The asphalt shone bright from the cold rain as he stepped out to his porch, and as he had been told, a black Yukon sat in the driveway, idling like a lion at rest. The passenger-side door opened, and out stepped a skinny man dressed in a black hoodie and white jeans, his baseball cap studded in a multitude of glittering gemstones.

"You the man?" the blond boy called in his thick Russian accent.

"I am," said John, his hands down at his side. He scanned his street, the old industrial buildings of Raleigh's south side looming like the close-up hills of a place he fought not to think of. Loading into the backseat of the Yukon, John leaned his head to the right to get a look at the driver. A bald man with a snarling wolf tattoo inked into the flesh of his brawny neck, he wore a pair of square "shade" sunglasses, the pink kind that many kids in the techno clubs wore when they were bombed on ecstasy. He stared ahead, rubbing at the irritated flesh around his nostrils.

The blond retook his front seat on the passenger side. "You like music, bro?"

"I like it fine," John said. "Why?"

"What you want to listen to? We love all the tunes here from America."

"Got any Cash?"

"We have fucking everything, bro." The blond lightly nudged the driver with his fist. "Right, Sergei?"

The driver said nothing as he pulled out into the streets. As the soft thrum of a guitar vibrated out of the speakers, John watched through the window as empty roads dotted in wet lamp posts and old brick warehouses passed by, quiet against the deep voice that started to speak.

As God began to sing, his soul calmed for the business ahead.

If tonight was an indicator, business was booming.

The midnight riders arrived at the Gold's Gym on Capital Boulevard, long stretch of road crammed with shopping centers, motels, and vice. Men in deep coats stood at corners, hands in their pockets, shivering in down as they kept on the lookout for potential buyers. If one wanted to find a hooker in Raleigh, they went online, and if they went online, most of the better-looking ones were usually at those motels.

Pink and white neon lights bathed John's face as he stepped out of the black Yukon, a dead man's words fading from the speakers in the door. Carrying his gym bag low at his side, he entered Gold's and glanced at the attendant manning the desk.

Tall and eastern European, he met John's gaze and pointed in the direction of the locker rooms. "He has tribal tattoos on his arms."

Straight ahead, John passed by tweaked-out junkies and jacked-up bodybuilders who worshiped their bodies into the wee hours, and entered a small hallway that led back to an exit and two doors set to the left. Checking behind him one more time, he fished out his cell.

Sergei answered on the other side, the first time he had spoken at all. "Ja?"

"Bring the car around the back to the exit on the northwest side."

The call ended.

Pushing open the door to the locker room, John marched inside, taking his time to make sure his steps did not echo off the tile intersection where people dumped their used towels or weighed themselves on the scale. A shower sprayed somewhere in the back, moistening the air with a warm, clean smell.

No voices.

He wove through the interconnected labyrinth of showers, sinks and mirrors. Finding a bench and an empty cell of open lockers, he quickly opened his gym back to extract his pistol and screwed on the suppressor. Down a short hallway of stalls and toilets, John saw the first showers within the next passage, their glass doors clouded to a bright blue color. Edging the corner, he peered around.

Steam rose from only one of the shower stalls, the tile beneath flooded with water and a shadow to accompany its mirror.

He waited a few more minutes for the man to exit, his tanned body dripping wet. Heavily muscled and dark haired, jagged streaks of black ink covered his arms in geometric curves and spikes. Paying no attention, he sauntered toward the nearest alcove of lockers, out of John's sight.

Gun in both hands and crouched low, John breached the shower hall and crept, his boots quiet against the plastic floor. Reaching the next corner, he found the target sitting on a bench before an open locker, busying about with a pack of cigarettes.

John held his breath, pivoted, and fired two rounds. Blood flowered from a well-formed chest and smooth forehead, followed by an explosion of brain matter, the thud of a body and the smell of gun smoke.

Dawn tinted the sky pink as John leaned against the window of the Waffle House outside Apex, North Carolina, a little town that had somehow lasted in a place bereft of the rustic soul he had grown up with. The tobacco fields were replaced with suburbs and schools, the old forests curated for little more than the supposed happiness of well-off America.

Shit like that didn't matter to him as Veronica came by, an angel's smile on her face and a pot of black coffee in her hand. Dressed in the requisite diner uniform, the pale blue button-up and stained brown smock did little to hide her beauty. Her mane of dirty blonde hair pulled back in a ponytail, she leaned close as she refilled his cup.

"Morning," she said in the chilly quiet of the diner. The old cook worked over his flat iron behind her, sizzling the hash browns, eggs, and bacon that John had ordered with his waffle. "Up late?"

"Had issues with some permits in the new buildings. Found an inspector friend of mine who was up," he replied, his throat warmed from the first sip he took. Their eyes met, and sneaking his hand across the speckled black laminate, he touched his fingers to hers.

Veronica's smile widened. "I'm off at two today. Will you be busy?"

"Probably not."

"I was thinking we could go to your place," she said. "My roommates think we're starting to get too noisy."

He chuckled at the assessment, letting it provide cover while he considered the situation. He lived in an empty warehouse, with only a bed, a couch, a table to eat and work on, and a kitchen that took up an eighth of the space. Everything else, left bare, bore the silent anguish of the years in the desert. With only that cold bed to offer her, he preferred the warmth and safety of someplace else, swaddled in welcome darkness of someone else.

At some point she would push.

"Maybe," he said. "Let me see if I can get it cleaned up. I have to warn you, there isn't a lot in it."

"Well, of course not," Veronica replied, shaking her shoulders. "It hasn't had a woman's touch yet."

John simply closed his eyes and smiled as she laughed.

He flipped open the burner as he stepped into his truck, checking to see if any messages had arrived. The blue screen glowed empty. Slipping it back into the pocket of his coat, John drove down US-1, back toward Raleigh. First to the bank, then off to some furniture store to find a coffee table to place between the TV and his couch.

Did he even have clean sheets?

He went to one of those ridiculous shops at Crabtree to buy new linens and a coffee table, something the sales girl promised would be very attractive. So, with fresh bed sheets and a red-painted coffee table, fourteen hundred rolled to his front door. A goddess in a white daffodil sun dress, leather knee boots and a smile that would draw a sniper's eye appeared.

Out the door, through the streets, lips brushed and fingers tangled in gentle twines over local brews and simple dishes, until curious conversation and glances led them back to John's home. Gunshots and bloodstained lockers were replaced with the smell of cold night, the char of an ineffective heater and the silence broken by the tap of Veronica's boots on the bare floor.

John watched her the first half hour after she walked in, saying nothing as she surveyed the sparse condo. Barefoot on the cold concrete between the kitchen and his couch, Veronica asked the simple questions civilians always asked: "How long have you been here?"

"Where's the bathroom?"

"Well, what do you want to do?"

He gave her everything she asked for, answered every question, until at some point they sat on the couch at midnight, held close beneath the afghans John had— maybe his mother had bought them before she died. A bottle of beer rested on his thigh as he set his naked feet on the new coffee table, he relaxed, content as Veronica's warmth eased the old pains carbines and IED's had pounded into the joints.

"John?" she whispered, sleepy.

He buried his nose into the soft tresses of her honey hair. "Yeah?"

"I like your place," she said. "Maybe we could come here a bit more?"

John stilled, the scattered noise of his flat screen faraway.

He had known she would push.

He *knew* better than to let her.

"Okay," he said.

Lips met, clothes slipped off in the push and pull to the cold bed, and there in a lightless world, Veronica swaddled John in warmth and safety.

It was the first time he felt at home.

The burner buzzed.

Groggy, John blinked a few times before the pre-paid phone rang a second time, its alert expanding past the first vibration into a grating melody. Snatching it up, he flipped open the clamshell and checked on Veronica to make sure she had not awaken. Still in the moonlight cutting through the large windows on the eastern wall, she lay like a statue of some forgotten goddess, the kind he had seen shattered in the ruins of old valley temples by the hammers of the devout, acts made for a failed god who had replaced the failed gods that came before him.

He placed his ear to the receiver.

"Go to Vitali's stall at the fish mart. Eight o'clock," Sergei's thick Russian voice said. The line died.

His breath caught in the air, chilled to visibility as he knocked a cigarette loose from the pack he had drawn from his pocket. Leaned against the white wall near the entrance to Raleigh's fish mart at the Farmers Market, Vitali's stony expression remained as impassive as John had always known it to be as the old man's faded blue eyes slid up to look at him, the orbs bulging in his skull like his stomach did over the band of his sweatpants. Clad in a white apron stained with fish guts, he fished inside one of the pockets, his heavy brow pinched in confusion.

"Shit, you always forget," John said, pulling a red lighter out of his jean's pocket. "Here."

Vitali smiled at him as he flicked alive a flame, lighting the end of his bit. Taking a deep draw, he blew rancid smoke through his nose. "But you always remember, Ivanovich."

John grunted. Standing between the white brick building that held the fish mart and the next one that held the produce and meat sellers, they watched as farmers from all over North Carolina unloaded their pickup trucks and trailers beneath a clear winter sun.

Vitali finished his cigarette and threw the butt on the asphalt, grinding it beneath his shoe. "You're work recently was good. Very good. But there's a new problem."

John pulled his hands from the pockets of his jacket, blowing heat into his cupped hands. "Not for me. I did what I was told and you gave me my money. Beyond that I know nothing."

"It is not that simple." Vitali rubbed his fingers in his sunken eyes. "At least not now."

The weight of his Sig felt heavy stuck in its holder, and hands on his hips, he leaned back. "Who was he then?"

"A client's son. Some Raleigh corporate pimp. We pressed him to pay his dues for the protection we provided and he reneged." Waving John to follow, Vitali led them back into the fish mart, going to his stall where salmon and halibut lay frozen in their ice boxes, their scales gleaming under the fluorescent lights. Grabbing a cleaver from his cutting block, Vitali retrieved one of the halibuts and hacked its head off. "We've not received his surrender yet."

"So?" John asked, watching as his old mentor dressed the fish of its bones.

"You know how our business is, Ivanovich," said Vitali. "Money talks, and if he has not started to talk with us, then who is he talking to?"

"There's no one left in this city besides the Bratva with enough sway to make any of it matter."

"This client is a New Yorker."

John paused at the information. Few of the cartels and old families paid little attention to North Carolina beyond its banking and business-friendly atmosphere, and the attention of a northern contingent coming south would cause often deterred those from wars with the Ukrainians. Killing a snot-nosed son of some local businessman who failed to pay his debts offered even less of an incentive.

But New York was New York. Those folks thought they played by a different set of rules.

"Where are those two kids you had pick me up?"

"Sergei and Antoni?" Vitali rolled his eyes and coughed. "Probably in one of those ugly little clubs in the city. Those boys spend money like its water."

Walking through the doors, John set a deep frown as the pulsing beat blaring out of the speakers reached his ears. The girl behind the glass window by the entrance paid him little attention as he slid past the booth, too busy with her game of solitaire to charge. The inside of Pure Gold in Cary, North Carolina, was cast in purple neon, the lights lurid as the lone dancer gyrating on the stage in room's center. Behind the stage, sitting at a table littered with empty liquor bottles, Sergei watched the girl shake her bare breasts for his offered dollar, turning around slowly and lowering them to present the band of her G-string.

John passed through the murkiness, coming within five feet of Sergei's table before the driver noticed him. His hands out at his sides, he approached slowly. "Pistol's in the belt."

Sergei looked at him, the circles around his eyes made darker by the purple lights. He used his foot to push back the third chair at the table, offering the seat. "On my hip."

Taking the black chair, John scooted up to the table, his hands on the round, black surface. The two sat there, watching the girl dance to Motley Crue and then Master P, saying nothing until Antoni stumbled out of the bathrooms, his gait crooked and unbalanced.

"Hey, it's the midnight rider," he said, his reddened face opened in a wild grin. He clapped John hard when he retook the leftover seat, reeling in drunkenness as he tried to steady himself. "What are you doing here, my friend? Get bored in that cold home of yours?"

Unsmiling, John met the skinny Ukrainian's pale gaze, cold against the foolish happiness of the blond and the terse stoniness of his companion. "Did you two know who I took care of?"

"What do you mean?" Antoni asked, squinting at the question. "We talk to lots of people. Pretty girls, funny guys, like Sergei here," he said, nudging his friend in the arm. Wordless, Sergei poured more vodka into the empty shot glass set between them. Somehow the trickle seemed louder than the music in John's ears as he watched it fall.

"You picked me up two nights ago, boy," John replied, gruff. "Do you know who I was supposed to meet at the gym on central?"

Sergei's dull brown eyes shifted toward Antoni.

His smiled faded, Antoni took the vodka shot and pounded it back, wincing as he swallowed. "Some rich man's son. Does it matter now?"

"Someone might approach you looking for information on what happened that night," said John. "Call me if that happens."

"Or?" asked Sergei. His voice, a deep, rough baritone, rumbled out of his broad chest.

"Or what?" said John. He rose from his chair, his stare bored at the driver. "We're just talking, aren't we?"

"For now," Sergei answered, his hand floating at the each of the table.

The tension between the two thickened over the sickly-sweet smell of the stripper as she wiggled her ass, the pulsing beats through the speakers, the flashes of her movements. They stared at each other, neither cowed by each other's grim sincerity. Antoni remained silent, too drunk to care and too infatuated with the girl.

John opened the door of his home to find Veronica sitting on the couch in front of his television, wrapped in the comforter from his bed and wearing only the shirt he had worn the previous night before during their date. She smiled broadly as he entered, turning her attention away from the football game on the flat screen.

"Hey, you," she called. "Get the pipe fixed in your tenant's bathroom?"

"Took a bit longer than expected, but everything should be fine," he replied, an easy lie built on another. He plopped down on the couch beside, somewhat amazed by the angelic woman sitting next him. He wished he could have told his friends back in Afghanistan how he had ended up here—if they hadn't all died. The grim thought did little to drag at this unexpected happiness. Reaching over, he laid a calloused hand on her thigh. "What have you been up to?"

"Just watching TV," she said, sheepish. "I may have eaten your leftovers in the fridge."

"That's okay. I hear we can replace those," he said, amused.

"Oh, can we?" She twisted on the couch and laid back, her head in his lap. "This has been a perfect weekend, you know."

"Yeah, save for a faulty pipe."

"So what now, Mr. Mint? There are still hours in the day."

Rubbing the black stubble on his chin, John looked to one of the large warehouse windows set in the northern wall. Outside grey clouds streaked a pale blue sky, and try as he did, he could not think of a single thing to do other than what he was doing now. He chuckled at the absurdity of life.

"What if we just stayed in and ordered a pizza?" he proposed, hardly serious.

Veronica smiled her white grin at him, a picture of redemption that promised that, perhaps, the damnation he had brought back from the desert might be lifting. Turning her body against his, she curled under the flower comforter and shut her eyes like some satisfied feline. "Somewhere local."

A half-eaten pizza laid flat on its open box, the cheese mottled and yellow after hours of letting the air dry until it was hard and rubbery. Neither John nor Veronica cared, twisted in a post-coital embrace upon the couch. The sunlight dappling the concrete turned the gray to gold, and stretching across the floor, it streaked the white walls.

Gunfire shattered the windows, spraying shards of grass.

John covered Veronica with both arms as rounds powdered the wall behind the couch, raining down bits of dust and dry wall. Hundreds of rounds snapped the evening air before chaos died to an absolute silence, which filled with the baying of neighborhood dogs, screeching tires, and a young woman's terrified sob.

"Are you hurt?" John whispered, looking to the floor for where he left his gun. When he felt her shake her head he let go and went for it. One hand on the grip, he ran towards the front door.

Outside the cold fogged his breath, and searching the street, he raised his gun at a black Yukon as it turned away at the end of road, but held his first shot as it disappeared.

For John, it was simple math.

Charging back into his home, he found Veronica still huddled on the floor, searching her cloths for her cell phone. "Don't," he said in a voice he had never used in front of her, a voice that hearkened back to grim days under the sun.

"We have to call..." Veronica sobbed again, her hands shaking. She looked to the iron in his hand. "Why, John? Why do you have a gun?"

Unflinching, John walked past the weeping woman on his floor, headed for his armoire. "Because I need it."

She followed, stepping gently over the glass. "Why? Why would you need it? Did you bring it back from the war?" Veronica reached for his arm, stopping him as he pulled out a fresh T-shirt.

He glared.

Shrinking back, she stood silent before him, wearing the face every civilian wore when they saw him for who he really was—a man with the devil in him.

She had pushed, and as John had known all along, there would be no home for him when he returned.

"Stay or go," he said, tugging on his shirt. "You won't like my answers."

Vitali had called after sunset, a rare thing for a man who never spoke to John unless they met.

"Come to the fish mart, Thresher. We have them."

The drive had been quiet beneath the graying skies, filled with a silence that spelled something worse than any form of hell John had heard spoken from the lips of the blessed, a void of life, love, and a future. Down the black highways sandwiched between forests of skeleton branches and dull, dark hills, he yearned for the sound of gunfire, of mortars and desert winds.

His gun lay light on his lap, a tool readied for a work he would relish.

Veronica had begged him not to leave. She had cried, and screamed, and pounded on his chest, whispering every promise she had that they could make this work, that whatever happened was by mere chance, not something to pay back with anger, hate—all the things John knew so well.

The farmer's market was empty when he pulled into the parking lots, save for a few cars he recognized.

And that black Yukon.

Vitali answered the back door, silently waving him in before bolting it shut. In the center of the concrete floor that made up the fish market sat Sergei, bound and bloody on an old wicker chair. Antoni's corpse slumped forward in the seat beside his, blood running from the hole in his forehead to stain his white pants and neon-sprayed shirt. A few of Vitali's lieutenants stood in a circle around them, smoking cigarettes and playing on their smart phones.

"What's going to happen now?" John asked.

"We'll have a war," Vitali answered, tired. He shook his head. "They gave us up for twenty grand, Thresher. Is there no honor anymore?"

"Never was, old man." John went forward, drew his gun from his coat, and entered the circle.

"Fucking American," Sergei screamed when he saw him emerge into the light. "Fucking ugly, dumb, American! I hope they rape your whore! I hope they rape her!"

John fired two rounds into his skull. Without another moment of attention to the bodies, he returned to Vitali's side. "Call me when the fireworks start."

Unlocking the door to his house, John had not expected to find Veronica there, but to his surprise there she was, seat on the couch before the television, her naked feet on the recently bought coffee table. She did not look his way, deciding to stare forward in silence. The glass on the floor glittered in the light of the fluorescents set in the ceiling.

He drew his gun and unloaded it, leaving it on the table by the door. "Did you stay here all day?" he called to her, monotone.

She said nothing. Looking to her chest, John noticed that her breasts did not rise or fall. Slowly he inched forward. "Veronica?"

No answer. Waking into the space between the TV and the coffee table, John stopped when he noticed she held something in her lap. A frame picture leaned against her stomach, and behind the clear plastic smiled a father soon, one a well-dressed businessman, the other a muscle-bound man with his arms covered in black tribal tattoos.

Red dripped from a clean bullet hole in Veronica's forehead.

Wordless, John's breath caught in his chest, and his knees gave out. Drowning in rivers of tears, clenched teeth, and damnation, knew then and there a single truth:

He should have pushed her away.

Ain't Livin' Long Like This
Bobby Nash

Jamie Southern grew impatient.

She hated waiting...for anything. That included a table at her favorite Hollywood bistro, the cinema, or police headquarters when she needed information. So, naturally, her profession of choice involved sitting around waiting for someone outside of her control to do something that was also out of her control. It frustrated her no end, but she tried to cope.

Jamie Southern was a private detective and a good one at that. Before taking over the agency started by her late father and his late business partner years earlier, she had already begun to make a name for herself as the "P. I. to the stars." It was a misnomer, of course. While it was true she had a couple of clients in her files that could be considered Hollywood royalty, she also had just as many files, if not more, from small businessmen, families, and local politicians. Jamie got results, which was usually of the utmost concern of her clients. She was discreet and worked fast because no one liked having their dirty laundry aired publicly.

It was a sentiment that Jamie understood well. Her father's high-profile death had brought all kinds of unwanted attention. At first it had been well-wishes and condolences, but once she made her plans to continue Southern and North Investigations, it turned to questions of competence, threats, intimidation, and conde-scendsion. While those tactics might have scared off another her age, twenty-eight-year-old Jamie Southern was made of sterner stuff.

Not only did she continue her father's business, she thrived in it and carried on the proud name of Southern and North Investigations. These days there were cases around the block, sometimes more than she could handle alone so she kept a few freelancers on call. They came in handy at times, but not tonight.

Tonight, she was flying solo.

The job was simple.

Jamie's client was Alexander Bishop. As far as she could tell he was a sweet, kindly old man. A successful businessman, Mr. Bishop was wealthy and influential in both business and politics. Once he had even run for office himself but lost the election. Feeling that the people had spoken, he opted not to run a second time. For good or ill, he helped shape and mold Southern California into what it was today. Like most successful men in his position, Alexander Bishop had more than one skeleton in his closet, secrets that he did not want to get out into the world. The funny thing about buried secrets was that they almost always found a way into the light.

Someone had discovered some of Bishop's secrets and he was being blackmailed for them. Two other men, David Westerfelt and Roland Carter, both well-known members of society and wealthy businessmen, were also being blackmailed, presumably by the same person. The three men had known each other since their twenties and they all belonged to the Ravenwood Club.

She wouldn't be much of a P. I. if she discounted that as a coincidence.

Although Jamie had suggested finding the blackmailer and stopping him or her, Mr. Bishop and his friends opted to simply pay what he wanted so the problem would go away. Such thinking was nonsense, but he remained adamant that she handle things his way.

She was simply the bagman—or was that bag-woman?—on this one.

Her job was to follow the directions the blackmailer had sent for the drop. Whoever was behind this was good. The blackmailer had Jamie bouncing from one location to another where new instructions were waiting for her. She had seen the tactic before on a similar case. The blackmailer wanted to make sure that she was acting in good faith, that she had come alone as instructed.

She had.

Her first instinct had been to set up a tail to follow her and the money or to put a tracker on the money. She had considered reaching out to Sam Hunt, a freelance investigator she used from time to time, but her client would hear none of it. For a moment, she considered ignoring Mr. Bishop's request, but then thought better of it. She could handle a simple drop on her own without any trouble.

After reaching the blackmailer's final stop, she waited.

And waited.

And then waited some more.

After almost an hour, she grew tired of sitting on her can waiting for the bad guys to make their move.

"This is ridiculous," she muttered, climbing out of the

car and stretching. Ordinarily, a late night rendezvous would have called for a glamorous dress and high heels, but when dealing with criminals, Jamie found that black slacks and low-heeled shoes were the way to go. It was so much easier to run that way and in her line of work she did more than her fair share of running.

"You the money?" a voice called from the darkness.

Show time! Jamie smiled. "That's what they tell me."

"Hand it over," the man who stepped out of the shadows between the buildings said. He was dressed in brown corduroy pants, a blue denim shirt under a green jacket that was zipped up halfway, presumably to allow him easy access to the gun he was fondling inside it. A black ski mask under a golf hat fraying at the edges completed the ensemble. The man was about as nondescript as he could get without wearing a burlap sack.

"Now, you know better than that, mister," Jamie said in her sweetest tone. "There are rules for these sort of things. I believe you have something for me as well?"

"Yeah. I got it." He stepped closer, next to her car, but out of arm's reach. Smart. He had clearly done this before or been coached by someone else who had.

"You'll pardon me if I don't take your word for it," Jamie said. "My client is paying a lot of money for this so I want to see it before I hand it over."

"Okay," the stranger said, pulling the gun from his jacket and pointing it at her.

If he had been expecting her to flinch, she was happy to disappoint him. This wasn't the first time, nor did she suspect the last, that someone would point a gun in her direction.

"Here's your envelopes," the man said, setting three large manila envelopes on the hood of her car. "Now...your turn."

Jamie pulled a suite case from the car and held it out toward him. "All yours."

She could just make out the toothy smile through the mouth hole in the mask. "Nice try, toots. Open it. I want to make sure that thing ain't booby trapped."

"Whatever you say, dear," Jamie said, sugar dripping off every syllable. She sat the briefcase on the hood next to the envelope and entered the unlock code. With a double snap, the locks popped loose and Jamie opened the lid so the man with the gun could see the money inside.

He whistled.

"One hundred and fifty thousand dollars. Fifty for each," Jamie said. "In small non-sequential bills, as requested."

The man reached over and shut the case before picking it up. He was no longer out of arm's reach. It would have been so easy for her to get the drop on him. Whoever this man was, be he the blackmailer or a hired flunky, the latter being her best guess, he wasn't a pro. She was fairly certain she could drop him like a hot potato without breaking so much as a sweat, but out of respect for her client's wishes, she resisted.

"I take it this concludes our business?" Jamie asked.

"Yeah. We're done."

"Good. Before you go, there's just one more thing."

"What's that?" he asked nervously. He glanced around as if he had stepped into some sort of trap.

"Against my better judgment, my client instructed me

to follow your guidelines to the letter and I have, but let me be clear here, okay? This ends here and now. If you decide later that fifty thousand apiece wasn't enough, I will be very upset."

He snorted a derisive "heh!"

Jamie took a step forward and lowered her voice, venom having replaced her earlier syrupy tone.

"Trust me when I say you wouldn't like to see me upset," she said. The threat was plain. "Am I understood?"

"Y-yeah," he stammered. "You got it."

"Then get out of here before I change my mind and do something rash."

The man disappeared back into the shadows. She could hear his footfalls against concrete as he ran down the narrow space between the buildings once he was out of sight. Seconds later, Jamie heard a car door slam, then another. Unlike her, the man in the ski mask had not come alone. She was more convinced than ever that he was simply a hired flunky. She wouldn't be surprised if whoever hired him disposed of him now that his part was done. She hoped not, but ski mask boy wasn't her problem. Tires squealed as their car speed away into the night, blocked from view.

Jamie picked up the first envelope. She had an idea what was inside, but she looked nonetheless. Inside she found several photos, each easily twenty-five to thirty years old featuring a young Alexander Bishop and his underage lovers in multiple compromising positions. She recognized most of the men in the photos, but not all. Bishop ran in powerful circles in his youth as well as now. In addition to the photos, the negatives were also inside.

The second envelope contained several photographs of David Westerfelt in the company of several different ladies, none of whom was his wife. Some were shots of meals whereas others were more intimate, with him and the ladies in various states of undress. Some of the photos were quite old, others more recent.

She opened the third envelope and found more of the same inside. There were also group shots featuring multiple men and women enjoying one another's company, including Roland Carter, mixed in with the others, including her other two clients. To say they were close would be an understatement.

Jamie didn't judge. She herself had met many couples that had unique arrangements. Her client's indiscretions didn't matter to her. She had been hired to get the incriminating evidence and she had done just that. It was not her place to pass judgment on what consenting adults did behind closed doors. She, herself, was known to throw caution to the wind from time to time.

Her clients weren't ashamed of the photos, but they also didn't want to deal with any type of scandal should they go public. Paying off the blackmailer was the simplest solution.

Jamie got in her car and headed back to the office to wash up and change before meeting with the client to deliver the photos and the good news that it was over. In an hour, she would wish she had gone straight to Alexander Bishop's home.

Had she done so, she might have saved his life.

* * *

There was no answer when Jamie Southern rang the bell.

Unlike her previous visits to her client's home, this time there was no one on staff around to greet her, no pitter-pat of expensive shoes against the marble floor. This time there was only deathly silence.

It made her uneasy.

Jamie turned the doorknob carefully, surprised to find it unlocked.

Pushing the door open slowly, Jamie stepped inside. There were no lights on in the house. The only way she could see was by the moon outside streaming through open curtains. Since she had visited Alexander Bishop at his home on multiple occasions to discuss the details of his case, Jamie realized immediately that something felt *off.*

One of the first lessons she learned as a private investigator, and one of the things she had heard her father say on more than one occasion, was to always be on guard and to always protect yourself.

Ain't living long like this unless you're prepared, he often told her in regards to the business. It was advice Jamie took to heart. She pulled her trusty .32 handgun from her clutch purse before sitting it down beside the door. She needed both hands free.

Jamie eased into the foyer and into the hallway that led deeper into the house. Off to the right, a set of stairs ascended to the second floor bedrooms. Without a word, she passed the stairs and headed for Bishop's study. The house had been ransacked. Papers littered the floor along with broken pieces of glass from picture frames and assorted glass and ceramic baubles her wealthy client kept on display. She heard shards crack and pop beneath each step she took.

The study door was closed, but not all the way. She pushed against it with the toe of her shoe, the .32 firmly gripped with both hands. The door swung open on well-oiled hinges. Jamie stepped inside. The condition of the room resembled the rest of the house. She righted a toppled desk lamp and snapped it on, glad to learn that the bulb had not blown. A pale glow filled the study, forcing the shadows to the far corners of the room.

That's when Jamie found her client.

Alexander Bishop lay on the floor, a small pool of blood radiating outward from beneath him. From his albino pallor, she knew he was gone, but Jamie had to make certain. Mindful of the debris and her short skirt, Jamie knelt next to her client and felt for a pulse. Not surprisingly, there wasn't one.

"Damn," she muttered.

Bishop had enemies. He had told her as much when they first met. A successful businessman, he had climbed over many others to reach the top. That left a lot of potential suspects in his wake, including her other clients, considering what she had seen in the photos she'd recovered from the blackmailer's bagman.

After a moment, Jamie stood and searched the rest of the house.

It was empty.

She picked up the phone from the study floor and sat it back on the desk, the one piece of furniture in the room that hadn't been upended. She assumed the solid oak frame had proven a bit too much for whoever had torn the place apart. She dialed the number by heart.

"This is Jamie Southern for Lieutenant Chase, please," she said once the desk sergeant at the local precinct answered. "It's an emergency."

The smart play would have been to call 9-1-1 and let the system work the way it should, but then there was no way of knowing who would be assigned the case. With Chase, she knew what she would get.

Once Lieutenant Chase got on the line, Jamie laid out the situation for him and he promised to be right over. Before hanging up, he told her to get out of the house and wait for him outside by her car.

"And don't touch anything," he finished.

She lied and told him she wouldn't touch a thing, but did just that as soon as she hung up the phone. She knew there wouldn't be much time before the police arrived. Chase and his people were good, but this one would have eyes on it from higher up because the victim was part of the city's wealthy elite.

"What were you looking for?" she asked the room.

Lying near the body were several pieces of paper and a couple dozen business cards. She knelt and looked to see if anything about them stood out. The papers were a bust. Nothing jumped out at her.

She could hear sirens approaching and was in no mood to listen to another one of the Lieutenant's lectures about disturbing his crime scene. Not tonight. Jamie was about to head outside to meet him when something caught her eye.

One of the business cards looked out of place compared to the others. Most were white or cream colored with lots of letters, addresses, names, numbers, the usual, but this one card had none of those on it. It was all black with a white border.

Curious, Jamie picked up the card and turned it over. She couldn't believe what she was seeing. She rolled the card around in her fingers before dropping it back to the carpet so the police could find it.

"Just when you think you've seen it all," Jamie said.

She walked away, leaving the card next to the body. It was a simple card, but it spoke volumes. Three words in white text on a black card leapt out at her.

The Ravenwood Club.

In this case, all roads led to Ravenwood.

Jamie Southern was tired and irritable.

She wanted nothing more than to head home for a long soak in a steamy hot bubble bath, but police Lieutenant Mark Chase was doing everything in his power to make sure that didn't happen anytime soon. Most of the time, she found his tenaciousness adorable, both on the job and at play, but this was not one of those times.

"Okay, let's go over this one more time," he said.

"What do you think I'm going to say that I haven't already told you the last five times you asked," Jamie said, no longer bothering to hide her irritation. "Alexander Bishop is..." She caught herself. "...was my client."

"What were you doing for Mr. Bishop?"

"You know I can't tell you that, Mark. You know that's confidential."

"Damn it, Jamie, this is serious," Chase said, his voice

rising slightly. "I've got a dead man and no clues."

"And I've got a little thing called ethics," Jamie fired back, her tone sharper than intended. From the look on his face, she had scored a direct hit.

The Lieutenant softened a bit, his tone lowering to just below normal. "Look, Southern, you've got to give me something I can work with here." He pointed toward the house where the coroner's people were starting to load the body into a plastic bag opened atop a gurney. "Your client is dead. I stopped caring about his confidences the moment he stopped breathing," Chase said.

"But I didn't," she said as the body was rolled past them. "And neither did he."

Chase opened his mouth, but then thought twice about what he was going to say and shut it just as quickly. The last thing either of them wanted to do was fight each other. There was a murder to solve.

"Did you find the card I told you about?" Jamie asked.

"I did."

"And?"

"And what?" The Lieutenant blew out a breath and reigned in an outburst.

"I've heard stories about The Ravenwood Club all my life. So have you. My father used to tell me about his early days as a P.I. and some of the things that used to go down in that place. That's where we'll find our killer."

"They're just stories. Not real."

"Most stories have some basis in truth."

Chase held up his hands in mock surrender. "Maybe,

but even if you're right what do you want me to do? No one gets in who isn't a member. Not if they want to keep their police pension intact. That place is a who's who of people who tell my bosses what to do. I ain't kickin' that hornet's nest without some damn hard proof."

She smiled. "You mean you aren't a member?"

"I look old and rich to you?"

"Can I have the card?" she asked, hand outstretched. "I've got a hunch. You boys in blue aren't the only ones allowed to have those, you know."

He chuffed a laugh even as he pulled the card from his shirt pocket. He rolled the card around in his beefy fingers, looking it over. "Fine." Chase handed it over. "It's all yours."

Jamie reached for the card, but he pulled it away from her touch. "One condition," he said.

She scowled. "Somehow I just knew you were going to say that. What's your condition?"

"On the off chance you do find something, you call me and let me know."

They stared across the card between them, neither wanting to be the first to blink. Finally, Lieutenant Chase flinched. "Deal?"

Jamie plucked the business card from his grip. "Deal. So, I'm free to go?"

Chase smiled. "Yeah. Get out of here. I'll call you tomorrow in case you jog any other details while sleeping. Or, perhaps I could pop by your place first thing in the morning to compare notes."

"It might be better if I come to you," Jamie offered.

"Fine. Just make sure you don't leave anything out."

"Why do you always assume I'm hiding something,

Lieutenant Chase?" she asked, pouting playfully.

"You private eyes are all the same, Southern. You're always holding something back."

"Heh," Jamie chuckled. "And we all know how much you cops love to share, don't we?"

Chase stepped away, arms out to his side. "I'm an open book, Southern," he shouted. "Nothing to hide."

"We'll see about that," Jamie muttered as she turned and headed back to her car. She tucked the evidence into her purse next to her gun. Mark Chase was many things, but he was fair. He would follow the evidence wherever it may lead. Alexander Bishop had not been killed with a .32 so he hadn't tried to take her gun, although he knew she always carried it with her. There were more than a few of his colleagues who would not have afforded her such a courtesy.

The Ravenwood angle was a long shot, she knew, but it was not the only card in her arsenal, so to speak. Urban legend or not, if the club was still active and that somehow led to the death of her client, Jamie Southern was determined to find out the truth.

But that would start in the morning. It had been a long day and she was ready to call it a night. A nightcap and a soak were waiting for her back at her place and she planned to enjoy both to the fullest.

Right after she fed the cat.

Jamie Southern woke to the sound of a ringing phone.

Before taking over the family business, the thought of starting her day before the sun came up was laughable. One of the hardest things she had to learn as a private investigator was how it was all but impossible to keep a set schedule. Late night, and often overnight, stakeouts were the norm, but so were morning meetings with clients. It wasn't easy to juggle all of those things alone, but so far she had managed. The thought of one day bringing on a partner was one she toyed with from time to time, but she always discarded the notion as something to worry about another day.

She hadn't even rolled out of bed yet when the phone rang on her nightstand jangled again. Eyes still closed, she reached for the bedeviled machine.

"Jamie Southern," she answered, trying to stifle a yawn. She was not surprised to hear Mark Chase's voice on the other end of the line.

"Morning, beautiful," he said. "Did I wake you?"

"Of course not," she lied. "What can I do for you, Lieutenant?"

"Told you I would call. I thought we could get together and compare notes. On the case, that is," he clumsily added. "I can be at your place in...half an hour..." He let the invitation hang there for a moment, hoping she would invite him over to her place. While the idea had its merits, she had a murder to solve and having Mark Chase in her house for breakfast was not the best way to stay on target.

"Let's make it my office," Jamie countered. "One hour?"

"Sure thing," Chase said. He didn't bother to hide the disappointment in his voice. "See you in an hour."

Five minutes later, Jamie rolled out of bed, ready to face the day. After a shower and getting dressed, she fixed a small breakfast, toast with peach preserves and coffee, before rushing out the door on her way to the office.

No sooner had she gotten off the elevator than her favorite police lieutenant jogged up the stairs with a case file clenched in one hand and a box of donuts from his favorite breakfast stop, Donut Explosion, in the other.

"You're late," she joked, leaning against the door frame.

"Nonsense," he countered. "I'm always right on time."

She nodded toward the box he carried. "I see you brought breakfast."

"Cop's best friend," he said with a laugh. "Can you think of any way finer to start the day than hot coffee and warm donuts?"

"I can think of a few."

"So can I, but you wanted to meet at your office so this is all I could manage," he said, a big goofy grin on his face. "Come on, Jamie. This is brain food for detectives."

"I'll try to remember that," Jamie deadpanned. "Seems like you've forgotten the coffee."

Chase took on an air of mock hurt. "Now what kind of partnership would this be if we didn't both bring something to the table?"

"Come on in," Jamie said before turning on her heel and walking into the office. "I think there's a coffee maker in here somewhere."

Breakfast with Mark Chase didn't yield any new leads.

At least not in terms of the case.

The Lieutenant had made no secret his desire to be

more than friends and Jamie knew it would be a lie to say that she hadn't enjoyed being chased, no pun intended, but there was a time and place for everything and eating donuts over case files in her office was neither.

It had taken a bit of time to get his mind on the task at hand, but Jamie was quite persuasive when she wanted to be. They discussed the case in generalities at first. It seemed like he was more interested in learning what she knew than sharing information with her, but she managed to pull a few details out of him. While she wanted to keep things purely platonic, Jamie had no problem with using her feminine wiles to her own advantage. Mark Chase thought he had the upper hand, but he was putty in her hands. He just hadn't realized it yet.

The ME had retrieved the bullet, a .22 caliber. It was a mighty small weapon comparatively. There were certainly weapons that pack more of a punch. Beyond that, they exchanged a few additional details, but nothing of substantive value. By the time Chase left her office, Jamie still had more questions than answers. Someone had blackmailed Alexander Bishop and then killed him. Was the blackmailer and killer the same person? Alexander Bishop had followed the black-mailer's demands and paid the money without any fuss. Killing him made no sense.

These thoughts and more bounced around inside Jamie Southern's pretty blonde head as she drove through the city, enjoying the warmth of the midday sun. She had the top down on her new Jaguar, a treat she had allowed herself recently after concluding a rather lucrative case. The client had insisted on giving her a bonus and she happily accepted and put the money toward the new car. It handled like a dream.

Once this case was behind her, she planned to take a long ride up the coast to really break in the new car.

Before leaving the office, Jamie called David Westerfelt and asked to meet him and Roland Carter outside The Ravenwood Club instead of back at her office. Her clients were hesitant at first, but relented when she reminded them that the evidence pointed to someone at the club being involved. She needed to check out the club on her own, which wasn't going to be easy. Gentlemen's Clubs like Ravenwood were notoriously close minded when it came to the fairer sex.

No girls allowed.

It seemed that some boys never really grew up.

It wasn't a hard and fast rule, though. Women were strictly forbidden to be *members*, but the waitresses, and professional companions were always women, always leggy, always young and usually eager to curry the favor of a wealthy patron. Jamie had seen too many places like The Ravenwood pop up over the past few years and disliked them greatly. She wouldn't admit it aloud, but Jamie took a perverse thrill in pushing her way inside the club on official business.

She walked into The Ravenwood Club on Westerfelt's arm, with Carter following behind them. Carter was always following his friend's lead, she noted, but he did not seem happy about it, especially not today. Carter reminded her of a volcano, pent up and ready to blow.

She wondered if it was the blackmail that had him on edge. Carter was nowhere near as wealthy as Bishop or Westerfelt. He hadn't had the fifty thousand to pay off the blackmailer and had to take a loan from his friends. That must have stung.

The club was not what she had expected. It was like stepping back in time to an old library. Bookshelves with thick, old tomes lined the walls, broken only by the occasional picturesque window or painted portrait of one of the founders of the club. The first she saw was of a handsome man named Ravenwood so she assumed the club was named after him.

It was quiet, with men, mostly over fifty from the look of them, sitting around talking softly while others sat alone reading the newspaper or a book while others sat staring widely off into space. She recognized many of them, business leaders, pillars of the community, and a few politicians as well. The club served as a refuge for them, Jamie assumed, a place to escape their daily lives and relax. Begrudgingly, she started to sympathize, until she realized that, if not for blackmail and murder, she would never have been allowed inside. Her sympathy began to fade at that point.

Westerfelt motioned toward a secluded room where they could talk privately. Like the rest of the club, the room was nice, although a bit more modern than the public area they had walked through. There was a couch along one wall and three large chairs spaced perfectly for conversation. A table filled the center of the room. A young lady wearing a cocktail waitress outfit two sizes too small for her supermodel thin frame sauntered in behind them and placed a decanter and three glasses on the table. Smiling at Westerfelt, she poured all three before asking if they required anything else. Jamie imaged that at least one of them only drank top shelf booze.

"I assume you have some information for us, Miss Southern?" Westerfelt said as he reached for a glass. "Have you figured out who is behind the blackmail or who killed poor Alex?"

"I believe I have."

"Oh?" That brought both men upright in their seats.

"Who...who is it?" Roland Carter asked, a stutter in his voice.

Jamie smiled. She had suspected, but now she knew. "It was you, Mr. Carter."

Westerfelt let loose a big belly laugh. "Don't be ridiculous, girl. Roland here couldn't hurt a fly, much less a friend like Alex. And he doesn't need the blackmail money."

Carter shot him the dirtiest of looks.

"What?" Westerfelt said. "Tell her it's ridiculous."

"You old fool," Carter said. The words were soft, but enough to shut down Westerfelt's boisterous defense. The volcano was ready to erupt.

"Roland? What are you...is she right? Is that what you're saying? How could you? Did you kill poor Alex?"

Carter shot to his feet. "Poor Alex? Poor Alex? Sure, why not? Poor Alex who used to torment me...torment both of us. Is that the poor Alex you're talking about?"

Westerfelt set his glass back on the table and stood. "You little cockroach," he said, anger burning red in his cheeks. "Torment? You don't know the meaning of the word, Roland! We were kids! Kids prank one another. That's all it was."

"Not to me!" Carter spat.

"That's because you're weak," Westerfelt said with a dismissive wave. "You always were."

Carter lowered his voice. "Not always. Just ask Alexander."

"You sonuva—" Westerfelt took a swing at his friend, caught him on the chin, and knocked him against the wall.

"That's enough," Jamie said.

Westerfelt backed off.

"Why?" she asked.

"I've lived with this so long. I thought all of that was behind us, just kid's stuff. Alex was my friend. I loved him."

"But..."

"He kept photographs. One night, he brought them out and showed them to me and he laughed. Some of them...some of the photos I'd never seen before. Things they did while I was asleep or passed out drunk. I never knew. I never..." he looked at Westerfelt. "I thought you were my friends!"

"They were just pranks," Westerfelt said.

"No," Jamie said. "I saw the photos. They weren't just pranks."

"What happens now?" Roland asked.

There was a knock at the door.

"That will be Lieutenant Chase," Jamie said. "He's here to arrest you on charges of blackmail and murder."

Carter nodded. He knew he'd been beat.

"And I'm sure he'll want to talk to you as well," she

said to Westerfelt. "You should be ashamed of yourself."

"We were just being funny," Westerfelt pleaded.

Jamie opened the door for Chase and his men.

"Do you hear anyone laughing?" she asked Westerfelt.

"Getting your own clients arrested isn't a smart way to run a business, Miss Southern."

"No it is not, Mr. Chase."

They sat on the balcony outside her office and watched as the sun started to set on the horizon. She was on her third glass of wine. Chase was on his fourth beer. It had been a long day.

"Reminds me of something my dad used to say when he ran the business and a client didn't pay...Ain't livin' long like this."

"Your old man sounds like a smart guy."

"He was," Jamie said.

Chase clinked his bottle against her glass. "Here's to living to fight another day."

"I'll drink to that."

Danger and Dread
Delilah S. Dawson

Daddy always said ugly don't hurt—it's the teeth you got to look out for. He was the one who taught Emma Lee how to raise a dog mean enough to kill. Most good game dogs were ugly, whether by birth or brawl. Some grew into their teeth, and some turned into bait. But ugly ran deep, and it never went away.

Emma Lee was born pretty, but then...something happened. Daddy said it was Mama's fault, letting a juicy little baby toddle out among the cages at the wrong time. He said that was why Mama was gone—because she didn't do her job. But Cousin Jerry sometimes chucked Emma Lee under her scarred chin and called her Bait, so Emma Lee had her doubts about where to lay the blame. *Mama* was just a word she'd learned on the TV, along with things like *school* and *reading* and *illegal.* Emma Lee didn't like being pointed at, so she didn't mind staying home.

The dogs didn't care what she looked like, so long as she kept feeding them.

She walked past the cages at first light dragging a big plastic bucket, same as every morning. As she passed each chain-link kennel, she tossed a package over the top of the fence. Old men's shirts and pillowcases tied tight around Ol' Roy dog food and chunks of whatever Cousin Jerry brought home from the chicken plant. The dogs went crazy for it, their crazy barking going quiet, one by one, as they fought through cheap fabric to get to their food. Crazy-Eyes, Killer, Grill, Murdergirl, Snaggle-tooth, Shovelhead, Ripper, and then the pups from Murdergirl's most recent litter, all cowering together in cage eight. They hadn't even earned names yet and still whimpered at being separated from their mean-as-hell mama. They'd either learn to get mean like her or become supper. Either way, they contributed to the family.

At the end of the row, the bait dogs in the shed woke up, pawing at the padlocked door and whimpering. She did her best to ignore it.

Sitting on the trailer's rotting step, Emma Lee watched each of her charges, looking for weakness or unfortunate sweetness or a collar of heavy chains going loose or cutting too deep into bunched muscle. Every-thing was as it should be, half falling down but still held together with duct tape and more chains. The birds were waking up, the cicadas were droning, and the hills were filled with the sound of slurpy swallowing and the clink of weighted chains. One of Murdergirl's pups whimp-ered, and Emma Lee walked over to check on the white pit poking his nose through the fence, his scabbed over, stubbed tail wagging and his eyes big, black pools of something that Daddy wouldn't like. She glanced back at the house, real quick, then rubbed his nose gently.

"Girl, you know better. You make 'em hate you, or they get soft and turn into meat."

Hearing that voice from the kitchen window, a chaos of growls went up along the line. Emma Lee swallowed and pulled her hand away from the pup straining toward her.

"Sorry," she whispered.

"Go on and do it."

Her eyes closed for just a second, holding back tears. Pulling back her fist, she punched the white pup in the face. He tumbled back, whimpering, butt tucked as he cowered and pissed himself. It was the first time he'd been beat, but it wouldn't be the last. Just last week, she'd been allowed to hold him right before Daddy took off his tail, and he'd licked her with a black-spotted tongue.

"Good, girl," Daddy called. "Now come inside and help me with these goddamn kittens."

Emma Lee wiped up her tears and went inside.

The day got hot quick, and Daddy stayed mad. Hornet mad. Emma Lee was too slow taping the bait dogs' mouths, and she got slapped. She accidentally dropped Daddy's can of beer while he was working the jump pole and got slapped again. She almost got bit holding Ripper down for his shots, and Daddy popped her so hard she saw stars.

"It's a hard life. Get used to it," Daddy told her again. "Gotta be tough if you're gonna be dumb."

"Yes, sir," she said.

She didn't want to get popped again, so she grabbed the hose and went to spray out the kennels without being asked.

When she came back, Daddy was in the kitchen. On his best days, he joshed around and gave Emma Lee a stick of gum and told her stories about when he was a boy and they'd lived up at the big house Mr. Gooch had bought from the bank. Sometimes Daddy would pull a ripped photo out of his wallet and show her what she'd looked like as a baby, when she was still pretty and he still smiled, and she'd draw a sweaty finger over the faded picture and leave a wet streak over the other pair of hands holding her, their long nails painted bright pink.

Today was not one of his best days. Daddy had a big pile of pink hamburger on the counter and was wet up to his elbows, making smushed-up patties. His white undershirt was the color of old bone and ripped in the underarms, and his gray sweatpants were splattered in rust-red stains. Sweat dripped down his shaved head, plunking onto the pile of meat.

"Go wash up, girl. We got company tonight. I put out a dress for you. Look as pretty as you can."

She watched him, considering. "Daddy, how old are you?"

Daddy's head slashed around like a snake. "Why are you asking?"

"Because I don't know."

"I'm twenty-five. And you're nine. And that means that you owe me for nine years of putting up with your ugly face. So do as I say." Daddy turned back to the rickety old oven, opening the door and pulling out two wads of cash wrapped in rubber bands. A heavy black gun squatted on a burnt cookie sheet on the bottom rack. "I said move!" he shouted, kicking the door shut with his bare foot when he caught Emma Lee watching too close.

Emma Lee ran for the bathroom before he could pop her with wet-meat hands. She shut the door quietly, turned on the shower, and stepped out of her old tank top and shorts and worn-out panties. The water never got very hot, and the soap was just a slippery sliver, but she got as clean as she could and rinsed her hair with baby shampoo. The towel was still wet from Daddy's shower, and when she wrapped it around her middle, it hung to her knees.

The mirror was speckled and dirty, but she had to look at herself as she combed out her hair. She tried to figure out how the dog must've bit her to leave the marks. One rip from her forehead down over her eyebrow like a flap, always making her look surprised. One rip up her jaw and cheek, a white line curving her mouth up stupidly. The traces of old stitches, ragged and pink. She could almost picture the jaws opening in slow motion and closing on a baby's head like it was an old football. Silver claw marks raked down her neck, up her shoulder, over her belly. Whenever she asked which dog it was, Daddy said it was long dead, and that was that.

Emma Lee had seen what a good fighting dog could do in the pit, and she figured that if she was still alive and had all her parts, somebody must've loved her enough to snatch her away from a dog in a killing frenzy. If that wasn't love, it was something close.

Back in her room, she closed the door and locked it and knelt to check the box hidden deep under her bed. Everything was where she'd left it, and she sighed her relief and checked the door over her shoulder and shoved the box back in with the dustbunnies and outgrown shoes. The dress Daddy had laid out on her mattress was a thin, flimsy thing with straps that tied over her shoulders, but it fit pretty good. She tiptoed into the kitchen holding up the ties, feeling foolish. The oven was on now, and the kitchen was hot, which meant Daddy was baking a frozen pie, which he normally only did on Christmas. The money was gone, and the gun was in Daddy's waistband as he chopped up a watermelon and cussed to himself.

"Daddy?"

Daddy jabbed the big knife into the melon and turned to face her. "What?"

Emma Lee held up the ties on her dress. "I don't know how..."

With a sigh, Daddy wiped off his hands and took up the ties and made tight bows that dug into Emma Lee's shoulders something fierce.

"Who's coming over?"

Daddy shook his head and stood back, inspecting Emma Lee like she was a dog about to go in the ring. "We're gonna have us a fight tonight. Uncle Jerry's bringing some big men up from Atlanta, thinking about buying some of our dogs. We do good enough, we might could get out of here and move to the city. Wouldn't that be good?"

"Yes, sir," Emma Lee said, not because she wanted to go to the city, but because she knew that was the right answer, and Daddy had plenty of wooden spoons within reach.

"Now you get on out of here. Don't mess up your dress, but don't be around, either. I don't want you to scare 'em off."

She took a few steps toward the laundry room where

they kept stray cats or unwanted kittens, whatever the local rescue needed to get rid of. Taking care of the kittens was Emma Lee's favorite job, and she had a few weeks yet until the current litter would be big enough to give the dogs any kind of challenge.

"Let them kittens be. You get too attached. It's bad, to do that."

Emma Lee nodded and hurried out the door, past the long line of snarling dogs, and down the curving dirt drive. It got quiet, once she rounded the corner, just tall pines and the hot sun. She scurried across the cracked black asphalt of the road and ducked into the trees across the way. There was a small path here, made by her own flip-flops. Daddy didn't know, but Mr. Gooch was a nice man, and he had given her permission to be on his property, so long as she didn't bother the cows or get in anybody's way. He even gave her a butterscotch, now and then, when he caught her sitting quietly, watching the new calves. When he called her Honey, it felt more real than when Daddy and Uncle Jerry did.

As she picked her way down the narrow deer path, she pretended she was something that belonged in the woods. She touched a fuzzy bumblebee on a purple flower and twirled around a yellow butterfly and laughed when a blue dragonfly tried to sit on her hand. When she saw a copperhead sunning on a flat stone, she walked wide around him. Emma Lee had a clear understanding of what was and was not dangerous. She knew how not to provoke.

The stream was mostly dried up, and she hopped over the mucky trickle and squeezed through the wooden flap-door into the cow pasture. She took a deep breath and pushed it back out, and it felt like the whole world floated up off her shoulders. Here among the gentle cows with their sweet, dark eyes and big, twitching ears was where she felt the most herself. Even the bull was a tender sort, settling his mighty bulk down by the most tired mama with the newest calf and watching over his herd with sharp but still kind eyes. He could've trampled her to guts, but instead he just blinked at her and chewed his cud, and she loved him for it.

Emma Lee had named every critter in the herd by now. Her favorites were Dove and Chocolate and Velvet and Lacy and Baby Bones and Mrs. Butterworth and her new, toasty-brown baby, Pancake. The bull she called Sweet Daddy. She'd been coming here for a couple of years, and she knew that, like the dogs back home, the cows had jobs to do. You couldn't get attached to 'em. They came and went, and new calves were born, and when Daddy brought home a big tray of hamburger meat for the fights, she hoped it wasn't anybody she knew personally.

Time passed strangely in the bright green pasture. Emma Lee didn't know how long it had been, but she shivered when the sky went purple and she heard the sounds of big trucks burning down the road, breaking the quiet up into sharp, glittery shards like what was left of the mirror taped to the back of her door. Her legs prickled when she stood up, and she could tell that there was a wet spot on the back of her dress from sitting too long on ground that was wetter than it looked. If she'd gotten grass stains on the dress, Daddy would make her fetch a switch. Or worse: Make her be the one to hang kittens and weak pups from bait chains and so he could dangle them into Killer's cage to make him jump high.

When she ran to the gate, the calves danced along behind her, ever curious. She slipped through the gate and ran back up the path, leaping over the sleeping snake and pausing only at the edge of the road to make sure she didn't get mowed down by the men from Atlanta. A big, shiny black Ford rumbled up with a cage chained in back, and Emma Lee hid behind a tree until it had passed. She didn't run up the dirt drive behind that scary truck; she cut a longer path around the rear of the trailer and darted in the back door.

It was loud again. The dogs were barking and growling and throwing themselves against the rattling chain link fences as men laughed and taunted them from the safety of the other side. The trailer shook with swaggering footsteps, and the air stank with cigarettes and the skunk-smell of weed smoke. Emma Lee checked the short hall before dashing for her room and closing the door gently so it wouldn't make a sound, her back falling against the flimsy door as she caught her breath.

"Well, ain't you a sweet little thing?"

Her heart just about hopped out of her mouth when she saw a shape sitting on her bed in the low light, tossing something from hand to hand.

"This is my room," she said. "Daddy don't let men in here."

He turned on her bedside lamp and smiled at her with crooked teeth. "Maybe he didn't used to, but maybe he changed his mind. What's your name, honey?"

Emma Lee put her hand on the doorknob, and the man stood, whipping out a knife. "Shh, honey. Don't wanna do that. Just turn around now and let me get a good look. Let's have us a chat. Your Uncle Jerry says you're good with the dogs. Says you respect 'em."

Lamplight flickered off the dirty knife, and Emma Lee took her hand off the doorknob and put her back against the door. The man nodded like she'd done good and sat back down.

"I don't like it," she said, referring both to the dogs and to what the man was doing in her room, his knees spread wide in too-big jeans and his work boots rubbing red clay on the gray carpet.

"If you don't like it, maybe it's just because you ain't had it done good enough," he said. "I know my business, honey."

Emma Lee shivered, feeling like the sundress was the flimsiest thing in the world and wondering if her Daddy had dressed her this way on purpose. "I'm ugly," she said. "Everybody says so. You don't want to mess with me."

His smile was all wrong and sideways. He put down the knife and held out a scarred hand. "Maybe I do, though. It ain't all about your face. You wanna come stay with me? I got a nicer place. We got a pool. You like to swim?"

"No. I wanna stay here."

He'd set down the thing he'd originally been tossing around, and now he picked it back up again, holding it out to her. "I'll let you keep a kitten for yourself. How long you had this one? You didn't take good care of it, did you?"

Emma Lee's stomach flipped over when she saw it lying there, floppy and still. She'd stolen it from its litter the night before and slept with it, soft and warm and milky-smelling, under her chin. She hadn't even named it yet. When she'd gotten up this morning, she'd put it in the shoebox under her bed with Dixie cups of food and water, and she'd checked on it, and now...

The man must've seen the dread slash over her ripped-up face.

His grin went dark. "Does Daddy know you steal from him? You be good to me, and I won't tell. It'll be our secret."

Emma Lee reached behind her, fingers skittering over the broken mirror. When she found a shard, she smiled and nodded.

"Okay."

The man smiled back. He set down the kitten and held out his hand. So shyly, hands behind her back, she walked toward him, flip-flops quiet on the carpet, and let him wrap his big fingers around her waist.

As he pulled her close between his knees, she slashed straight across his neck with the shard of mirror.

The blood spray didn't surprise her; she'd seen enough dog fights to know where to strike to end something fast. She stepped back to watch him thrash around on her bed, his blood soaking into the faded checkered sheets as he tried to hold it all in. It was strangely quiet, just gurgles and dripping, no growling at all. As he fell still, she picked up the kitten and rubbed a thumb over its tiny ears. Its head flopped sickeningly, and she had no trouble imagining this man hunting around under her bed for a little girl's treasures and laughing as he wrenched its neck.

She looked back at her door. The mirror was missing several shards now, and she remembered to check her hand. It hadn't cut her too bad, just a little scratch. She wiped it off on her sheet and picked up the man's knife from where he'd dropped it. He was done with needing it, but she sure as hell wasn't. She knew he had a piece on him, somewhere; they all did. But she didn't trust guns. They were unpredictable. Emma Lee trusted what she knew.

The barking picked up around front, signaling the beginning of the fight. Emma Lee licked her lips and sat down on the floor to trade her flip-flops for a ragged pair of sneakers. Picking up the dead kitten, she scurried back outside and found Daddy's pile of old tools from when he'd tried to grow a patch of weed to sell. The grave was shallow and small, but so was the kitten. Her hands shook as she covered it with crumbly red dirt and a brick. They just fed the dead dogs to the ones still alive enough to fight, so she'd never seen anything get buried before. There was no one around to tell her if she'd done it wrong.

Peeking around the trailer, she saw about what she expected. All the men were gathered around the fight pit down the hill, which was just a big hole in the dirt edged in plywood and stained with years of blood. Most of the time, Daddy kept an above-ground pool over it with just a scant bit of rainy water in the bottom, but now it was moved aside and two dogs were down in the pit, going at each other in a flurry of teeth and fur. She didn't know who was down there, and she didn't want to know. She didn't need to know. But she checked that every pair of eyes on the property was aimed down into that hole, including Daddy, who was standing over the pit, his frenzied face lit by floodlights, spitting every curse he had as a beer dangled, forgotten, in his hand.

Emma Lee ran back into the empty trailer, climbed up on the counter, and snatched Daddy's key ring from where he kept it hid, in the Snoopy mug on the highest shelf. Each key had a number written on it, and each number matched one of the kennels outside. One to one, two to two. She unlocked each padlock, leaving it dangling on the chain as she moved on to the next cage; only Ripper's kennel was empty. Most of the dogs had never seen an open door, and they were too busy barking at the fight and the strangers, so they didn't even try rattling their cages open. Once all eight locks were undone, Emma Lee looked from the kennels to the fight pit. What she was about to do—it couldn't be undone. Once those doors were open, she couldn't close 'em again. Down in the floodlights, Daddy threw his head back and whooped, and the man standing beside him in a leather vest held out his hand to shake.

The first kennel door opened, and then the next, and the next, all down the line, as fast as a little girl's blood-slick fingers could go, fumbling with the locks and chains and the rusty gates until all the dogs had rushed out into the night, baying their rage and aimed for the scent of blood and grilling meat. Emma Lee picked up a rusty hatchet from the firewood pile and backed away into the shadows to watch.

Killer was the first one to hit the crowd, and he went straight for Daddy, just like Emma Lee would have, if her teeth had had any bite. The Atlanta men scattered, but Uncle Jerry headed over with a break stick to help. Ol' Killer was latched onto Daddy's arm like a snapping turtle, and Murdergirl rounded on Uncle Jerry, her torn-up ears and long, pink nipples flapping as she lunged and caught his leg, shaking him to the ground. Emma Lee realized her own teeth were bared, a growl coming up soft from her chest.

She didn't wait to see what would happen next. She held on to that hatchet and ran.

Down the dirt drive to the asphalt, across the road, into the woods, over the creek, and into the moonlit pasture. The cows were sleeping peacefully, shadowy blocks snoring softly, gentle as a dream. Emma Lee curled up behind the cows' round bale, hidden by scratchy hay, to listen. And to wait. If another Atlanta man came looking for her, or if Killer found her first... the hatchet was in her fist, and she'd be ready.

Like the cows, she was accustomed to the sounds of death. Barking and growling she knew, and diesel trucks roaring down the road, and the punch of gunshots. But there were sharper, newer, sweeter sounds, too: the screams and shouts and pleading cries of grown men dying in the jaws of dogs they'd trained to kill.

Things went quiet for a while, just like it did when the dogs were eating breakfast every morning. By the time the sirens and flashing lights arrived, it was too late. The cows rustled sleepily and lowed their displeasure at the interruption. There were more gunshots, and Emma Lee couldn't help wondering how many bullets it took to put down Killer or Ripper or Murdergirl when they were in a frenzy. By the sound of it, plenty. It was a long time before the night went silent again and Emma Lee felt safe enough to drift off.

Mr. Gooch found her the next morning. Emma Lee was deep asleep, snoring through scar-twisted lips, the cows stepping daintily around her as they nibbled their hay. Sweet Daddy lay near, watching her like she was one of his calves. In one arm she held a white pit-bull puppy, torn to shreds and barely breathing. She held the hatchet in her other fist.

He did not wake her.

Ain't No Grave
Ryan Sayles

"I'll be damned if that don't do it," Riggs said as he lets the hammer off his revolver and walks away.

I lay still, face down and listening to the crunch of dead leaves under his boot get softer and softer until I knew he was far off. The dirt between my teeth tasted clean compared to the bits of burnt gun powder drifting down onto my lips. I didn't blink. Not once. The night's frigid and I can feel the snakes of heat rising from my body cool instantly in the air. I try to breathe. It's hard. My left eye is filling with blood that the January cold is working overtime to coagulate real fast.

I owe Riggs sixty large. I robbed his card game. No sense in sugar coating it. I just strolled in there and blasted Keith, his muscle. The four players stared, Keith's blood all over their kings and sevens. I approached them and you'da thought I was a beam of light breaking up some cockroaches. They scooted back from the table and I slung one hand down, snatched up the kitty. Pocketed it. Rolled out. Counted it later and never woulda thought it woulda been so damn huge.

I needed seventeen grand for Emilina's trust. Emilina, my mentally-handicapped daughter. My *tard*, as Riggs calls her. Her mamma was the type of woman I always courted. Drunk. Trailer queen. Died about four months after birthing Emilina. Seems she finally found a rail of coke she couldn't handle. Took her long enough. I held the baby and fell in love right then and there. Didn't really miss her mamma, though.

If you knew me, you'd know I'm not good enough to care for my Emilina. She's six now, and doin' as good as she is thanks to her grandma, which is my own mamma. My pa went to the state pen for robbery and hurtin' some people. Never made it out. Found on the shower floor, bleedin' from everywhere, I hear. Cocksucker had it comin' every which way. But I'd leave Emilina with my own mamma for months while I went and chased work or tail. It was a fine arrangement. So my mamma raised her for all this time and then she upped and died a month back. Heart attack in her sleep. God rest her soul. That leaves Emilina to me, and what that really means is Emilina is in trouble.

A church-goin' friend of mine got Emilina into an assisted living home. Seems she had some pull there. Seventeen grand wasn't going to cover Emilina's life, but it would get her by until other monies showed up. So I robbed a damn card game. Simple plan. I ain't a worthwhile man, but I do want to be something different for that little girl.

Riggs knows about Emilina. I didn't think he did. You don't want Riggs knowin' 'bout anything important to you.

I used to work for him. He runs the dope in the town, as small as the town is. Cops either take a couple of bills from him, they don't care enough to get involved, or they got squeezed. Riggs isn't shit, but he struck light-ning somewhere, sometime. Now he runs his own show. I acted in it.

So he finds me, pistol-whipped me in the bar bathroom not an hour ago. Drug me out here to the edge of the woods. I woke to a shovel falling on my face, the metal flat striking the bridge of my nose. "Dig," is all I heard. So I did. I got about a foot down and Riggs was impatient. Probably the cold leeching into his bones just as it was mine.

Down on my knees, me thinking Emilina was going to be okay because she's already in the home. I hear him cock back his hammer and when the bullet punched me in the back of the head all I did was think about my sweet little angel as I fell over, face first. It was a good death.

But then Riggs says, "That tard daughter of yours... you ain't worth sixty grand. Hell, you ain't worth the shit I took this morning. But she is. I'll get my sixty grand from her."

He waits around for a minute, me trying to stifle the tears I felt. Only blood ran from my eye, drizzling down my head from the hole in the back of it.

"I'll be damned if that don't do it," Riggs says as he let the hammer off his revolver and walks away. Guess I don't warrant a second bullet. But I ain't dead. The left side of my head hurts in a way I can't even put words to, but I ain't dead. Soon, ain't no doubt about that. But not yet.

Got a new lease on life through a gun shot.

I drag my arms up, put 'em underneath me. Weird sensations firing off through my head, my body. Like my brain's trying to figure out how to do all the things it did before now that I got skull-popped.

I push up off the ground. Leaves falling off me, drops

of blood dribbling like I was flicking the hairs of a paint brush. Stand up on shaky legs. The left half of my world is dark and blurry. Bullet must be there. I lifted a hand and my fingertips met the bloody clumps of hair around my skull. I had the urge to reach inside there. The bullet hole is behind my left ear, and just skirted inside the bone. I can feel a trail of fire underneath the skin as it traveled around my head.

Who cares? It's a ticking time bomb now.

"I'm coming, Emilina," I say, light a smoke and walked out of the woods. Feels good to smoke. Burns. Feels like inhaling hate. There's enough vengeance rollin' around in my guts to where I don't even feel cold no more.

I chain-smoke six coffin nails before I reach the outer edge of the bar's parking lot. It's like stepping from hell and across the threshold to heaven when I met that pave job, as cracked and weathered as it was. They musta heard the gunshot. I wonder what Riggs said to 'em as he drug me out the bar. Probably *Leave well enough alone.*

Tony's cab is right where it always sits; at the far end of the one cone of light working over the bar's front door. The glow of his cigarette cherry is like a beacon; bright red, dulled to shadow, bright red, dulled again. A flashing buoy to lead me in.

I try not to look like I was shot in the head as I move over to the door. Rap a knuckle on the window. Tony's half-asleep, slumped in his driver seat but slides right up, grabs the steering wheel.

I get in and a blast of agony rolls across my brain. Feels like the first wave of tissues in there shit the bed. I gotta move before I get that same sensation in the center of my brain. The underlying reek of fake leather and a mishmash of smoke, liquor, vomit and breath mints don't mix well with the way my stomach is roilin'.

I grit my teeth and fight off a groan. Takes a second. "Tony, you know where McCray lives?"

"McCray?" Tony stubs out his smoke and looked in the rearview at me. Recognizes my face, says, "Riggs' right hand man?"

"Yessir."

Narrows his eyes, sounds concerned. "I do. Why?"

"I gotta get there."

Tony's eyes in the rearview mirror; search my face in the dark of the back seat. "I'm not a big fan of those parts."

"They ain't the ghetto or nothin'."

"I know. It's just that...you look like you got a score to settle and I don't want—"

"The association?" I try to laugh and it don't work. "You don't want to be on my side?"

Tony takes a long moment. "Truth be told...yeah. That's it. I got a family, you know."

"Me too," I say. Follow it up with some lies. "It'll be fine. No score. No trouble. Just real quick, eh?"

Tony sighs, "I dunno. I kinda was waitin' out here for a quiet night of driving drunks is all."

I reach into my pocket. Grab some bills and toss them up front. Tony looks down, does the math, drops it in drive. Sighs. "It better be fine."

"It will be," I say and rest my hand on the knife I

always keep tucked down in my boot. I like it because it's long and thin, and has no problem making its way between two ribs.

"Drop me off two doors down and I'll come meet you back at that cul-de-sac we just passed," I say. "Shouldn't be but a minute."

Despite his greenback courage, Tony's all too happy to pull over and let me out. Tony knows I lie, and he knows I cause trouble.

The neighborhood is hushed. Cold. The only one street lamp is a few more doors up the road, and its light is piss yellow. About as half-dead as me. The dead grass and leaves underfoot crunch with that hard, crusty sound where you expect snow. We ain't gotten any this year. Not yet. Just a wind that steals the life outta all the things it rolls over. Emilina keeps watch for snow. I shoulda moved her to the Dakotas or Alaska. She loves snow.

I walk, feeling how my walking was gettin' off rhythm. You know how when you was a baby and learned how to put one foot in front of the other and you've used that skill without thinkin' about it for the rest of your life? I noticed strollin' through the two yards I gotta go through that mine—wherever my old brain stored that rhythm—is dyin' off just a tad. Like, if it were a long math problem where the equal sign pointed to walk straight and good, now I'm missin' a plus sign in there somewhere.

McCray's driveway is empty. I'd rather see Riggs' wheels sittin' there, runnin' on idle like he always does.

Seems the dude has an allergy against turnin' off his truck. Just lets it rumble in lots and driveways as he goes inside to conduct his business. But it ain't there, and that ain't a good sign for me.

On the front porch and I can hear voices inside. I knock twice, just the way Riggs does. The door swings open and it's my lucky day. McCray standin' there, wife beater and jeans, his long hair tucked back behind his ears like he was some porn star givin' a blow job and wanted to make sure the camera can see his face.

"You—ahhhh..." he says, staring at the left side of my swollen head.

"McCray," I say. "Riggs around?" And I swing that boot knife right up under McCray's chin and it don't stop until it hits the top of the inside of his skull. He twitches but I shove him inside as I yank the pistol out from his waistband. His is the third man's blood on that blade.

In the front door and two dudes I ain't never seen before are on the couch, sharing a joint. They got two fresh beer bottles on the end table in front of them. Point and shoot, point and shoot and two blasts kick them boys back into the sofa. Blood and whining. I shake McCray's twitchin' face offa my knife and his skin slides down the blade. He rolls off and I step over him, mindful of how I ain't steppin' quite as good as I was. Glad to see I still got my hands.

Darlene shoots out from around the corner, her sawed-off 12-gauge starin' me down. "My livin' room look like some card game to you, you turncoat fuck?" she asks, violence in her tone.

"Nah," I say, lumber forward. Them beers look good

right about now. "Lookin' for Riggs is all."

Darlene freezes, lookin' at my face. She musta been in the kitchen when I knocked on the door. The gruff shouts of men dyin' and the gun shots somethin' she prayed to avoid but knew would come to her living room one day. Figured she'd go out fightin'. But now, seein' a man she recognizes, as fucked up as I am, she don't know what to do.

"What happened to you?" she asked, nudgin' the sawed-off at me. Pointing.

I pick up a beer, swig it long and slow. I feel the booze work around in my mouth and mostly spill out the side. The gunshot numbed that whole half of my face. Hard to drink beer that way.

"I picked my daughter over Riggs. He executed me and now is goin' after her. I was hopin' he was here."

Darlene, one of the crew just like I was until the card game, she knows the life. Our life. Crossin' Riggs was at best, death. At worst, war. I chose war by not dyin'.

"Yeah, I guess he hinted around to all that over the past few days," Darlene said, lowering the gun.

"Thanks for the head's up."

"I got nowhere to go. I ain't choosin' against Riggs. I can't win," she said.

"I know." I finish the beer, best I can. "Know where he is?"

Darlene looks at me with those unremarkable brown eyes she has, and scrunches those heavy brown eyebrows she has. Right here and now I can see if she had a little different upbringing, she'd never walked our path. Settled for a matchbox house that Riggs used to shelter and move dope. She's pretty in a way. Condemned to this life instead. Choices. We all make 'em. We all pay for 'em.

Finally she speaks. "I think...I think he started his rounds over."

"So he's over at Fat Cat's?"

She looks at her dirty carpet. "That's where I always knew him to start, yeah."

"Thanks, Darlene." I turn around shamble a few steps, then stop. Over my shoulder I say, "If I botch this and he comes here, you just say you hid in the kitchen while I whacked these fools and McCray talked. Not you. Got it?"

"It'll have to do."

Out the door and I do my crazy man shuffle to the cul-de-sac.

"This is as far as I'm willin' to go, paid or not, just to be up front about it," Tony says. His tone's like what I'd expect a man to use when he's leaving the mother of his children and expects her not to bug him for help.

"I'm glad you drove me this far," I say. I'm about tired of watching the haggard world pass by through these finger-smudged windows anyhow. I stick my hand into my jacket pocket gain and feel it start to tremble like electricity's starting at my elbow and sparking at my fingertips. I don't like that. Harder to shoot well. Behind my eye I got shooting pains and a pulsing sensation. My mouth's gotten dry. Tacky, wanna-close-your-throat-off dry. "I don't think I gotta 'nother trip in me anyhow."

"Get out quick, okay?" Tony says as he pulls right up in front of Fat Cat's house where Riggs' wheels are parked. In my pocket I pinched the two last bills—both sporting Mr. Franklin on them—and toss 'em up front with the others. It bothers me to watch how my arm warbles as it moves. No good.

I step out. Tony's quiet. So am I. No need for last words. Parkin' this close is goodbye enough on his part; two hundred dollars in exchange for risking his life was mine. My feet on the driveway and Tony's nearly to the next block. I didn't notice 'til now but he doused his lights at some point.

Riggs' wheels—a souped up two-door truck with the flashy paint and chrome add-ons—is idlin' in the driveway. Idiot. Five-gallon can of gas in the bed amongst trash.

I touch it, try to wiggle it. It don't want to. Full. I hear that voice right then. His voice. I try to duck, don't do it very coordinated. Hit my head on his wheel well and jiggle that bullet in there. It sends a surge of agony down my spine and I can feel it trace out along all the nerves branching off, hitting every fiber of what God stitched me together with. I want to cry, but my eye is too mangled up to make a tear. I piss myself, though. Can't have shame when you're walkin' around with your brains for the world to see.

Fat Cat's back door, some cheap metal screen door, slams shut. Fat Cat and Riggs outside. When they smoke rock they go outside. Fat Cat lives with his grandma and that woman straight up calls the cops when he smokes cigarettes in the house. She don't care that he sells dope for Riggs out of her house, but she'll be damned if he smokes anything inside. People are the strangest.

I get an idea.

I managed to slowly, steadily walk my way along the side yard, still hearing Riggs and Fat Cat make their slow, crackling inhales as they smoke up.

That lighter poised under the spoon, staying lit to melt the rock. Me trying very hard to not spill as I round the corner. Inch by inch. There they are, one guy smoking and the other guy stuffing his hands in his pockets in the cold.

My vision's gone real bad, but I think I got it. I wait until one silhouette passed off the spoon to the other. I figure the other's gotta be Riggs, and before anything can foil my dumbass plan I move.

Life freezes in time. Both dudes stare at me, not moving an inch but realizing what's happening. Maybe it's that Riggs sees me and knows he shot me dead a few hours ago. Maybe Fat Cat does the same. Maybe it's the empty one liter soda bottle I pulled out of the trash in Riggs' truck bed, cut off the top and filled with gasoline.

Maybe it's when I toss that whole bit at them.

Only problem is I don't see the gun come out of Riggs' coat pocket. His hands are free. Fat Cat is smoking, that big, bright lighter still sparking under the spoon. Just as all that gasoline splashes Fat Cat and makes out with his fire, Riggs yanks that trigger. A bunch.

The world gets warmer as Fat Cat torches up. My guts get warmer as bullets pass through them. Fat Cat screams and scrambles, a burst of oranges and reds engulfing his chest and face, him hitting Riggs and they both fall over.

Riggs hollers frantically, trying to roll the burning guy who has earned his plump nickname off him. I collapsed. A different kind of fire in my belly. Whatever time I had left just got cut down to a few minutes. I can feel the loose blood filling my guts, swelling. I have a wild fantasy about kissing Emilina's forehead one more time. The damage to my brain probably helps me think it was decent idea to begin with. But I have it anyways. My lips caressing her gentle skin, that bit of love that goes between her and me when I do. Never said I deserved her. I don't. But I got her. I want to kiss her again. I wanted that one more time. Maybe before I go to hell, God will let my soul kiss her.

"Fuck you," Riggs says. I lean over to where I can see him. Fat Cat ain't movin'. He's still on fire just enough to keep Riggs warm through the night, but his bulky ass ain't goin' offa Riggs. Some crackles like the crisp skin on a burnt hog. The smell is bad. Meat and burnt fabric. Glad I'm over here.

"Pinned?" I ask.

"You better hope you're dead before I get up from under here, you piece of shit."

"That's the Riggs I know."

He squirms and tries to roll. Burns himself on Fat Cat's smoldering coat. Shouts a bunch of swears. Settles down, lying on his back with a dead man on top of him like they was forming a cross.

"How'd you live?" he asked, out of breath. "I saw your brains fly out when I shot you."

I try to laugh. It don't sound good. "Not enough, I guess."

"You're dead now."

"Yeah. But Emilina is goin' be okay."

Riggs laughs. "You think I'm goin' die here too? Bullshit. And when I get up here in just a minute, I'm goin' tell McCray he doesn't need to kill that tard daughter of yours anymore. I'm goin' do it myself."

"You told McCray to do it? It was his gig?"

"*McCray wanted it,*" Riggs said. "Wanted to prove he could take your place in the organization."

Now I laugh for real. I can't describe the relief. It gives me strength and I wiggle around the corner of the house just enough to grab the stuff I stashed there.

"McCray ain't gonna be much good to you now, Riggs."

"Why is that?" he asks, scooting enough of Fat Cat around to add a strong drop of boldness to his voice.

"Same reason you ain't gonna touch my little baby." I get up on an elbow, ignoring how my vision had dimmed down to a pinpoint and I can't get enough air anymore.

"*Tard* baby."

"*Babies* are babies. They're wonderful. Emilina is wonderful. She's perfect." And I use every last ounce of my life to throw the rest of that five gallon gasoline can at Riggs. The nozzle off, fuel spilling everywhere as it closes the gap.

Riggs starts to say something as that liquid heat splashes across his face, his eyes. In his mouth. Some bit of it somewhere touches the remaining fire on Fat Cat and that paints a line to the rest and with a *whoommffttt*

Riggs is screaming and whipping around and beginning consumed in a blanket of flame.

"I'll be damned if that don't do it," I say. I fall back. Let Riggs lay to rest in his own grave. I ease down into the cold, bitter dirt of Fat Cat's backyard and think about my perfect baby and hope she'll get something better than me when I'm gone.

I hear the sirens coming, and they follow me down into my resting place as I go.

Cooperhead Road
Ken Lizzi

"Well, ain't that some shit," Earl Stevens said to no one. He clicked off the TV news, the anchor silenced in mid-sentence after delivering the disconcerting report.

"Legal? Fuck me." Earl digested that, easing back into the creaking leather of his dad's old recliner. Oregon voters had legalized marijuana. What was a pot grower to do? A conundrum. One probably best tackled with a bit of herbal assistance.

He worked his way noisily from the depths of the recliner, fixing to roll one. He paced through the wood-paneled living room, past the wet bar that retained his dad's shrine to Rainier, Oly, and Henry Weinhard's, and across the swept clean, but dingy linoleum of the kitchen. Earl had almost reached the basement door when he heard the gunshots.

Earl flung himself down, sliding along the floor atop an oval rag rug. The basement door brought him up short.

"Shit," he said, disgusted with himself. It was only pistol fire from somewhere. He wasn't taking incoming from jihadists in Ramadi. Probably one of the neighbors breaking in a handgun. "Get a grip, Earl."

He made his way back to the living room and out the front door. *Don't be a pussy. Scared of something? Face it like you've got a pair in your Levis.* What his old man would have told him. And hell, he wasn't scared. Reflex was all. Get shot at enough, you learn to duck.

Earl left the white-washed house of clapboard and river rock his great grandfather had built in the early 1900s. A long gravel drive led out to the mailbox along Aldershot Road. The gunshots, still popping off in ones and twos, came from Earl's left. The Mikovsky place.

Bud Mikovsky and Elvin Stevens had been old, on-again off-again friends as long as Earl could remember. They'd be drinking buddies for months on end, then Bud would discover a few of Elvin's plants on his land, hidden beneath a trellis of hop vines. Bud would come over and bitch out Elvin, not talk to him for weeks. But he'd never call the cops. Elvin would shrug, explain later to Earl as how copper choppers couldn't spot the pot beneath the hops, and point out how the two plants were actually related. Bud and Elvin were on good terms when the emphysema gummed up Elvin's lungs perma-nently, sent him to meet the previous Stevens genera-tions, the old man fear-eyed and clawing uselessly at his chest while Earl watched helplessly, pressing the call-nurse button and yelling for help.

Elvin's on-again-off-again friendship with Bud was a pattern he'd repeated with Earl's mom, Stacy. The two fought and separated as often as they made up and cohabited. The final separation occurred when Stacy took up with a Hell's Angel for what would probably have only been a fling had the biker not ridden his Harley Davidson into an oncoming log truck while Stacy sat helplessly behind him. Bud had been there to provide what clumsy, stoic comfort he could to both Elvin and Earl. Earl owed him for that. Always would.

Earl hiked through the ankle high fescue of his front lawn, cutting across to the Mikovsky place, toward the sound of gunfire. Faster than going out to the road then over to Mikovsky's driveway. Not a long walk, really, but it would add a couple more minutes. Not that he was in any hurry. Earl remembered hiking out to Aldershot Road to join his old man at their roadside fruit stand, Elvin Stevens half-stoned, taking the occasional surreptitious toke while he waited for a carload of day-trippers from Portland to drive by. Earl liked to think of him that way, content, maybe even happy. Would that make *him* happy as well?

He wondered if Elvin's death had triggered fears of mortality in Bud Mikovsky. Mikovsky had changed, no question. He'd sold off the hops entirely, moving on to chicken farming, then trying his hand at raising rabbits for the pot. Like he was trying to find something easier to do, but unwilling to cash in his chips and retire. Despite knowing there ain't nothing easy about farming or ranching. His latest project was alpacas. And heavy drinking. He was doing better at one than the other.

Earl felt a twinge of guilt. He'd not been over to see Mr. Mikovsky in weeks, the stench of despair coming off the man pushing him close to his own bout of depression. That slick-walled, grim pit lay too near as it was, his discharge and his dad's death following one after the other, leaving Earl at loose ends. Easy to misstep and fall right in with nothing to occupy the mind but memories. And the recent ones mostly bad.

A closely spaced rank of hemlock trees marked the property line. Earl could smell the tang of gunpowder and hear the pop-pop of side arms. He heard laughter as well, raucous, male. And something else. A mewling. Extended "emmmm's," like children crying.

He crouched, duck-walked to the tree line. He thrust his head between two hemlock trunks, keeping beneath the lowest boughs. A half-dozen men leaned against the cheap wire fencing—a bare step above chicken wire—that Bud Mikovsky used to corral his alpacas. The men dressed alike, in a sort of uniform of filthy denim jeans and dark brown leather vests adorned with some insignia Earl couldn't make out. Most had a pistol in one hand and a bottle of beer in the other.

Small, crumpled, furry heaps interrupted the clean swath of close-cropped grass within the corral. A couple of the heaps still thrashed about, emitting piteous bleats. Three alpaca remained on their feet, darting about the confines of the corral while tufts of grass erupted around them from missed shots. Two of these were already bleeding, dark red staining the cream-white of their fleece.

"Motherfuckers," Earl muttered. He looked about for Bud, didn't see him. Lights were on in the house, but that told him nothing. A section of Mikovsky's drive was visible past the corner of the house. Earl saw a pair of motorcycles, and what could be part of a third. Hogs, not rice racers.

Another alpaca went down on its back, legs kicking, still crying that almost human "emmmm."

"Motherfuckers," Earl said again.

"You think you're getting another fucking beer, think again," Charlene said. "Keep up your bitching, see if that's gonna help." She wrinkled her nose. "Fuck, you smell like piss."

Bud Mikovsky sat in a recliner, his arms and legs duct-taped to the plaid fabric upholstery, the seat cushion urine saturated. A hard-plastic baseball hat fitted with cup holders on either side rested on his head, two empty beer cans in each, flexible rubber straws swaying against Mikovsky's unshaven jowls. The chair faced the television in the corner. The remote control lay on the floor by the recliner where it had slipped from Mikovsky's hand earlier that afternoon.

"'Course I smell like piss, Charlene. You won't let me go to the bathroom. What you expect?"

"Last time I let you tinkle you tried to run, Bud. Your own fucking fault you gotta sit in a puddle of piss." Charlene lit a cigarette, took a long drag. *Jesus H. Christ, would they stop shooting already?* The pop-pop-pop was frying her nerves.

"At least pick up the remote for me. I can't watch another goddamn infomercial."

"Pick it up yourself. Seem to think you're good at picking things up. Me, for instance. Shit, that's so pathetic, you old fart, hitting on chicks less'n half your age."

"Half my age, shit. What mirror you looking at, Charlene?"

"Fuck you, Bud. I'm not even thirty."

Bud's laughter turned into a choking cough. Charlene stomped across the thick, gray carpet—what color it was originally was anybody's guess—and slapped Bud, sending one of the empties soaring from the beer helmet. She kept moving, into the bathroom, slamming the door behind her. *Let the fucker stew in his own piss.* At least the gunfire was slightly muted in here.

She kicked through the layers of unwashed towels on the linoleum, the empty toilet paper rolls, empty bottles of bargain value vodka, whiskey and tequila. She stooped to snag a towel, then wiped through the accumulation of filth that formed a thick skim over the vanity mirror's glass. *I'm still pretty, aren't I?* Her auburn hair could use a wash, looking a bit stringy. And, *Are those gray hairs?* Maybe her skin had coarsened a bit. But she was thin, really thin, except where it counted up top. Men liked that. And she still had most of her teeth. She probed around a cuspid with her tongue. Felt a bit loose, but not in danger of falling out anytime soon.

Charlene had seen worse, women hitting the pipe too often, beginning to care about nothing but the gack. She retained her will power. She decided when to indulge, let that exultant heat flow through her. The Speed Demons might think she was just one of their bitches, willing to suck their cocks and serve them eggs and sausage every morning so long as they provided the meth. But that wasn't the way of it. She made the choices, not the crystal, not the men.

She stubbed her cigarette out in the sink. She took another inspection tour in the mirror before leaving the bathroom. *I've still got it. Enough to pick up horny old dipshits like Bud Mikovsky anyway.*

The gunfire ceased. Charlene entered the kitchen, picking through a maze constructed of Spanish language labeled cartons of cold medicine, boxes of ammunition, motorcycle parts, and stacks of money bound with rubber bands and plastic wrap. She selected one of the half-full bottles of vodka from the litter atop the kitchen table. She found a tolerably clean glass, hesitated, then snatched up a second. She returned to the living room, filling both glasses. She slipped one into the empty cup holder on Bud's hat and inserted the straw.

"There. Friends again, right, lover?" Charlene raised her glass in a toast.

"Friends? When were we ever friends?" Bud asked, but sipped at the straw anyway.

"How about those first couple of nights? You seemed pretty friendly."

"Yeah, then you ask if some friends of yours can come over for a party. Next thing I know, the fucking Hell's Angels invade and I'm taped to my own chair. How's that friendly?"

"You had a good time," Charlene said. She finished her drink. She retrieved another cigarette and lit it. The basement door banged open down the hall past the bathroom. "And they're not Hell's Angels. Don't let them hear you say that."

Down the hall sauntered Boar, one of the Speed Demons. Over his vest, jeans and boots he wore a rubber apron and thick yellow rubber gloves, like Charlene's mom used to wear when she'd finally sober up and get around to washing dishes. Green tinted goggles rested on Boar's head, and a painter's respirator hung around his neck.

"Shut the fuck up, Charlene," Boar said. "You don't need to be talking to our host." He stripped off the gloves, the process sounding like someone stretching a handful of rubber bands. "Go get me a beer. I'm thirsty and I'm probably four or five beers behind already. Shit, Bud, you stink like piss."

Earl considered calling the cops, the idea not even surviving the walk back to his house. The Stevens did not involve the police in their own affairs, a position Earl wished the cops reciprocated. But the calculation was simple. Shit wasn't right at the Mikovsky place. Bud was Dad's friend. More than that, Earl owed Bud. Therefore the shit was Earl's to clean up. And the topper—fucking bikers. No better than the shit stain that had killed his mom.

First thing to do was figure out what exactly was going on. He needed to get eyes on the problem.

Earl drove his dad's late-nineties model Ford F-150 the nine miles into town. He ought to get something newer, something of his own. But the truck still worked. And until he figured out what he was going to do for a living, making a major purchase was off the table.

He'd always assumed he'd follow in his father's footsteps. Keep the orchard in semi-decent condition. Same with the berries and the tomatoes. Enough to look legitimate. Meanwhile, keep growing the cash crop. He knew his dad's prime spots in BLM lands. Could raise a few plants under grow lamps down in the basement among the arsenal of long guns his dad and granddad had accumulated over the decades through sources that didn't generate paper trails. Trick was to manufacture an excuse to be burning that much electricity. Christmas decoration was a good one. Grow during December, have a jillion bulbs and a sleigh on a motorized carousel ready to switch on at the first hint of Federales.

But now? Hell, it was just farming now. Legal farming. What would legalization do to the prices? What sort of hoops would the State make him jump through? Licenses, agriculture inspectors crawling up his ass. Taxes. Would the reward be worth the effort? And, *well, shit, it ain't exactly* outlaw *anymore, is it?*

He drove through the farmland, the fertile fields held by generations of Willamette Valley settlers, the houses modest but in good condition. Then the truck rose and fell as the road meandered through hills newly planted with grapes. Mansions sprawled across the hill tops, the freshly constructed homes of millionaires playing at being vintners. Recent model SUVs shared the road, before turning off left or right to reach the faggoty tasting rooms of Domaine this or Chateau that. Out of the hills, nearing town, he passed through the belt of manufactured homes and trailer parks, the abode of the agricultural poor and the out-of-work.

Hell of a difference a mile can make.

He drove through the bistros, bottle shops, and antiques stores of the quaintly charming, Main Street America tourist blocks, then on to the big box store the other side of town. He tucked a ball cap low over his eyes, noting his hair was getting a bit long and deciding he didn't care. Twenty minutes later he was driving back, his purchases—paid for with cash, of course—on the seat beside him.

Dusk neared by the time he got home. At the kitchen table he assembled the quad-copter drone and familiarized himself with the manual and remote control. He fitted the tiny, box like video camera to the drone, tested the batteries and the video link to his tablet computer.

Earl wondered what his dad would make of a pot farmer getting a chopper in the air to spy on a biker gang. *Tell me I had my priorities ass backward.*

Earl had helped launch his infantry company's Raven UAV a few times in both training and in practice, even got a few minutes at the stick. The quad-copter was less frustrating, more intuitive. A high altitude pass showed the corral as a slaughterhouse kill floor. Alpaca corpses formed little hummocks in the close-cropped grass. One of the bikers clumsily butchered a carcass, hacking away with a boot knife. Another added wood to the fire in a burn barrel, while four others stood around swilling beer. *Some half-assed attempt at a barbeque,* Earl figured.

He worked the drone close to the house, angling for a look in the windows.

Fuck. You old fool, Mikovsky, what have you gone and done now?

The drone's camera picked up images of Bud Mikovsky, strapped into his armchair, wearing nothing but sweatpants and a T-shirt. That and a cup holder hat. The place looked like shit. He counted two, no three, others inside. One looked female. So, not counting Mr. Mikovsky he was looking at an op force of nine. Better add a fudge factor, in case he'd missed a few. Figure on a dozen Ali Babas.

A pass around the house to count the choppers tended to support his original count, but there could be a few riding bitch.

All right. For the moment, Bud Mikovsky—fucked up soup sandwich of a man or not—was family. Time to

teach these asshats not to fuck with the Stevens on
Aldershot Road.

Earl could hear the bikers whooping it up as he low
crawled through the hemlocks. Dense clouds hid the
stars and the thumbnail of a moon. Back of the house
the burn barrel lit up a circle of laughing, swearing,
drinking bikers. Only the varying brightness of the
television from inside provided any illumination out
front. But it served Earl's needs. His old man had taught
him a thing or two about booby traps. As had Uncle
Sam. And, second-hand, the Ali Babas with their fucking
IEDs.

"It's a competitive business," Elvin Stevens had told
Earl, showing how to rig a spring gun with an old, piece-
of-shit twelve gauge. "Ain't the Feds I worry about out
here so much as other growers."

Earl wrapped a couple loops of wire around the front
door, eased down the front steps, checking the tension.
He dropped to his belly, sighted along the barrel. *Front
toward enemy*, he thought, remembering the helpful
printing on the convex side of a claymore mine. He elevated the shotgun another inch with a hunk of sod
ganked from Mikovsky's lawn.

He turned his attention next to the row of parked
motorcycles. *A damned shame*, Earl thought, getting to
work.

A silence momentarily fell upon the party out back. A
bleated "emmmm" filled the space. Incredibly an alpaca
still lived. *Okay then, fuck the bikes.*

Charlene woke. Something wasn't right. A concussive *whooomp* rattled the bedroom windows. Red flared beyond yellowing curtains. She pushed away from the stinking, unwashed body of the Speed Demon who'd been fucking her that night.

"What the fuck, Charlene?" the biker asked. She couldn't remember his name and ignored him, walking to the window.

Pushing aside the curtains revealed a tangle of blazing Harley Davidsons, flames leaping and dancing ten feet in the air. The explosion had blown the machines in all directions. The high grass of the front yard steamed and flared about the burning hulk of a hog. Another motorcycle, leaning upside down against the house, gouted flames toward the eaves, its spinning wheels adding a touch of pyrotechnic whimsy to the conflagration.

"Goddamnit!" the biker behind her swore, thrusting himself into his jeans. Charlene heard doors opening, boots hammering down the hallway. She heard the front door open, heard a shotgun blast. Then screaming and more swearing.

The biker tore out of the bedroom, barefoot, shrugging into his vest, a pistol already in hand.

The hell with this. Squatting in Bud's house had run its course. Time to move on. If she could get out alive. A rival biker gang? The cops? Didn't matter to her, so long as she escaped.

Charlene pulled a canvas travel bag from beneath the bed. She snatched up a handful of the clothes strewn about the floor and stuffed them in the bag. A twisted baggy of crystal meth lay on the nightstand, next to the clock, the LED display of which read 3:16. Charlene swept the meth into the bag, slipped into a skirt, jacket and shoes and left.

She stopped in the kitchen. An exchange of gunfire outside told her she didn't have much time. She shoved as many of the stacked bundles of money into the travel bag as it would hold, overstuffing it to the point it wouldn't zip shut. She slung it over her shoulder and crawled on hands and knees into the living room.

The light of the burning motorcycles showed figures outside, crouching and creeping. Muzzle flares and the *cracks* of pistol shots indicated only chaos and danger. Maybe not that way, then, not over the sprawled body of one of the Speed Demons, his chest nothing but a red mess of closely spaced craters.

"Charlene, get me out of here," Bud said. "Please." His eyes were huge in the flickering glare, terror in his voice. He stank of shit now as well as piss.

Charlene leaned back into the kitchen, snagged a butcher knife from the knife block. Loose ends.

"Fuck you, old man," she said, and stalked toward him.

Another explosion rocked the house. The front wheel, forks, handlebars, and mangled remains of a fuel tank rocketed through the front window behind a torrent of glass shards.

Charlene staggered, lost her balance, and fell forward across Bud's lap. The stench rolled over her like a wave. She gagged. She shook her head, trying to shake off the concussive effect of the explosion and the debilitating smell of the man she'd kept marinating in his own filth for days.

She pushed herself to her feet, to find Bud Mikovsky slicing through his restraints. And behind him, from down the hall, marched a roiling onslaught of fire and smoke.

Earl's position among the rank of hemlock trees farther up toward Aldershot Road provided an excellent angle on the front door. The bikers rushing out the front door fired into the darkness in front of them, assuming a head-on assault, not the oblique attack he employed. The Ruger Mini-14, one of his dad's collection of disposable, un-traceable, long guns, fit comfortably, cupped against his shoulder. Felt little different than a day at the range, or another patrol in Ramadi gone tits up. The brass sizzled past his ear, joining a growing collection. The minutes he'd spent wiping down the cartridges, along with the rifle itself, might have been wasted. Then again, might not. Fingerprints could be pesky, persistent little shits.

He put a .223 round through another alpaca-murdering biker. Center mass. Earl waited, heard no return fire. Saw no movement. Had he got them all?

The illumination from inside the front door increased. *Shit!* He hadn't meant to burn down Mr. Mikovsky's house. Especially not with Bud inside it. He hated to break cover, but he had to risk it.

He rose to his feet and ran a crouched, zig-zag pattern toward the burning house.

A shadow erupted from the corner of the house, from the direction of the corral. A biker hit Earl in a flying tackle, jarring the rifle from his grip. They fell to the grass, rolling, limbs tangled. The biker emerged on top. He slipped an arm across Earl's neck, leaned forward, pinning him. His free hand reached down to his boot, then came up with a knife. The boot knife descended. Earl caught the wrist. *Fucker's strong.* For the first time that night he felt fear grip him. The blade drew inexorably closer to Earl's chest, inching steadily downward until it dented his T-shirt. He felt the first prick of pain. The pain banished the fear, leaving only a cold desperation.

Earl bucked his hips, dislodged the biker and rolled him off. As Earl rose to his feet, his gloved hand came in contact with the Mini-14. The biker came at him in a lunge. Earl secured the rifle in both hands and brought the buttstock around, connecting with the man's forehead. *Just like basic training.* The biker went down and stayed down.

Inside the house, backlit by a hellscape of fire and smoke, Earl saw Bud Mikovsky struggling with a woman. As he ran into the house he saw a knife blade raised high, then plunge down. The woman screamed.

Earl dropped the rifle next to the overturned easy chair. The woman wasn't moving. Bud Mikovsky dropped to his hands and knees, coughing. The plastic wrapping of bundles of cash inside a duffle bag reflected the light of the approaching fire.

"Mr. Mikovsky," Earl said. He slipped an arm beneath the old man and helped him to his feet. With his other hand he snatched up the duffle bag. Bud Mikovsky reeked, even over the smell of smoke, and the smell of something else burning. *What was that?* It stunk like cat piss. *Methamphetamine?*

The two men staggered down the front steps and down the driveway, heading for the road.

The bag over Earl's shoulder was heavy, nearly as burdensome as Bud Mikovsky tottering along, leaning against Earl's other side. How much money, in large-ish denominations, would it take to weigh that much? Enough to get out of the pot business. Is that what he wanted? Did he really want to give up the outlaw lifestyle? The Stevens' tradition? It was only pot the State had legalized, after all. That left a world of banned, recreational pharmaceuticals for an outlaw to deal in. Hell, judging from this bag alone, these bikers must be pulling in a shit-ton from meth.

Could he do that? Deal with the sort of people who'd do this to Bud Mikovsky? Was that the sort of man he really was?

No. Money like this tempted a man to go legit. He'd stash it in one of his dad's hidey-holes in the woods, buried deep, and wait for the heat to die down. Then dig it up, spend it on the farm. Hell, maybe he'd grow grapes.

Earl smiled at that thought as they reached the road. He could smell the meth burning down Aldershot Road.

Drunken Poet's Dream
Trey R. Barker

"Three months."

"Three weeks? But I thought you loved me."

The harmonica tight in her fist, she bashed his nose. Thunder exploded in his head, a crack of cartilage and blood, an extreme burst of pain. Tears sprang in his eyes, nausea in his guts. His legs wobbled and he sank to her kitchen floor.

"Three months, asshole. The fuck took you so long?"

A tower of rage over him, she hit him in the nose again. Her fist came away bloody and warmth drained down over his lips and chin.

But he kept his eyes open, staring at the tarnished harmonica, cobwebs in some of the mouth holes. "The...fuck did...you get...?" She held it out but he didn't touch it. How could he touch an illusion, a conjured trick? That harmonica had left with Christine when she'd walked out and left him bloody and alone so how could it be here now?

"I do love you, Aubrey, I do...you are my best friend ever. But with him it's...different."

Aubrey shoved the past outta his head and took deep breath. Pain whistled through his skull as though she'd punctured him with an icepick and he was leaking out of himself. Her expensive two-story adobe ranch-style house hid off an empty of back road and smelled of west

Texas dust and cow shit, of the rotten eggs and struck matches of hydrogen sulfide and sulfur dioxide from the oil refinery burn-off, of the same desperation and loneliness he'd smelled every moment of the quarter-century since Christine had walked out.

"You hear me? Three months ago." The woman, a striking Latina beauty with sizzling dark hair and blazing dark eyes, shoved the harmonica closer to his face. "She's been dead three months."

"I heard you."

"Her savior." She snorted. "You ain't nothing but another used up drunk."

The pain in his nose now dull, Aubrey stood. Blood dotted his shirt. "Who are you?"

The woman's eyes blazed. "Elena. Mariah's best friend. The only one who loved her."

"But I love you, Christine. He doesn't...he's a piece of shit. He'll hurt you."

"Mariah?"

"Christine. She changed her name when she got married the last time."

"The last time?"

"Well, she's dead now, ain't she? Ain't getting married again. Seven musta been her lucky number."

Aubrey had just sat on the back stoop at Wylie's, a bar on the wrong side of the tracks in Midland, his back against the cracked brick, his ass on the stained asphalt, when Elena's letter had found him. Aubrey hadn't wanted to get it, though he hadn't known it—specifically—existed. He'd always known it—generally—would find him and when it did he wouldn't want to read it.

"Where'd you get my harmonica?"

Trey R. Barker

"Who do you think? A wino? Maybe some junkie dropped it off after Mariah died?" Elena glared "I got it from her. Just like these."

She yanked a couple of black and white pictures from her hip pocket and for a moment, his heart soared. When he and Christine had been together, he'd spent hours taking black and whites; her running and laughing, her in the old claw foot bathtub in the place he rented, her naked and seductively splayed across his bed.

I love getting naked, she had said. *I love being looked at.*

Of all the pix he'd taken, and there had been hundreds, he only had one left. It was creased and sweat-stained, folded and refolded every night of every one of those years.

These new pix were different, though. She was heavier, older, the mileage obvious and painful in her face and body and in the sag of her breasts and the veins on her legs and the tracks on her arms; the setting a cheap apartment trying for sophistication. The picture in his pocket was sexy and playful where these were rote and mechanical. It was Christine but at twenty-five years removed...it was not Christine.

"He's not good for you, Christine, he's a user. He'll hurt you. I can give you what you need."

"Baby, you can't give me anything except love."

Elena snorted and nodded toward the pictures. "He took these."

"I took some, too."

"They all did. Every boyfriend...every husband. Larry, *Laurence*, took these. He took these and then he killed her and it was three goddamned months before you

193

showed up. Wassa matter? Couldn't get outta the bottle?"

"Huh? Killed?"

"Murdered." Spittle, angry as the sandstorm outside, dotted his face, warm likes the blood from his nose. "He shot her in the *face*." The woman pounded her open palm against her cheek. "He told her all the time...'You ugly...you stupid,' then he shot her in the face."

"Her last husband."

Elena rolled her eyes. "Finally...lightning strikes. Yeah, dumbshit, her last husband. Larry. *Laurence*."

Slowly, his hand shaking like an old man's—and wasn't he an old man now?—he took the harmonica. Maybe he expected it to be hot with the promise of love like when she bought it for him and he played for her. Or maybe he expected her hand to wrap around his while his wrapped around the harmonica like she had when she was naked and lusty.

Instead, it was hot with summer heat. And silent...one of the keys long since broken. Instead of seduction there was a gaping hole through him, the dust of memory beneath the crushing emptiness of life without her. It was the same instrument but like the pictures it had lost the magic she had imbued it with.

"Love's not enough?"

"No. I'm sorry, Aubrey. I need adventure. I need excitement. It sounds stupid, I know, but I grew up out here in the dust and I want something different. We're moving to Midland."

"Bright lights, big city."

"What?"

"Why'd take you so long? She always said send it to

Wylie's and you'd get it and you'd come for her."

"I was...gone."

Aubrey had been lost between Fort Hancock, Texas, and Los Lamentos, Mexico. Not even sure what he'd been looking for, but convinced, in his mescaline haze, that he could find it on the road between those towns. He'd wandered for six months, killing and eating rabbits, downing huge amounts of mescaline. In the end?

He hadn't found shit.

"Said you'd come back for that fucking harmonica and rescue her. All those years and you never did."

"Well, goddamnit, until this—" He shook the letter. "She never reached out to me."

Elena's eyes stabbed him. "Asshole, she reached out to you every night. Thought you'd hear her heart or some bullshit."

"I never knew."

"No shit. And when she finally wrote that fucking letter where were you?" Elena came in close, her breath hot and violent. "I know what happened. I know what that night cost you. She never stopped counting the pennies and nickels and dollar bills that left you empty."

"No one knows what it cost me."

"Christine? What happened?"

"Nothing, Aubrey, I'm fine."

"Did he do this?"

"No, I tripped."

"Bullshit. He did this...just like I told you he would."

"No, Aubrey, it was my fault. He had to hit me, I didn't give him any choice."

"Whatever." Elena glared at him. "It cost you the rest of your life and you been lost ever since. You saved her and lost yourself and now she's dead and I wanna know what you're going to do."

He blinked against the sun pouring through the open window, against the dust blowing through the world, the physical pain forgotten in the spiritual pain of Christine's death.

"What. You. Gonna. Do."

"About what?"

"Larry. *Laurence*. You know how to find people, skip tracing and muscle for cheap gangstas. Go find him. Avenge Mariah."

He shook his head. "But I don't—"

"Settle your bill."

"Huh?"

"Put paid to the debt you started paying twenty-five years ago."

He stared at the harmonica, at the picture Larry had taken.

"Gotta kill yourself some Laurence. For her. For you. For me."

"For you? What? You want it done then why haven't you done it?"

She grinned, all teeth and acidic sweetness. "*I'm* not a killer."

"Dammit, Christine, what did he do to you?"

They were Christine's Teotihuacan.

Oil rigs, towering a hundred and fifty feet up, pipes clattering in the stand, the hum of the rotary drill twisting to get deeper, were elegant to her. The metallic clank and bang, the grease-stained platforms, the industrial stink, all seduced her. Christine's mother had been to Teotihuacan in Mexico and had always spoken in reverent tones of the pyramids. Whenever Christine got drunk, a diet of whiskey and Oreos and thirteen donuts from the baker who gave her the dozen and a *lagniappe*, she would tell Aubrey her mother's stories of dancing with the dead along the Avenue of the Dead on Teotihuacan. Her mother had found the dead in the dry breezes and arid winds and pyramids, in the scent of the desert, and the dead were always Christine's father, killed in an oil rig explosion near Marfa in 1969.

"Bobby do this? Again?"

"Aubrey, stop it! This is none of your business. This was my fault. I jumped on him first."

"That's shit and you know it. How many times are you going to let him do this to you?"

"Shut the hell up. You don't know anything about it."

"Yeah? Then why do you run to me every time it happens? Christine, please, lemme help. He's going to kill you."

Christine found her own dead, maybe her father and maybe her soul, in the dancing pipes stacked at the rigs' monkey boards, waiting for derrick men to manipulate them and the drills to spin them into the ground searching that oil that became gasoline. Christine would tell her mother's stories and then drive her and Aubrey until she found a rig in the desert. She'd dance, naked, in the dark just beyond the reach of the workers' eyes, to the sound of pipe tripping and motors howling.

This was the cemetery where Christine's mother and father were buried. Right now, the cemetery was sandwiched between two rigs. One worked, the din exactly what Christine loved. The other was shut down; empty of workers while long sections of pipe lay broken on the ground outside the bent and battered metal fence that kept the dead from escaping their kingdom.

"More than a beating this time, huh?"

"Aubrey, stop it."

"He do that to your cheek? With an iron?"

"Aubrey, it's fine. I shouldn't have argued with him, I know better than that."

"It's never your fault, Christine."

Aubrey found her grave quickly, the marker exactly where Elena had told him. Christine, Aubrey's only love, was dead. Shot in the face by her most recent husband, a man Elena had called a pimp and panderer.

Laurence Petit.

Who immediately fled but who, according to a couple of quick phone calls Aubrey had made this morning, was in Odessa, about twenty miles west of Midland. An electricity account, a sewer and water account, a job in a cheap bar all bright and clear on his credit report. The bar was bullshit. If he was a pimp, then the bar was a cover job to sell his women.

Christine's marker was simple; no name, just a cross. She was next to her parents and when he and Christine had been together, that plot of land, a few feet wide and a few more feet taller, had been the one constant. She had kept it clean. She had prayed at their feet more often than not, and found a calm in the midst of her chaotic soul.

The harmonica was stiff in Aubrey's pocket. Christine had kept it all these many years, since the bloody night she'd left him, unable to face him anymore. He had never forgotten the harmonica or stopped wondering where it had ended up. Through all the boyfriends and pimps, through the husbands and abusers, through the convicts taking whatever money she managed to hoard, she'd managed to keep this broken harmonica safe.

And believe that someday it would lead him back to her.

"I'm sorry, babe. I should have been there."

Bullshit. It wasn't that he should have been there, it was that he should never have left. *Spilled whiskey*, he thought. *Broken cookies. No use crying. We loved how we loved. I did what she secretly wanted but couldn't ask, and she couldn't bear to know it.*

So she had left, had hooked up with someone as bad for her as Bobby Trimble had been and standing here now, trying to feel her through the ground over her, Aubrey wondered if they all had become Bobby Trimble for her like they did for him. Every face he saw in a bar or on the street or in a cell with him, was Bobby Trimble. In all his dreams and nightmares, in every single goddamned shot of whiskey he'd knocked back. In every poem he wrote in his head but refused to commit to paper, in every song he wrote in his heart but refused to lay across his guitar.

"I didn't know who else to call."

"You did fine, Linda. I'm glad you called me."

"Aubrey, it was awful. There was so much blood. Is she going to die? I called the ambulance but then...I couldn't stay...they would have asked me stuff and... Aubrey, I'm so sorry, I cain't afford no other arrest."

"Linda, hush, you did good. Thank you for letting me know. I'm sure she'll be okay."

"She still loves you. She told me so."

"Yeah? Then she should come with me."

Aubrey could almost smell her lavender scent, almost hear her laugh in the breeze. He hadn't known any of the other bastards she'd filled her life with since Bobby Trimble. She'd slipped away and except for the occasional word from a mutual friend, he heard nothing.

Now she was dead.

All the bastards had become the first and now Larry...*Laurence*...was the last.

And Aubrey would kill him just as he had killed Bobby Trimble.

The bar was on Nuevo Street, the street itself a dive that ran for miles, populated by bars and head shops, by tattoo parlors, by a battered and bruised police substation next door to a Salvation Army kitchen, by resale shops and mom and pop groceries offering nothing but scratch-off tickets. People with worn-out bodies were scattered afterthoughts all over the street, between broken buildings, under cars and in alleyways; clusters of cancer eating away at the body human.

Aubrey, his head banging, his hands shaking, his heart as resolute as the weakest coward, stood in a parking lot. A few cars, a handful of trucks, broken bottles, used condoms and syringes. On the far side, he saw a '14 Expedition with tinted windows and wheels that spun when the tires turned. The plate was the same as his friend at Midland PD had given him.

So Larry Petit...*Laurence*...was here.

Which meant so was Bobby Trimble.

"I thought he was going to kill me, Aubrey."

"I know, baby. Don't talk right now."

"I'm scared. I tried to leave him but—"

"Shhhh..."

"Aubrey...he—"

"What, Christine? What did he do?"

"He...raped me. He beat me and he raped me. I'm so scared. He's never going to let me go."

"Yeah, he will. I promise you that."

Everything since Bobby Trimble had been shit; bottles and cheap women, fights and skip tracing for low-rent bondsmen up and down west Texas. Everything since had been self-recrimination and attempts to beat the memory out of him, or to drown it out, or even burn it out the night he set himself on fire while cooking meth.

Inside, this bar was the same as every other one he'd been in for twenty-five years. The same stink of piss and blood and stale booze and vomit and hopelessness and who gives a shit about redemption anyway. The same dull neon beer signs that offered little or no light and the same groan of tired country and seventies arena rock.

"I can save you, Christine."

"No one can save me. My soul is lost."

"I can save you. I will save you."

"What are you going to do? What kind of savior are you?"

"Get'cha something?" She was a dirty blonde, her breasts tired, her eyes empty. She smelled of big box store discount perfume and cheap soap beneath that. Her hands were scarred and her skin gone leather.

"Looking for Larry. Owe him a few bucks." Aubrey winked conspiratorially. "Heard I could catch him here."

"Who?"

"Larry? Runs the ponies?"

Her face clouded and he knew that look. For a second, she'd thought he was something different, but he opened his mouth and she decided he was exactly like everyone else who came into this place. The truth was, Aubrey felt like everyone else. Sometimes, in the midst of a bad night, in the midst of a fisticuffs or two, Aubrey knew he'd spent too many years in shitty bars with bodily fluids as the decorating motif, too many nights between buildings with blood leaking from his head or spitting teeth.

He could blame Bobby Trimble all he wanted but at some point, didn't he have to be a man? At some point, didn't he have to stand up and be who he was supposed to be? Who the Lord above wanted him to be? Or was this it? Dissolute in a bar, hungry for the next crap-tacular job that would replenish his stash of whiskey and fast food burgers and seeing Bobby Trimble in every face?

"Ponies, huh? You a rider, cowboy?"

"Hard to say."

She frowned. "You owe him or not?"

"Yeah."

Aubrey could see the caution in her face. "Well, I don't know no Larry. Might check the backroom, all kinds'a shit back there." She nodded toward a doorway behind the bar.

Silently, Aubrey slipped a ten in her apron as she headed for a trio of rig workers playing their hard hats like drums.

The hallway was short and narrow and as dingy as he'd expected. Dirty bathrooms were on one side and a cubby-hole kitchen, probably shellacked in grease, on the other. A back door was closed and a lock bar thrown across it, an EXIT sign half lit above it. Just before that door, there was another. Aubrey checked the .45 in his pocket and went in without knocking, banging the door against the wall.

"The fuck're you?" A man sat behind a desk, face startled at the intrusion. A pile of brunette hair never stopped bobbing in his lap. "Get the fuck outta here, I'm busy."

"Be careful of those teeth, boy, cut you up."

The man grinned. "No teeth. Like my women best with no teeth."

Aubrey tapped the door. "We got business. The beezer can wait."

The man laughed but pulled the woman off his cock. "A good blow will never wait, but I get what you're saying." The woman stood, wiped her lips, kept her eyes well away from Aubrey. The man patted her ass. "Keep that mouth wet, honey, and them lips warm. Get your ass back in here the second this dude leaves."

She must not have answered quickly enough or submissively enough. His hand flashed out quick as a blade, landed hard against the side of her head.

She rocked sideways, "Yes, sir," and waited for whatever was next.

"Get the fuck out."

When she was gone, Aubrey kicked the door closed. "You're a cartoon."

"Explain that."

"Cliché. Nothing redeeming about you at all."

The man grinned but it was a predator's face, lips pulled back and teeth shining nicotine-yellow in the dim light. "Whatever. I got the ponies and you wanna ride. Guess that kind'a makes me king, don't it?"

"Alpha male."

The man's grin spread like a bloodstain across his face. "Goddamned right. Alpha."

"Alpha and omega."

"Huh?" The man frowned. "Who you?"

"Aubrey."

The man's eyes scrunched and his head craned. "Sounds awfully familiar."

"We got mutual friends, Larry."

Putting himself away, the man sat, leaned back in the chair, and lit a cigarette. The air was hot, saturated with dust that hung like meat in a butcher's shop. He propped his feet on the desk. Scuffy boots, dirty jeans, a white t-shirt with sweat stains dried yellow beneath his armpits. "Larry? Got the wrong man."

Aubrey shrugged, felt the weight of the .45 in his pocket. "Your world, boss. Me? I'm just trying to get me a little ride for tonight."

"Like the ponies, do you?"

"Wouldn't be standing here otherwise, would I?"

"The fuck do I know what you'd be doing and not doing?"

"Fair point. Can I get one?" Aubrey mimed smoking.

"Ponies *and* my smokes? You ain't got enough for a smoke, how you gonna have enough to ride?" But he lit a cigarette with his own and handed it over.

Aubrey dragged deeply and blew the smoke into the sunlight. "I got what I need. Got me a taste, too... Laurence."

The man stood slowly. Aubrey saw him glance over Aubrey's shoulder, then down to the middle drawer in the desk. His leg moved just a bit beneath the desk.

"'Cause I've never seen *that* before." Aubrey went to the door and just as it started to open, he slammed it shut and threw the lock. Someone on the other side grunted and banged a fist against the door.

"The hell is going on? Boss?"

Aubrey looked at Larry. "'Boss?'" He laughed. "Boss is indisposed. We'll be done directly."

Sitting across from Larry, Aubrey said, "I had a girlfriend once. Chrissy. She was a hard-riding woman. Loved being naked, loved having her picture taken, loved being Daddy's little girl. If you get where I'm drifting."

"Drift where ever you want, but you don't let me outta this room, and I mean now, you're in for a world of hurt."

Aubrey laughed. "Man, you do anything that ain't a cliché? Talking like that ain't bad ass rockin'...it's pussy. Then again, so is beating on women."

"Aubrey you said?"

Aubrey stared at him. Eventually, the understanding came. He skinned the .45 and held it loosely, pointed at the floor. "Yeah, Mariah's friend."

"Easy, friend. I don't know what you think you know but you're wrong."

"Easy enough to clear up. Did you or did you not take pictures of her?"

"Yeah."

"Did you or did you not beat on her?"

"Well...yeah...women need to be taught."

"Did you or did you not shoot her in the face?"

"It ain't like you think."

Aubrey pointed the gun directly at Larry's face. "If you beat her, if you raped her, if you took her picture and posted it online, if you sold her to shitbags, if you put a gun in her face, pulled the trigger, and killed her...then it's exactly like I think."

"Yeah, but it ain't. I didn't do it just 'cause I wanted some bloodsport. You kidding me? She was grade A pussy. Bitch made me and my partner a fortune...a fucking mint up that cooter. Why would I—"

But Aubrey had already fired. The bullet, two hundred and eight grains moving at who even knew how many feet per second, was twisting out of the barrel almost before Aubrey realized he had fired. He wouldn't take it back, but the quickness of killing this man surprised him.

Killing Bobby Trimble had taken forever. It had taken three shots, each anchored with hesitation and doubt. It had taken hundreds, if not thousands, of heartbeats pounding in Aubrey's chest before Bobby Trimble was actually dead.

This was quick. A single shot, a rose blooming on the man's chest, surprise in his eyes for a split second before he crumpled beneath the desk.

Shoot and done and he didn't realized until nearly three hours later what Laurence had said before the blood.

"He dead?"

Elena's blazing eyes were dark and satisfied now, a smirk across her face.

"That's what you wanted, right?" He gripped the harmonica tight with his left hand. "Put paid to that long-standing debt?"

She drank sweet tea while they sat at her kitchen table. Through the kitchen window, they could see the wind had died. The dust that had been swirling was now piled in and around mesquite bushes and rocks and outbuildings.

"Alpha and omega. The first and the last."

"You killed them both. Easier the second time?"

"Easier every time, I guess. But I made some calls when I was done. Well, after I let Miss Amber take control for a while."

"Used up drunk." Elena shook her head. "Don't get what she saw in you."

"Didn't see it deeply enough, I guess, did she? Not if she kept on with abusers and pimps and madams."

Elena held his stare, gently drinking her tea.

"Turns out Larry had a partner."

"So say the whores and junkies."

Aubrey smiled. "I'm better than that; my information is better than that. Turns out that partner was you."

"Fuck off."

"Thanks for the offer, but I'll pass. Turns out not

only did Larry marry her, but introduced her to you. Most of your whores married?"

Elena eyed him over her glass. "Just the ones whose husbands owe me a bank full of money."

"So Larry killed her, I'm guessing, because she finally wanted to leave. Because she'd had enough of two users and decided to smack you both in the face with some balls. But why have me kill him?"

She set the glass down and carefully kept her hands on the table. "You do muscle. Two birds one bullet."

"He decided to quit paying, huh? Didn't want some piece of gash telling him what to do? Likes his women under control but couldn't control his bookie?"

"Bookie...dealer...procurer...whatever."

"Why not kill him yourself?"

"'Cause now I got something over you, don't I?"

He pulled the .45.

"Terrible mistake, Aubrey."

"Mistakes are my best thing. And the killing does get easier every time. So the *lagniappe* won't be no kinda problem."

Her eyes were confused. "The what?"

"The Spanish is *la napa*."

"Okay...the extra. So what? The extra what?"

"Was a dozen donuts for Christine, but for me? It's the extra bit paid on the total debt. Alpha...omega...*la napa*."

"Ain't you the big man? Shooting everyone you come across."

"No, just those who hurt Christine."

"Shoot yourself, then, 'cause you hurt her worst of all."

"Yeah, I did."

He fired and it happened even quicker than it had with Larry. She was there, grinning contemptuously, then she was dead, blood spilling across the tiled kitchen floor from the hole in her head.

He looked at the gun for a second, made sure there was at least one more round, pocketed it, and left her house.

Just Along for the Ride
Michael Bunker

The moon is in free fall. I never would have guessed it, or thought that, but after hearing my dad talk about it I guess it's true. The term "free fall" has to do with what force is acting upon a body, not particularly what direction its going. If gravity is the only force working on an object, they say it is in "free fall." So that's what's up with the moon.

And me too.

I'm not as smart as my dad by any stretch of the imagination. He's the theoretical physicist and I'm the one in here. He surely would have never gotten himself into this trouble. I am a product of my own errors, a failure of my own construction, but one way or another his theories got me here.

And then there's another construction. Built to end my life. There's that too.

I can't see outside very well, but I can hear them building it. Hammers and hand saws been at it for eight hours, no less. Carpenters and handymen called in from around the county, I reckon. Here in 1884 there would have been a lot of handy folks around, and a job is a job I suppose.

But I'm not from 1884. I'm just visiting, I guess you'd say. Dropped through a wormhole that proved my father correct. And as far as I know, Dad doesn't even know I came here.

As far as I know.

Dad said to travel just right you have to be on a certain spot and you have to free fall at just the right moment. So there are two elements there. Just the exact certain spot...and free falling at the right moment. So where is the perfect spot? It depends. It changes all the time, but according to Dad, it's predictable.

He was right.

"Pressure points" in our reality open up on a regular schedule, if you can do the math and figure it out. Soft spots in the fabric of space-time. "Like when you wear through your jeans, son," he told me once. "After reality rubs in the right place for long enough a finger (or your knee) could just rip right through the fabric."

I can make it more confusing, because my father sure enough did.

"It's like a basketball, boy, only turned inside out while you're watching it happen. Without bursting or ripping in any way. It takes more than three dimensions for that to happen. If you can imagine such a thing...and I figure you can't."

And then there was this...

"...and inside to outside of the basketball, there are long, dripping cylinders of something like plasma. Like syrup stretching from one pancake to another. And if you are in the right place at the right time, you can travel with the syrup to the same place in another time."

"Free fall. That's the ticket. That's what makes it work."

I suppose I like the fabric comparison the best.

Only this time the fabric is space-time. The stuff that keeps stuff where it's supposed to be. According to Dad, a hole would open up and something could pass through. Something...a person, perhaps. It'd only stay open for a few seconds, and then it'd close up again. For exactly one week. Then a week later (to the absolute second) it'd pop open. Again for a few seconds only.

So I figured that there would be a way to get back. If only you knew where and when and could be there at the exact right moment. And be free falling at the time.

So it ain't a little thing. All those parameters would have to be just right.

He figured it all out with supercomputers and suppositions, and probably quite a few WAGS. *Wild-Ass-Guesses* he called 'em. Things that should be true, but no one had proved 'em yet. Like that a pressure point was going to open up in the city square of Jessup, Texas on May 4th at 12:01 p.m. local time.

That's the WAG that got me here.

I watched him do all the math. I looked over his shoulder as he plotted where the cylinder would open up. And when he was gone to get coffee with his professor buddies, I stole the map. Made a copy. Put the original back.

That was the first of my crimes, and the least of them too.

Jessup, Texas is only ninety-three miles from where we live, so you can imagine how the wheels in my mind started working. To me it was all too simple. Get to

Jessup on May 4th. Hang around town until noon. Then I show up at "X-Marks-The-Spot" at exactly 12:01. Right?

Wrong.

You forgot the important part (I had to tell myself). You forgot you have to free fall.

How far? How fast?

No clue.

I remember Dad saying that it was the fact that the body would be in free fall that made it possible for the other forces to work for Time Travel. So I read up on that. Just dropping from a building wouldn't work. Apparently there is wind resistance which applies an opposing force to gravity, nullifying free fall. Seriously. So when they tell you some parachutist was "in free fall" for X minutes, it ain't true. Not unless he's dropping from space. Once he enters our atmosphere it's not technically a free fall any more.

But my dad speculated that if the fall was short enough, atmospheric resistance may not add up to enough to matter.

So again...how far? My father's friends asked this over and over.

"Just jumping up and coming back down?" They asked.

"Probably not enough."

"From the top of a tall tree?"

"Maybe too much."

"How about a ladder?"

"That might work."

Wild-Ass-Guesses. Just another WAG.

So I decided on a ladder.

There were other questions. Most I couldn't answer, especially since I'm not a scientist and my father had no idea I was planning on testing his theory myself. Questions like...would the ladder come through with me? Who knows? I had to figure that it wouldn't, even if it might. I had no idea how big the cylinder would be, or what might happen on my way through time. And if I end up in the past or in the future, will I be able to find a ladder in a week's time so I can drop back home when the cylinder re-opens? Again...who knows? It's a crap shoot. Probably suicide. If it works at all. Worst case scenario (or maybe it's the best case?) I just jump off a ladder in the middle of the Jessup town square and twist my ankle and nothing happens and then have to tell people why I'm a stupid asshole.

Now that I think of it, I did consider worse things. But none as bad as what actually happened.

I landed in Jessup, Texas, in the middle of the town square in 1884. But then you know that already.

I'd set up my ladder on the X-marks-the spot and at precisely 12:01 I jumped.

In the time it took to hit the ground, I went back 132 years. With no ladder.

I couldn't tell you what all I felt. I didn't feel much at all. Just the feeling of dropping, then the ground blurred and I heard a snap...as my feet hit the ground.

Well, I should tell you that before I jumped, I put on some clothes that I figured were as time-neutral as possible. Nothing fashionable or trendy. A white button-up shirt with black pants, black boots, and suspenders.

My hair I cut short. I figured that wouldn't be too weird, unless I drop into 1970. I bought a tiny can of marking spray paint, too, that I kept in my pocket. I intended to mark the X-marks-the-spot where I land, just in case I get the opportunity to get back home.

Frankly, at that moment I didn't care if I ever came back.

At this moment, I do.

Bobby Wayne Atkins is my cell mate. He's a bad dude, so I try not to talk to him unless I have to. He's in here for murder, too, a bunch of them, but I reckon he did what they're accusing him of. He doesn't deny it.

He doesn't say much except to mutter threats and promise revenge on all mankind.

"Revenge for what?" I asked.

"Because every human of any society that can produce a Bobby Wayne Atkins, deserves to die," he said. Then he looked at me with stone, cold dead eyes that promised all that he hoped to deliver.

It was my luck (and probably the only luck I'd experienced since I jumped) that they kept Bobby Wayne Atkins chained to his bunk. He didn't strain against his shackles or rattle his chains. He'd been a bad dog for a very long time, and he knew the drill.

Me, they left unchained. Maybe they hoped I'd kill Bobby Wayne Atkins and save them the trouble. But not me. I'm not a killer, despite what they say.

* * *

When I landed in Jessup, only two people saw me. One was an old man, half-drunk who was surprised to see me appear but not overly interested one way or another. He took a pull on his bottle and stumbled on the way he was going. The other was Henry Carroll.

Henry was about my age, slender, and his dark skin and rough hands showed he didn't avoid work. He smiled and became my friend...and betrayer.

I was painting the X-marks-the-spot when he walked over. I'd committed myself to painting the X no matter what was going on. It was part of my plan. If I got distracted by trying to figure out where, or when, I was, I'd never find the exact spot again. So when my feet hit the ground and while my footprints were still evident in the brown, dry grass, I quickly sprayed a yellow X on the ground and then put the small can of paint back in my pocket.

Henry was sauntering over from the feed store when I stood back up.

He never said a word about the X.

"Don't know where you came from, stranger, but welcome to Jessup," he said through his smile. He was picking his teeth using a splinter as a toothpick and the wrinkles around his eyes as he smiled showed kindness... and not a little amusement to boot.

"I...uhh...I just got off the bus," I said.

"Bus? You mean the stage? You from England or something?"

"Yes," I said, "the stage. And I'm from overseas... Finland."

"Never heard of it," Henry said.

"It's near England," I said.

"Good enough," Henry said, smiling. "So you're new to this country. Dressed strangely, and I can only assume you need a friend."

And that's how I met Henry Carroll.

Henry straightened me out with some second-hand clothes and a hat from the Livery where he worked part time. He was new to town too, he said, and wanted to help others like he'd been helped.

Henry was staying in the stables and he put me up there, and it was from Henry that I learned that I was in the year 1884. He kept a small notebook in which he wrote things that interested him. He showed me the book my first night in the past. It was small, tan, and leather covered, with a hand-made hemp string tying it closed, and on the front of the book the year was written in Henry's own hand.

"You keep a notebook like this for every year?"

"I do," Henry said. "At least for the last several, I have."

In his book under the current date he'd written, "Found a passing stranger, and I think he'll do fine as a 'New Friend.'"

I asked Henry why 'New Friend' was in quotes and capitalized, and he said, "You never know how things'll turn out."

"Just a WAG," I said.

"A what?" Henry asked.

"A WAG...a Wild-Ass-Guess," I said.

Henry thought that was funny. He laughed and laughed.

"A WAG!" He said. "That's exactly what it is!"

I reckon I should get to the crime.

That's the reason I'm in here, and that's why there's all the construction going on outside.

After I helped him do his work in the mornings, feeding and watering the horses and hauling hay, Henry took me around town and showed me Jessup, Texas in 1884. He took me to the L.G. Swinney General Merchandise store, and to the Overton's Quality Goods shop. We had a small steak with an egg and coffee at Menlo's Fine Hotel, and Henry took me to see where the telegraph office would be installing a telephone switchboard "soon enough," Henry said.

Then he took me to the Prescott and Vance Transport Office. We didn't go in, we just looked at it from across the dirt road.

"That's a right peculiar place," Henry said.

"What's peculiar about it?" I asked.

"Well, most towns...the folk keep their gold in the bank. But in Jessup, the bank is clean as a whistle."

"Why's that?"

"Because people rob banks, you numbskull."

"So where do they keep the gold?" I asked. I shouldn't have, but I asked.

"Right there," Henry said, pointing with his ever-present toothpick splinter. "You see, strangers and out-of-towners, they don't rush in and rob the Transport Office. It's pretty clever. Unless you know the gold is here."

"And how'd you come to know this information, Henry?"

"Just a WAG," Henry said and laughed.

I looked at him sideways until he smiled.

"I do my best to keep my ear to the ground, New Friend."

Maybe you have enough smarts to have already figured out how things went down, but I sure didn't. Not beforehand. You know what they say about hindsight. I was having a good time, and as far as I was concerned I was just along for the ride. Henry and I went back to work, and by the third day I actually started to think about staying in 1884. Things are cheap in Jessup, 1884. I had steak and eggs with coffee every day. No one pressuring me or demanding much. So long as we did our job right we got enough silver to jingle in our pockets as we walked around town looking at the sights.

We got our picture taken one afternoon. "Developed and framed in one day," Henry said, as he hung the picture on the wall of the Livery stable. We looked like outlaws from those old Time/Life western book series. We laughed and laughed at that picture.

We bought candy one morning from Swinney's— something that Henry indicated was an exceedingly rare treat—and I bought a new hat and a vest with only one day's earnings in silver. Henry bought a harmonica and at night he'd play slow, mournful songs that fit the ambiance just right under the hiss and yellow-orange light of the gas lamps.

After playing for a while, Henry would put his

harmonica into a box with his private stuff (he never let me see what was in the box. I could see the notebook, but never the contents of the box), then he'd snuff the gas lights and we'd fall to sleep in the loft, just right as rain until morning.

Nobody talked to us too much except to tell us what they wanted done with their horses or saddles, and other than that we might as well have been invisible in town. Most people lived out of town anyway and only came into Jessup to do business. I suppose if I just zapped out of town again through the time-travel cylinder, no one in Jessup would have ever missed me except for Henry.

I thought life was pretty good, and I was enjoying being along for the ride.

So I was surprised when I woke up one morning to find Henry gone. His private box was gone too. I found his notebook, though. He'd dropped it near the big sliding door of the Livery. I loosened the hemp string, opened it and turned to the current day. *Today's the day*, it read in Henry's script writing, *I feel sorry for my New Friend, but only a little.*

I walked all over town and I saw him a few blocks away from the Prescott and Vance Transport Office. He turned when I saw him, almost as if he'd seen me first, and he walked directly into the building.

Curiosity overwhelmed me, and I couldn't imagine what Henry meant by what he wrote in the notebook, so I followed him in.

He smiled when he saw me.

"Howdy, New Friend," he said.

I nodded.

"You dropped your notebook in the Livery," I said. "I hope you don't mind, but I read it."

"I figured you would," Henry said, pulling the toothpick splinter from his mouth as he took the notebook from my hand.

"What—"

I started to ask Henry about the notebook, but his hand came up faster than I could have ever imagined, and in his gloved hand was a revolver. The kind you're imagining right now, I suppose, and it was frightfully scary to behold.

Just then, a young girl came out from behind a counter. She couldn't have been more than thirteen, and she obviously did not see the gun in Henry's hand.

"My name is Laura Vance," she said rather loudly. "My father and his partner are out of the office for the next full hour." She looked down at herself as she walked. Self-important at the moment. I noticed that she spoke authoritatively, with clipped words that emphasized that she knew what was what, and we'd just have to listen to her...even if we were grownups.

She was swinging keys in her hand, and when she finally looked up and saw the pistol, she dropped them to the floor.

It was like time just struggled to move forward. It stretched out before me and it was like I was stuck in that maple syrup cylinder. I could only watch.

There was the gunshot. It wasn't as loud as I thought a gunshot might be in that situation. It was muffled, almost like there was gunpowder going off over a longer period of time than just the BANG of the guns I'd shot before. And there was smoke too, that billowed outward like the announcement of death itself.

The girl hit the floor. Lifeless. For a split-second it was like every movie death I'd seen in all my years. But...then it started, and it was *unlike* every movie death I'd ever seen. The convulsions, and gyrations. She was dead enough, but her body twitched and flopped as her legs churned in an attempt to run. There was a death rattle that escaped her mouth. Blood soaked the floor and I could not...could not...take my eyes off of her.

She was the last thing I saw because the lights went out on me. I went from stunned paralysis to being instantly enveloped in black, Stygian darkness like a cloak. Then, I woke up in this cell.

The rest I've pieced together since then.

That was three days ago. The trial was yesterday. The hanging is today.

Apparently, everyone had seen me with Henry Carroll. Simply *everyone* testified. And I do mean everyone. People I'd never even seen before talked about Henry and I eating steak and eggs at Menlo's, and buying candy, and "casing" the Transport Office like proper, diabolical, practiced burglars.

They said, "I always did think those boys were the bad sort. Evil, you know?"

And, "You could tell they were up to no good."

They had the picture of Henry and me, smiling into the camera like we shared a secret. It was the perfect set-up. Framed for sure.

Henry got away clean as can be, but not me. The

prosecutor said that "a disagreement between the miscreants after the robbery and murder left us this guilty one to stand for the crime. But this one we'll hang for the both of them."

A disagreement, he said.

I...I was just along for the ride.

So maybe you beat me to this conclusion too. I always was a little slow. Nowhere near as smart as my dad. But from what I can see if I stand on my bunk and push my head as close to the bars as I can get and look through the leaves on the trees...well...it looks like they built the gallows over X-marks-the-spot. That's just a WAG though. I can only hope.

The only thing that'll convince me that God Himself had this all planned out perfectly all along, is if they pull that lever at exactly 12:01 today.

It's been a week since I got here.

They bind my hands behind me, and a priest comes in to see if I want help. I wave him away. I'm religious, but I never was a papist, and there's nothing he can do for me now anyway. All that matters for me is time and distance. It's just science from here on out.

The time looks like it might work out right. Five minutes until 12:01. One minute to get there. They have to fix the rope and all that. A tremor goes through me as I realize what a long shot this is. Then they have to read the charges and the sentence. That'll take a few minutes. It'll be close.

I look up and at first it seems like the gallows are way too big. Then I see...

...They're made for two. There'll be two hangings today.

That's when I hear Bobby Wayne Atkins shuffling behind me.

I turn and his dead eyes embrace me like we're kin.

Oh, Jesus.

I look around to see if I can find any sign of the X-marks-the-spot, but I can't. It's covered by the monstrousity of the gallows.

Twelve steps up, about the height of the ladder, and my hearing goes away. It flashes back, but the sound is like if I was deep in a tunnel. Under water, maybe. My head spins, and I stumble. A deputy catches me and pushes me until I'm standing over the trap door.

The deputy...the executioner...offers me a hood, but I refuse it because I want...I need...to look down at that moment of freefall and see that X-marks-the-spot right under me.

The charges are read, first against me, along with the sentence, then those against Bobby Wayne Atkins. What a monster he is. He deserves what he's getting, and maybe I do too.

And then I think...what if he's over the cylinder? What if the trap door opens and Bobby Wayne Atkins drops into my own time?

I take a deep breath and it feels like time dilates. It's my imagination, but I feel myself in the cylinder, my vision gets cloudy and I look down.

I look down.

I couldn't tell you what all I felt. I didn't feel much at all. Just the feeling of dropping, then the ground blurred and I heard a *snap*.

Blood Red and Goin' Down
Tommy Hancock

He filled the doorway of the bar room, if it could be called such. It had been the second building erected in what was supposed to be a town on the road midway between Atlanta and Augusta, Georgia. A town decided on by one of the landowners who thought he'd take advantage of the growing traffic along the trail cut out of the red clay. It became less town, and more roadside stop than anything, over time. But, now, the man whose broad shoulders occluded the setting Georgia sun from peeking into the door didn't care much about any of that. He only wanted to find out where someone was.

He stood nearly six feet tall, a black leather duster hiding a body made muscular by forcing life to grow out of unwilling Kentucky soil. The wide brimmed brown hat that shadowed the man's face had been faded by too many days in the sun and stained with sweat. He was unshaven, not too many days shy of a razor, but enough that the rough look added to a somber, almost angry air about him.

The four men in the single room draught house had all looked up from their distractions as the poorly hung door squeaked open. The barkeep, a sickly thin man with skin the color of dried corn silk, stood behind the bar, two planks sitting on empty wooden barrels stacked atop one another. The other three men sat around a table, only one of four between the canvas walls, supported by a rickety skeleton of roughened wood posts and a solid back wall. Each had an empty mug in front of him.

"Looking for someone," the man said from the doorway. His voice was low, but not harsh. A hard man who didn't have to sound hard to prove it. "Told he might have been this way."

"Maybe," said the keep, leaning on the makeshift bar before him. "More and more people come this way every day, most of 'em headin' for Atlanta. Some still makin' their way to work in Augusta though. Too many to ride herd on, really."

The man in the doorway nodded, looked at the three men at the table. "Bet you three get out more than he does. Maybe you've seen who I'm looking for. Been around here a few days, hear tell."

Two of the men at the table didn't respond. The one closest to the bar, a big man in his own right, leaned back in his creaking chair. "You," he said, his words leaking out through his nose, "ain't new here yourself. Rode into town on the back of a Ford truck rattlin' through here yesterday morning, didn't you?"

The man in the hat and duster nodded and took two steps out of the doorway. "That's right. Down from Atlanta. Been looking for this feller for a bit."

"You," said the nasal speaker, "and a kid got off the back of that truck. A little girl."

As if on cue, a mass of dirty blonde hair set atop an unwashed face peeked out from behind the man. She was ten, just a couple of weeks shy of being eleven, and had green eyes that shimmered like stars. She looked around the room, wrinkled her nose up at the smell of dirty men and bad beer, but said nothing.

The three men at the table looked at each other, the one who'd been speaking nodding at the other two. The bartender started to make his way out from behind the bar, waving his spindle like arms in the air. "Now, waitaminnit...No kids allowed in here! This ain't no place for—"

The large man slid his right hand along the lapel of his duster, pulling the coat open, trapping it behind his holster. The barkeep stopped short, his eyes falling on the black butt of the .45 Colt S.A.A. revolver nestled in the leather sheath. The three men at the table took notice as well, the man who spoke through his nose sitting upright again. All three of them lowered hands from the table to their own hips.

"She," said the man, "stays with me. Never leave her alone anywhere. Don't intend to be here long enough for it to matter."

The bartender ran emaciated fingers through a mess of filthy black hair atop his head and snarled, "All right, then, but you ain't gettin' a drink here. Not with her."

"Don't want a drink. Just to know where a man is. Heard tell he called this place home, was from around here."

The men at the table laughed raucously. "Ain't nobody," said the one on the right side of the table, a potbellied squat man in a dented bowler, "lived here long enough to be from here. Hell, town ain't even got a name yet, mister. Only been here goin' on a year."

"Yeah," said the man sitting opposite him, a gaunt fellow with a hawk nose. "Little places like this all over, dontcha know. Nothin' but out of work farmers and criminals end up in places like this." The three men all guffawed again, the bartender adding his hacking chuckle to theirs. "This dude you're after, he either one of those?"

"A rainmaker," the man said. "Travels town to town in a beaten up 1902 Model A Ford, words painted on the side. Claims he can fire a cannon, bang a drum, and make it rain." He moved forward again, the little girl following behind him, clinging to his duster. "In a painted up Model A like the one what's behind your little beer house here."

"Well," said the bartender, his laughter fading into a nervous twitter, "ain't no business of mine who parks their autos or whatnot around here. No law hereabouts, along with everything else."

"Don't need law," the man wearing the Colt said. "Just want to know where he is. And the woman riding with him."

"Woman?" the man in the bowler cocked a thin eyebrow. "Blonde, green eyed like the waif there behind you? A woman like that?"

The man nodded once.

"Nope," chortled the fat man, "Not seen her. Him neither."

The man in the duster crossed the tiny bar room in two great strides, leaving the little blonde girl by the door. Raising his right leg, he kicked the chair the man in the bowler sat in, hitting as much flabby skin as he did the chair with his dust covered black boot. The chair groaned and crumbled into kindling, the fat man trumpeting like a bawling calf as he dropped to the dirt floor.

As he kicked, the man in the duster drew his gun and jammed it into the hooked nose of the man now standing to his left. His almond eyes bore down hard on the third man, also wary of the barkeep frozen in place behind him. The thin man cursed as blood spurted from his broken beak nose, pulling one hand up to staunch the flow, the other going to his own gun on his hip. But only going near it, not gripping the butt. Not staring down the barrel of an angry man's hogleg.

"No law, you said," the man with the Colt restated. "That's good with me. I need to know where the man that claims to make rain and the woman he's with is. I figure you know."

"Yeah?" questioned the man on the ground, floundering around to climb off of his ass onto his knees. "What if we do? Who are you to come up in here—"

The man's foot lashed out again, catching the fat man in the temple, knocking the bowler from his head. As he collapsed back to the ground with a moan, the man in the duster said, "My name is Titus Malone. That's all you need to know." He watched the man who talked through his nose, looked at his gray eyes as they widened for a second, then settled back on top of a sniveling smile crossing his lips. "Unless," finished Malone, "you already knew that."

"He said you'd be along," the man in front of Malone responded. "Said he was tired of running, now that he was back where he belonged. Said we oughta make sure you didn't get no further than here. Paid good money for us to do that."

Malone's eyes shifted to the fat man on the ground, still out cold. "Money was wasted on this one." He looked at the hawk nosed man on the other side of his gun barrel. "This one's out of sorts too. Leaves you, I guess."

The man answered Malone by charging him, trying to tear through the table. Titus Malone pulled the trigger of his gun, splitting the hooked nosed man's head in two as the other man crashed into him. They both fell into the table, Malone still holding his gun out, trying to keep it out of the fray. The barkeep swore out loud and retreated back behind the barrel-supported bar.

The little girl stood across the bar by the door, her eyes taking in everything. She'd seen it before, too many times to count, in the last several weeks. Ever since she'd woken up that morning on their farm in Brownsville, Kentucky, the night after the big storm. The day after the rainmaker had come into town and promised to make it rain. The day after he'd left Brownsville, taking her mother with him.

The hawk nosed man's corpse sprawled backwards, hitting the ground. Malone and the other man rolled back and forth. Malone hammered his attacker in the temple twice with his gun. The man barked obscenities and raised up, as if he were going to howl skyward. Malone brought the gun around quickly, clubbing the man upside the head with it broadways one more time. The man who talked through his nose wheezed and fell on top of Malone, barely breathing.

Malone grunted and shoved the dead weight aside, pulling himself out from under. Working his way to his feet, he glanced back at the door. The little girl stood there, her eyes on him, her hands fiddling with the frayed hem of the white dress she wore, the one he'd worked a field the other side of Atlanta for all day to be able to buy her. Now little more than a dirty rag, she tugged at the threads, watching him.

"You filthy bastard!" The fat man was up now, one eye already swelling shut, blood pouring from two busted lips. He had a gun in his hand, a .38, and he shakily aimed it at Malone.

Malone swung his gun around, not firing it, but slapping the fat man with it. He blubbered as the barrel crushed his teeth, dropping the gun to the floor. He tried to scurry backward, to get away from the next blow, but could not move before Malone's boot connected with his head for a third time. Without a sound, he fell back-ward, crushing his bowler, his tongue lolling out of a toothless mouth.

As the last of the three fell, Titus Malone strode forward. The barkeep tried to get away, backing up against the only solid wall in the building. Malone upended the planks forming the bar with his free hand, sending the boards ass over end and knocking over one of the pillars of barrels. The bartender screeched, beg-ging and swearing in the same breath. The man in the duster lashed out, taking the keep by his head of filthy black hair and bringing his gun around to rest against his skull.

"Take a gander around," Titus Malone said through gritted teeth, the muzzle of his revolver pressed hard against the barkeep's jaundiced forehead. The man whimpered in pain, the barrel pressing a circular brand into his skin, as Malone continued. "You gonna die for this? Canvas and clapboard tied to hold each other up. A few broken tables and busted chairs. And three men too stupid to stand down because some bastard's paper money's burnin' a hole in their britches." When words didn't tumble out of the keep's mouth like frightened rabbits running, Malone shoved the gun harder against his skull. "Or will it be four stupid dead men?"

The bartender's sickly yellow eyes tore away from the man about to kill him and fell on the truth of Malone's words. The three drifters lay either dead or near enough, having fallen in a lopsided triangle. He gulped, and then he saw her. A hint of filthy white dress peeking out from around the dirt caked duster Malone wore. A green eye veiled by wisps of blonde hair, shimmering like filthy gold in the red rays of the dying sun filtering through the windows behind him.

"Why," the keep wheezed, his words whistling through three long broken front teeth, "you bring a girl out here? For all this?"

The muscles in Malone's jaw drew taut, peeling his raging leer back into something out of a nightmare. He pushed the gun again, forcing the bartender's head back farther. Whimpers became sobs as Malone's breathing took on sound as well, an almost feral growling. "I'm all she's got," he answered slowly, "all that cares about her." Malone felt a tug on the back of his coat as small hands tangled themselves in it. "And I won't never leave her."

The barkeep listened, nodding, slowly realizing he'd expected a bullet canoeing through his head instead of an answer. His gaze locked on Malone's eyes, the brown of dried, hard ground, glistening with madness. Or maybe something else. "She..." a cough strangled him, catching in his throat, "she said you'd not come. Told him he was crazy, thinkin' you'd come all this way for them. Said what you said. That you'd never leave the girl."

"Where?" Malone demanded.

"Two down," the sickly man answered, "this side of the street. Not the one on the road, that's a card house, empty until later. Behind it, a little two-room shack, never fully finished even, left from when a pastor tried to bring God here. Neither of 'em stayed. There."

Titus Malone grunted, his entire body shivering as tension along his muscles repositioned. He let go of the handful of greasy black hair wrapped around his gloved hand. The barkeep yelped as he fell backwards against the hard packed dirt floor, his pants now soaked more with urine than sweat.

Lowering the gun to his side, Malone turned, his free hand searching for the girl behind him. She moved as his fingers reached for her, forcing her father into an awkward half pirouette trying to find her hand. It was one of their games, one of those things that fathers and daughters did out of habit. She giggled, circling around his right side, bumping into his gun. She stopped, holding her breath. Malone turned all the way around, finding her staring at where the revolver had been, and took her hand in his larger gloved one.

"Let's go, Delta," Malone said gently. "Time to see your mama."

Delta nodded once. Turning to leave with her behind him, Malone brought the gun around, pointing it more than aiming it at the barkeep, still laying prone on the ground, a sallow worm squirming in its own filth. "Best not get up from there," Malone warned, "'til after dark."

Their backs to the men on the ground, living and dead, Malone and the girl maneuvered their way out of the claptrap room. Kicking the door completely free of its frame, Titus stepped out into the muddy clay street, the girl still struggling to keep up with his large strides beside him. No one paid them any mind. Not the two drunks by the trough across the street. They both sat in the clay, leaning against the water bin, mumbling to one another. Not the women haunting the bath tents to their left. Not the three men standing in front of what passed for a general store, each of them leaned against a rather well kept Lambert Model A truck. No one. Like every other makeshift settlement along roads carved by farmers, outlaws, laborers, and whores, this town was populated by the deaf, dumb and blind that wanted to keep on living.

"We're not gonna see Mama." The little girl's voice was quiet, yet each word hit hard like a fist.

Malone's eyes scanned over the building beside the bar they'd just left, watching the tent flap for movement. "Yes," he said, "we are. What we came all this way for. To see your mama."

"No," Delta countered, her steps growing slower. "You came to see him. To shoot him for taking Mama."

Malone stopped in front of yet another chaotic mix of canvas and tenant farmer's shack, this one with a roughly hand painted sign hanging from its roof down in front of the door. CARDS. Leaning forward, he saw the corner of another building, this one all wood, but slanted worse than most of the tents around it.

"Yes," Titus Malone said, looking down into the dirty, angelic face of his daughter. "I mean to kill him."

The girl looked back at her father, not staring, just simply looking. Her eyes found the tiny lines around his mouth that used to pull its corners up into a smile. They saw the ruddy red of his cheeks, a trophy won by hard work in the fields. And they saw the man he'd become, ever since they'd left their home, the man he'd be until all this was done.

"He didn't make her," Delta said, clenching her father's hand tighter than ever. "He didn't make Mama go with him."

Titus Malone's eyes narrowed. He took a breath, nodded once at his daughter, then turned and walked off of the street. As they stood at the left of the card house, Malone let go of Delta's hand, and pulled his duster open. Taking his time, he reloaded his gun. As he emptied the spent shell and worked a fresh one into its place, Delta stared at the house before them. A tiny box made of four tilted walls and a poor excuse at a pitched roof, now bereft of shingles. Tar paper crinkled as a dry Georgia wind blew over it, the same breeze that teased the little girl's unwashed, yet still beautiful blonde hair. Nothing moved in the house, no curtains hung on the two windows she could see. Two roughhewn wood steps rose from the ground to the door, no porch adorning the front.

"Our house was better," Delta said as Titus took her hand again, his gun raised before him in the other. "Lots better."

Titus moved cautiously the few yards between the card house and the misbegotten church. As he came to the steps, he stopped, listening. Noises played inside the house, filtered through two walls. But still, Titus heard them. The creaking and scraping of metal. A guttural gasping, somewhere between a belch and "Oh God." And soprano squeals of pleasure, punctuated by breathy demands for "More."

Malone turned toward his daughter and knelt down on one knee. "Stay here," he said. He watched as fear started across Delta's face and he raised a single finger of his free hand to her pink lips. "Shush, girl. I'm not leaving you. Just going in here for a minute. And you can't go. Not here."

Tears brimmed Delta's green eyes as she fought to keep her lips from trembling. As she nodded, Malone stood up, tousled her blonde hair with his open hand, and made his way up the two steps. He turned the door's knob and pushed it open, pausing as the hinges screeched like off key crickets. The sounds from the room beyond didn't stop, so Malone entered.

A faded purple settee sat in the center of the front room, whatever lace and glory it once had long faded due to age. Three tiny hand cut wooden pews dotted the room in a haphazard fashion, the only hints that this place might have been meant to be a church. Malone's steps across the floor raised tiny clouds of sawdust, shed from the unfinished beams and walls that made up the building. He walked quietly, not out of precaution, but simply because it was how he moved. The moans and yaps of sex entangled with the squealing of a hard worked bed frame grew louder, almost as if they knew they had an audience. The door to the back room was closed and Titus stopped in front of it. He clenched his empty hand into a fist as he held the gun barrel up and kicked the door in.

Light from the setting sun flowed from the only window in the room, set crookedly in the middle of the wall opposite Titus Malone. The two bodies entangled in each other on the bed were bathed in a halo of red, a scarlet glow. The man was on top, twisting his head around at the caving in of the door. Matted black hair stuck to his forehead as his ebony eyes widened.

Malone took a single step in through the destroyed door and leveled his gun at the man mounted on the woman in the bed. Rolling out of her, the naked black-haired man opened his mouth, a rumbling yell rising out as he pitched to the left, going for a gun sitting atop an overturned crate.

"No more banging the drum, rainmaker." Titus Malone allowed the man to get one foot on the floor, mostly clear of the woman. He squeezed the trigger, the gun struggling to jump in his hand. The bullet planted deep into the man's neck, the fingers of his left hand splayed out desperately for the gun they'd never reach. The woman, still lying in the bed, shrieked. Blood and flesh spurted, mingling oddly with the sunlight from outside. The man turned his head slightly, as if trying to look back at the woman in the bed, and tumbled forward clumsily. Falling first on the left side of the bed, then sliding down the edge of the mattress to the floor, face down in his own blood.

Titus stepped fully into the room and up to the iron bed. The woman, her face stricken with terror, had crawled up from flat on her back, now cringing against the headboard. She made no effort to cover herself, leaving the sheets puddled around her sweaty, naked body like melting snow. Her eyes, green like her daughter's, fell on the gun staring at her chest with its single ominous, lifeless eye.

"Titus!" Her voice was high, like her carnal comments had been, but lust had given way to insane fear. She leaned forward, rocking onto her knees, a slender alabaster arm outstretched to him, pleading. "Titus, don't!"

"You left, Lizzie," Malone said flatly, his gun not wavering. "All the other men, I let that go. Because I still had you. You were still there." His right cheek twitched as the anger moved toward a fevered pitch in his voice. "But then the rainmaker came. And you left with him, with a con man. You left us."

"I'm sorry," she pleaded, advancing toward him on the bed, scuttling on her knees. He didn't waver, didn't lower the gun. "I'm so sorry, Titus. I didn't know...I didn't know..." She leaned closer, just a few inches between them now. Her fingers teased, then pressed against his unshaven chin. Still, he didn't move. "I didn't know how much you loved me."

She leaned closer to him, brazenly pressing her body against the gun, caressing his bristly cheeks with lithe strokes. Her tongue played along smeared red lips as they neared his, teasing him to taste them again. Fear still haunted her face, but hints of passion, of desire flickered along her features. Yet he did not waver. His eyes glared coldly ahead. His mouth remained pulled into a narrow frown. And, even as she played with him and seemingly ignored the barrel now resting between her breasts, the gun remained still.

"Take me home," she breathed, her whiskey-laden breath mingling with the raw smell of flop sweat and interrupted sex filling the room. "Take me back, Titus. So, we can be together. All three of—"

She bit back the next word as she glanced over Titus' shoulder in the midst of her obscene attempt at seduction. She looked into a reflection, almost. Eyes as green as hers. Blonde hair, too, dirty and unwashed, but still something else they shared. The delicate turn of her nose, the high cheeks. Lizzie Malone hesitated, at first thinking she was still drunk. Then, realizing that Titus would never have left her alone, Lizzie gasped.

"Delta."

A tremor rumbled through Titus Malone as he yanked the trigger of his gun. Lizzie's back exploded, painting the wall with gore again, splatters of blood falling on the bed sheets like wretched rose petals. Lizzie spasmed, the force of the shot staggering her, sending her backwards, still on her knees. She wavered, almost as if she might try to stay upright, but pitched hard to the right, turning at her waist. She fell almost languidly, her arms and head hanging over the bed.

Titus followed Lillie's descent with his eyes and the gun. As her head came to rest, she looked back at him, wide open green eyes, vacant, yet accusing. And still her. Titus fired again, the bullet piercing her left eye, carrying most of that side of her skull with it.

Titus Malone lowered his gun, sliding it into its holster on his hip, and he stood, studying the room. The way it smelled now more of gunpowder than fucking. How the dying sunlight now seemed more precise, sliver like needles of red striking on Lizzie's pallid, naked body.

The bodies. Two people dead to him from the morning he woke up to find Lizzie gone. It was then it had become up to him to make sure they paid for what they'd done to him. To Delta.

"Daddy." The voice was still small, only because she was, but there was nothing girlish about it. It was hard, empty, and firm.

Titus heard her speak, but didn't turn immediately. He'd watched Lizzie's eyes move and surprise enter them just before he killed her. He'd also heard the opening of the front door and the shuffling of feet across the floor. And then he'd shot her. She was already dead to Delta, too. No need for her lying words to pollute his daughter's ears ever again.

"Daddy," Delta walked up beside Malone and took his hand. "Let's go home, Daddy. Our house is lots better."

Titus nodded and looked down at the little girl. Her eyes were not looking up at him, but straight ahead, where the two corpses lay, just heaps of flesh, like so much trash. And both red with their own blood, dripping off of them and mingling with the sawdust on the floor to make a horrific mud.

"Yes," Titus Malone said, tugging at Delta as he moved out into the front room. "Let's go home."

Delia's Gone
James A. Moore

Carl Price didn't much like taking vacations, but sometimes a man just had to get away. It was the stress of the job. Sheriff of Brennert County meant he had a lot on his plate and lately it had been getting to him so, despite his personal desires, he listened to his doctor and agreed to take a week to himself.

The fishing was supposed to be good at the lake and his family had a cabin there. It hadn't been used much by him, but he paid for a groundskeeper and the man was honest enough to keep the place in order.

Back in his living room, a rather Spartan affair, there were exactly four framed pieces on the wall to the right of his recliner. A picture of him with his parents as a kid, a picture taken at his wedding, long before his wife left him of course, a picture of his folks together on their fifteenth wedding anniversary and a frame that held three different sheriff's badges: One for his great grandfather, one for his grandfather and one for his dad. It was a bit of a tradition in the family.

Sheriffs had to be elected, but so far the traditional values of his family and their reputation for getting the job done had worked well enough to keep him in office.

Of course, times were changing. The county was the same size but the population was growing. People from Atlanta were moving up his way and that was all right with Carl. New blood kept the area alive. Traditions kept it in order.

There were some traditions that were fading from the area and he was fine with that. Not all of them left as quickly as they should have. Despite his love of his family there were a few members he was ashamed of these days. Some folks who had gone around wearing white hoods and burning crosses back in the day. The world changed and sometimes the change was for the better.

The Waffle House served up a fine breakfast. Not as good as the usual fair he'd have had in Wellman, but good enough for breakfast on the road. He knew the waitress, Nancy, well enough and, like always, he flirted with her and like always she flirted back. Then it was off to the lake house and a week of fishing. He called in to let the gang know he was on the way and to call if they needed him.

They wouldn't bother him. Not a one of them would even consider calling him back from his vacation. It was the first he'd taken in five years. Somehow the business of being the sheriff got in the way of relaxing. It had been that way when he was a kid, too. Things came up and the family forgot to get anywhere for very long. Hell, most of the trips to the old house on the lake had been scheduled to last a week and lasted two days.

Carl reckoned that was all right, too. He had some mighty fine memories from back in the day.

When he got to the house he made a quick visit to the groundskeeper, a man in his seventies who worked hard for his money, and paid him for a couple of months more work.

"Ain't it a little late in the season for fishing, Sheriff?"

Carl gave him his best boyish grin and winked. "Never too late to sit down with a six pack and hope you get a nibble or two, Deke."

Deke couldn't disagree with that and the two men parted company. The air was brisk, but that was okay. He liked the cooler air. Beat all sin out of working up a hard sweat in July or August.

Likely the boys he knew were camping up this way had worked up a mighty fine sweat when they were killing Delia Greene. He planned to have a little chat with them about that. He shook that thought off. There was plenty to do before he met up with the trouble-makers.

Then he unloaded what little he'd brought with him and examined the house. It was still in excellent shape.

Carl set out his fishing poles, carefully laid out the tackle box the way his daddy had showed him, and the left the house. He locked the door. There weren't many people around but he was leaving behind his phone and all forms of identification and a man couldn't be too careful.

The old ten-speed bike was in fully working order and enough to take care of his needs.

He couldn't risk taking the car. Cops looked for tire tracks at murder scenes. They didn't often bother with bicycle tracks. At least he didn't. Not often any way.

It wasn't that far to the Newland Campsite. He wasn't checking in himself, but he'd been around the area enough times to know that there were a few dirt trails that led to the right spot.

It took a while to get where he was going, but he

wasn't in a hurry. They wouldn't come out just yet. It was too light for them and they were too sober.

The Huntley family was well known and influential in Brennert County. They'd been socially active as long as the Price family had been in law enforcement and that was a long stretch back.

Carl settled in and waited. He was a patient man when he had to be. Besides, he was on vacation. He had a week of nothing to look forward to.

He didn't have to wait a week. It was Friday night and the football game was in another town. That guaranteed a quiet time. There weren't enough people around the lake to cause too many parties. Oh, a few to be sure, but they were mostly on the other side of the lake, where his fishing cabin was. The weather was a mite too cold for most people to consider camping. That was okay. The office for the campsite, which was owned by the Huntleys, was the destination he had in mind.

Lester Huntley was the oldest at thirty-one. Les was a good enough egg for a while, but he'd gone overseas for a few years and when he came back he wasn't the same kid anymore. The families weren't all that close. They never had been, but they knew each other well enough that stories got passed around about how people didn't always stay bright and cheerful.

The Les that went away was a happy-go-lucky. The one that came back was bitter and seldom smiled. When he did pop a grin, it was most often the sort that was more a threat than a sign of happiness.

He had four younger brothers: Curt, Alan, Phillip and Michael. Mike was a good sort. Alan was a solid enough guy. Curt had been arrested several times for indecent behavior and liking to fight too much. Mostly that meant he got drunk and decided to hit on someone else's girl. When it didn't go his way, the fists started flying. He wasn't a bad looking kid, but he wasn't exactly gifted with any social skills beyond phrases like, "Hey, nice tits." Turned out most modern girls just didn't approve of that sort of thing and their boyfriends might agree, but they were obligated to beat all hell out of him for stating his drunken opinions.

Often as not it was Carl that tried to smooth things over and warn Curt to behave himself. If no one wanted to press charges, Curt got to spend a night in the drunk tank. They knew each other too well.

Phil was the big problem. Phil was a schemer. Schemers tended to start the ball rolling and see where it would go.

Phil was charming in a sleazy way. He could just about charm a person out of their wallet and watch and had on more than one occasion. There was no law against that, of course, but if he chose other things to work out in his head, it became a problem.

Carl thought about Phil while the brothers parked their respective cars on the gravel lot next to the campsite offices and the "Recreational Center" for the place. Georgia weather being what it was, there were days when the rains fell too hard for anyone to enjoy the lake. When that happened the rec center did good business with its three pool tables, four ping-pong tables and its big screen TV that was mounted to the wall. The TV and ping-pong were free. The pool tables were a dollar a game, quarters only, please.

Carl knew that at least half the summer the family

sold beer and harder stuff under the counter. He didn't care. They were smart enough to sell only to adults, which meant he had no reason to care, especially since the only people using the facility were also staying at the facility. Years of following that policy and there had never been a problem.

It was the off-season that caused troubles.

On four occasions over the last two years the three boys who were currently settling in to watch the Falcons pre-season game had been accused of rape. Different girls, all of them underage and all of them coming forward days or weeks later.

The problem with underage girls was exactly the same as the problem with underage guys: they always seemed to have something to prove. It had been that way when Carl was young and it was one of the elemental truths that never changed.

Mostly what they seemed to need to prove was that they were old enough to handle the liquor. It was a false glamour. The idea of getting ripped somehow came across as a good one and it usually took the ones that survived a few tries to understand that it was only fun until the morning after.

Carl didn't know if date rape drugs were involved or not. All he knew was that a few girls had come forth and made claims about being done wrong by three men who should have known better. In every case the charges were dropped when the girls suddenly had a change of heart.

Only one ever came close to saying she'd been bought off. She wouldn't actually say it, but she didn't *not* say it either. He couldn't force the young ladies to tell him anything and he didn't know *for certain* that they'd accepted money or been intimidated or shamed. That was the real problem. Never quite enough to pursue a court case after the ladies changed their minds.

That was okay. Each of the men in question didn't have enough evidence to prove that Carl had pulled them over when they were alone and explained how badly he would ruin them if they ever did it again, either. Hearsay works both ways. Proof is required in a court of law and none of the three had ever said a word to anyone else so far as Carl knew.

Phil was the one who gave him the most trouble. He'd pulled Phil over for speeding. Phil made it a habit. He liked going high speed on winding back roads almost as much as Carl liked busting the assholes that did exactly that. Too many wrecks he'd worked where people died to let him think speeding in the mountains was a fun sport. The exact figures changed every summer but it normally averaged in the low teens for serious, crippling injuries and anywhere between five and seven dead each summer.

Sometimes Carl thought his doctor was right about the stress of the job. Usually when he was thinking about watching the bodies hauled up the side of steep hills a day or more after an accident because no one noticed that car down in the ditch until well after a body had a chance to bleed to death.

So he was happy when he caught Phil.

Phil had been drinking. Not a lot but enough and when he was stopped he came out of the car full of righteous indignation until he saw that it was Carl. A lot of folks tried being angry as a defense for getting busted.

It tended to work better on the occasional new deputy than it did on the sheriff. Especially since the sheriff was slightly smaller than a bear and had a reputation as a hard ass. Carl was always glad to smile and he never had a problem with well-mannered people. Yelling was frowned upon.

"Say, Carl. How's things? Was I speeding?"

"Now, Phil, you know the posted speed here is twenty miles per hour. The road's just too damned curvy and the drop off is a nasty one." He smiled as he asked for license and registration. Phil twitched. He wanted so badly to argue, but there were the recently dropped rape charges and Carl's reputation for writing bigger tickets when people pissed him off was well known. It didn't take a rocket scientist to see the wheels working in Phil's head as he licked his lips and stared at the badge stenciled on Carl's Brennert County Sheriff's Department T-shirt. That was late July and damned if Carl was going to sweat to death in a uniform when he could wear the T-shirt.

Carl took great pleasure in making Phil wait while he pretended to look up all the information he'd already memorized on the privileged dick weed who liked to drive too fast.

Most of his record that stuck was moving violations. None of the rapes had made it to court. Not a one of them. But Carl had done his very best.

He was smiling when he crawled out of the cruiser. Being a stretch over six feet he couldn't just slide out. He preferred his truck for that reason, but it was in the shop. Again.

"Well, Phil, I guess I can let you go with a verbal

warning this time." As he spoke that smarmy smirk spread across Phil Huntley's face. Carl handed him back his license and registration with his left hand, and Phil started to work his way around to a "thanks" that would have taken several minutes. Once freed of the risk of a fine, he was downright pleasant. It was part of his MO.

He stopped trying to find the right words around the time Carl's fingers reached between his legs and grabbed hold of his balls. Phil let out a small squawk and then a soft whoop when Carl made a fist.

"No ticket today, Phil. But I'm watching. You *and* your brothers. Next time I hear a girl say you even looked at her funny, what happens will stay off the books." He made sure not to squeeze too hard, just enough to make Phil as docile as a newborn baby. "Tell me you understand, Phil. Tell me I don't have to repeat myself a little louder."

"I get it. We're good."

"This is a friendly conversation, Phil. Let's keep it between us, and I won't have to search your car for the shit you and me both know is there." It was a complete bluff, but not much of a stretch. Phil was that dumb on the best of days.

Phil nodded very hard and Carl gave one more squeeze before letting go.

"Nothing happened in the past that I can prove, Phil. But you're at strike four right now. I hear anything, it's going to be bad." Carl spoke with great cheer in his voice, as if he was telling a friend to have a great day. Phil was still looking sick and very likely considering puking on himself when Carl left.

Carl wore a cup for that reason. You just never know when some asshole is going to try to crush your testicles into dust.

That was his favorite of the three conversations. All three of the brothers, wisely, had failed to mention anything to the local police department or to anyone else, because all three of them understood that what Carl was saying was like their rapes. No proof it ever happened. No possible punishment would come of it, and Carl Price was old school enough to know other ways to handle people who complained too much.

Four generations of his family had been sheriffs. The dirt he had on everyone in the county was unsettling. A few times he'd handled disputes between some of the more influential families, including the Huntley's, merely by mentioning how he didn't want to air out any dirty laundry. Walter and Mary Beth Huntley, the parents of five rambunctious boys, were also on county committees, city committees, school committees and involved in social circles that were the envy of many. To them scandals were like kryptonite to the Man of Steel. And if Mommy and Daddy weren't happy, none of the Huntleys were happy.

So no, no one mentioned Carl's tactics, because shit rolls downhill and the family preferred the near scandals of the rape accusations be pushed aside and forgotten as quickly as possible.

What Carl hadn't expected was that the brothers would decide it was best to just kill the victims of their gang rape tactics.

He had no notion if the murder was intentional or an accident and he didn't give the least bit of a damn. All he had was hearsay that would never stand up in a court of law, not when the Huntleys had a few lawyers who ate smaller lawyers for breakfast.

Delia Greene had last been seen alive four days earlier. She and her family had been staying at the campground over the summer and there were no incidents, but two different witnesses that Carl had spoken to mentioned her hanging around with Curt Huntley, and they claimed Delia liked to talk a good fight when it came to the idea of partying, but that she never went through with it. She was fourteen and liked to brag. What kid didn't? Two different girls said that Delia'd been talking about her new boyfriend who was older. The only name that had been uttered was "C" and she'd been seen by two others hanging with Curt Huntley.

When Carl mentioned Curt's name the girls said "maybe."

When Carl mentioned his name after Delia's body was found, both of the girls said they couldn't remember. The way they said it, Carl knew they were lying. They couldn't even look him in the eyes.

She was fourteen and she was flirty and she had a pretty face and a slightly over developed body. She was, as Carl's mom used to say, "chesty," and when her body was found she had been "cleaned" with bleach, but the vaginal trauma still showed on the body. She had been sodomized repeatedly. She had been slapped around a bit, too. She had been strangled, but before that, she had been stabbed a few times with what appeared to be a sharpened stick.

There was no DNA evidence to be found.

Sometimes, the old ways are better.

Back in the distant past his grandfather had escorted more than a few people to the edge of the county and warned them not to come back. Some of them came back anyway and he drove them by a different route to a different part of the county line where he didn't have to tell them anything. They weren't coming back at all.

His father had done the same thing in cases where the person in question wouldn't listen. No one spoke of those things. No one. Not ever. It was understood that sometimes things had to be taken care of.

By Carl's count four of the six unsavories escorted away by his granddaddy had been suspected of inappropriate behavior with the youth of the area. Two of those youths dealt with the shame of unwanted children in an era where that sort of thing ruined lives beyond redemption. Their reputations were the least of their concerns. Some things you don't get past. Carl couldn't hope to imagine.

Delia Greene never had to imagine.

Delia was gone.

Her body was found down in one of those damned ditches alongside the winding roads in the mountain areas. She was naked. She was broken because whoever had tossed her out knew the area well and she had bounced off of rocky outcroppings several times along her way to the bottom of the gully. She'd have still been there, like as not, but a tourist was taking pictures of the foliage and spotted her body.

All three of them looked surprised when Carl walked into the rec center. He made sure no one else was around before he opened the door and stepped past the threshold.

Les half jumped out of his skin. He had never been very calm since coming back from his travels. The beer can in his lap dropped and spilled and frothed as he stood. He didn't say a word, but his hands clutched at his chest in a nearly comical gesture of shock.

Curt didn't stand up. He stared at Carl's form with wide eyes and his mouth pulled down in a sneer that had nothing to do with his dislike of the Sheriff.

Phil stood up too, and opened his mouth. "Hey now, this is private property and we're closed for the season." As was typical of the bastard, he hadn't even checked to see who he was talking to. He just knew he didn't want to be bothered.

When he did look, he paled.

Carl said, "What did I tell you boys? Each one of you? What the hell did I say to you? And now Delia's gone."

Carl wasn't sporting his service piece. He wasn't foolish enough to take a gun with him, because they make too damned much noise.

His hunting knife was much quieter.

Curt tried to run, but Carl was bigger and faster and before he made two paces Carl had kicked his knee hard enough to make it go sideways with a loud crunch. Some people might have screamed at that, but Curt fell quiet and pale. Carl stooped down long enough to drive the hunting blade through the side of his neck and to cut through his trachea. His throat belched blood and air in a wet mess.

Phil came for him and Carl blocked the drunken

swing that came for his head. One move to clock, a second to wrench Phil's arm around and with a little torque dislocate the man's shoulder. While Phil was screaming, Carl broke his neck.

Les put up the best fight. He nailed Carl once in the stomach and then drove his fist into Carl's side twice. Carl was a big boy. He could take a few hits. Les let out a groan like a wounded animal and tried to shove Carl backward. Instead he slid himself, his foot catching in Curt's blood.

One elbow to the face pushed Les back enough for Carl to finish things. The last of the brothers slipped back two steps and the blade came out again. He stabbed Les once in the side and once in the throat. After that Les didn't make any more noises. Like his brother, he bled all over the floor of the rec room.

Curt had a truck. Carl made use of it. The county line was only three short miles away. It wasn't even ten at night by the time he got back to his cabin and cleaned up.

Sometimes, the old ways really were better.

Don't You Think This Outlaw Shit's Done Got Out of Hand?
Levi Black

This road was a mistake.

I knew it the second you made the turn off State Road 17, wide rear tires singing as they left asphalt to chew on red dirt and gravel, but I didn't have the air to say it.

Damn Rodney's cousin Skeeter and his pissant .380 pistol. That's the one that got me. All those bullets they threw at us and it was his, the smallest one, that punched me right below the nipple, slipped between two ribs, and began to bounce back and forth inside, chewing my left lung into so much pulp.

So I couldn't say: *Don't turn on dirt, they can't catch us on asphalt, not in the Chevelle. I've put too much juice under her hood if we just stay on the road.*

Dirt's no good for running. Too twisty. Too narrow. Too rough.

Especially for you.

You were doing fine up on 17, but here? Here you're off your game.

I usually drive.

You hang in your seat belt like it's a parachute harness, fighting the wheel, the car under us rocking and bouncing, the ass end slewing left and right trying to wind us in a ditch and you *make* it stay on the road at this speed by sheer determination and you're beautiful.

Fucking stunning.

Hair soaked with sweat and pasted to your neck like we just made love on a summer night, outside among the cicadas and the lightning bugs as you are want to prefer. Brow furrowed in concentration, lips pulled in a snarl as you roar back at the motor that revs and ruts under your command. The tendons of your neck stand out like cables and your muscles are spring steel as you wrestle the damn car into submission.

Beautiful.

Fierce.

A goddamn Valkyrie.

On your own, you'd conquer this, leave the road and the car and the driving quivering at your feet as you rise in triumph.

But Rodney and his boys are right behind us, piled up in Skeeter's Silverado. The one modified and jacked up for off-road mudding.

And he knows this road even better than me.

The first night we met.

It's the first cool night at the end of summer. The first night it's not sticky on your skin just standing around. Four weeks into high school football season where the whole town turns out on Friday night in parking lots downtown to listen to the game on tailgates and drink beer.

Go Coyotes.

I'm leaning on the hood of my car, the one you're wrestling with now, and I just finished the last swallow of my beer when I *feel* your eyes on me, some jungle sense kicking in and making me itch between my shoulder blades. It takes a second to spot you in the crowd but when I do it lights me up like someone attached jumper cables to my pecker and hit the juice.

You're next to Bo McClintock and his crew of meat-heads but your back's to him and your witchy brown eyes are laser-locked on me.

All it takes is a smile and you start walking my way without a sideways word to Bo.

You come across that fucking parking lot, sleek legs under a short red summer dress, dark hair bouncing off your shoulders, and I know what it feels like to be stalked by a panther.

Goddamn, you were gorgeous.

Are gorgeous.

I'm so locked into your stare I don't see Bo until he catches up to you and grabs your arm right in front of me.

"Hey, where do you think—"

He doesn't finish the sentence before your hand makes a little hard fist and hits him right in the mouth. You have to go on your tippy-toes to reach that high.

He lets go and steps back, bumping into two of his crew, teeth stained red where they cut his lip when you hit him. He looks shocked, like he just got tasered and can't think straight. Then his big, square face goes mean and he pushes forward, reaching for you again.

"You little bitch!"

He stops short at the high, sharp crash of my beer bottle against the hood of this car.

I hold the wicked sharp end of it between us and push off to stand straight.

Redneck Switchblade.

You slide up next to me and stand there and I can feel the hard line of your body next to mine and it makes me go all loopy inside, like the things in me aren't anchored anymore and I want to start some shit.

"Turn around or I'll give her this bottle and let her cut you from balls to bullshit, Bo."

Everybody is looking at us.

Bo glances around. "This ain't about you."

"Ain't about *you* anymore. Walk away."

He stands there trying to make a decision. He's got three guys at his back the size of refrigerators and most of the people in this parking lot like him way more than they like me.

If the Sheriff gets here, Bo knows he'll be in the clear and I'll be in a cell and back on probation.

Dads look after their sons after all.

But everybody knows that Sheriff McClintock has a thing going with Becky Lou Shumacher on the other side of the county and Game Nights are their special nights because her husband, Coach Shumacher, is a bit tied up. Plus, Bo's unsure if anyone would've even called him yet. Deep inside he knows he's just enough of an asshole that the crowd around us might wait long enough to see if he'll back down or get cut.

They might want to see if I'd really do it. Am I just like all the other Rakestraws? Would I lay him open like gutting a fish?

I look deep in his left eye, pouring it all in there, letting him feel it.

The neck of the broken bottle is slick in my hand.

His boy, Trey, puts a hand on his shoulder. "Let it go,

man. That out-of-town whore ain't worth it."

Bo lets himself be pulled away.

I turn and you're smiling that crooked little smile of yours, dark eyes aglitter with something that makes me feel it deep in the valley of me. You tilt your head toward the bottle. "You got another one of those for an out-of-town whore?"

"That was my last one, darlin'."

You tilt your head toward the car. "I guess you'd better take me to get more."

I toss the broken bottle away and open the door, watching the hem of your dress climb you as you climb across the driver seat.

God.

Damn.

"Stay with me, baby!"

I bounce out of the darkness I didn't know I'd rolled into. My head careens off the glass window and leaves a smear of sweat that blurs it like Vaseline. I don't think much time has passed. We're still in the car, still on the dirt road.

The Chevelle shudders and jerks as we get tapped in the ass by Skeeter's truck.

I feel it in my kidneys like a bat across them. Soft tissue damage.

Bruising.

Rupturing.

My left lung hitches, trying to draw air in with the pain but it has no purchase, like trying to catch water with your feet. I cough and it feels like someone tried to pick me up with a tow chain attached to my asshole.

It hurts.

A lot.

You scream in anger and the car lurches as you stomp the gas and almost shoot us into the embankment on the left.

Everything goes up and sideways. The cardboard box full of Rodney's drug money slides across the backseat and tumbles against the door behind me and pain shoots up my leg all the way to my chest as the twelve gauge in the floorboard rattles around like dice in a cup and smacks my knee, blued steel barrel against my tendon and bone.

That'll leave a mark.

"I'm sorry, baby. I'll get us out of this."

I can't look at you. I want to look at you, but it's all I can do to watch the road. I know this road.

I know it.

This road takes you to Merscham's Field where I convinced Jenny Holliday to finally let me get my hand under her dress.

Down by the river.

Down by Deadman's Bridge.

I fight to stay conscious even though the black is squeezing my eyes.

Just get us there, darlin', and I'll fix this.

That first night together we stuck up Old Man Crenshaw at the Suds N' Stop for a case of shitty Miller High Life and two bottles of Mad Dog 20/20 using the .357 my daddy left behind when he bailed on Mom and me. We found a cutout on a back road like this one and drank our ill-gotten gains and laughed as the adrenaline of it all buzzed under our skin. You glowed that night, all lit up inside with excitement, sparks zipping around inside you. I could see them as you slid that red dress up your body and then your body up mine. We did it here in the front seat, our skin slick with passion and our mouths full of the too-sweet taste of stolen wine.

The fall and winter passed and we were together, like we are now, mated and fated. Outlaw married, living the outlaw life. Doing crime for money but mostly for the fucking thrill of it.

Nothing gets you worked up faster than when the guns come out.

It sounds like I'm saying you forced me to join you, coerced me in some way, maybe even seduced me to the dark side.

Bullshit.

I'm right here with you. Always have been even before we met. I don't fit the straight life and neither do you.

But we fit each other.

Goddam right we do.

And together, we are hell on wheels.

I'm drifting.

Shit.

Hard to think with no air in me, gimping on one lung in a '69 Chevelle doing a rocket impersonation on a shit red clay road while some white trash wannabe druglord chases us.

Rodney.

Pushrod Shubert.

Biggest dealer in the Tri-County area.

Biggest asshole too.

I didn't want to get back involved with him, but around here if you want to do some outlaw shit you gotta go through him. We wanted to pull stakes and head to Atlanta, but we weren't ready, not without some seed money.

So we went to work for Rodney.

Driving product to the next county, picking up tax-free cigarettes for him, a little of this and a little of that. As long as it paid and got you hot we were in.

Sometimes we were the ones who held the guns when bigger assholes came around to do business.

That's why we have the shotgun.

But Rodney got too comfortable around us. Under-estimated how much we want to go, start a new thing in a bigger town. He didn't think we were real outlaws, just kids playing at it.

He didn't know how you get around a lot of money.

He shouldn't have left that damn box full of it just sitting there with us holding guns.

The bridge looms ahead of us, looking like a rickety old barn that could fall in any second. It's almost a hundred years old, built by the mill that used to be at the other end of this road. It's not going to fall in, these timbers are oak soaked in tar pitch. Rock hard and waterproof, they'll never rot. They aren't going any-where.

But the planks across them? Those aren't so steady.

There's a big hole in the middle of the bridge, been there forever.

Big enough for a car to go through, falling into the river a hundred feet below.

You've managed to make some space between us and Rodney. They aren't far behind, but the straight part of the road back there and the gravel let you pull ahead, and they're out of our sight.

You keep pushing the car. The bridge keeps getting closer.

I yank on the seat belt, pulling myself forward, swiping at your arm. It hurts to do it but I need your attention.

"Slow down." I push out.

"What?"

"Slow....down."

You hit the brakes and it pushes me forward against the seat belt. It feels like I'm being cut in half. Gotta stay awake. This is the important part.

My hand flops out to the right. "That side." I flop again. "Hole."

You nod and twist the wheel, moving the car to the right side of the bridge.

I flop and gasp. "Closer."

Your mouth goes hard and you shimmy us right some more. The timber rail disappears from my sight and I know you're almost touching it with the car.

Damn, you're amazing.

I hope the fucking hole hasn't gotten worse.

We're down to a creep.

I'm watching you, trying to pray to God above, that we have enough room to squeeze past but it feels like I'm talking to dead air. Your eyes go big and you lean toward the window, looking down.

"Fuuuuuuuuuuuuuuuuuuuuuuuck." The word slithers out of your mouth.

I know when we pass it because your whole body relaxes against the steering wheel.

The sight of you like that makes me want to gather you up, fold you against my chest and hold you, tell you it'll be alright.

Instead I flop.

You look up.

"Over....and stop." I unfasten the seat belt as you do it.

"Baby?"

I don't answer 'cause I can't. I don't have enough left. Not for that and this. With the seat belt off me I slump forward, creasing to the left without the lung to support my ribcage. I grab the barrel of the shotgun. It's hot under my fingers.

Damn, my hand is white.

My other hand slaps at the door handle, fingertips catching it, the weight of my arm making it open.

"Baby, what are you doing?"

I want to tell you. I want to recite you poetry, to sing you a song. I want to tell you a thousand words how much I fucking love you, to describe in detail the perfection of your lips, the curl of your lashes, the line of your collarbone. I want to use every word for beautiful in the English language and then I want to start on Spanish...then French.

I want to breathe all these things into existence and to kiss you one last time, pressing lip to lip, twining tongue to tongue, drinking you, eating you, tasting you forever.

All I can do is croak out three words.

"Don't...look...back."

I flop right and roll along the seat, stumbling out of the car. My feet hit wood and I push with all I have, locking my knees, standing.

The shotgun is in my hand.

Good.

I forgot I was going to bring that.

I can smell the river wafting up through the hole in front of me.

My head has gone staticky and I hear you scream as if from across a field, just loud enough to hear that you're crying as you do it.

Skeeter's truck rumbles onto the bridge. I feel it through the planks under my feet.

You scream again and the Chevelle roars as you pull away.

The shotgun weighs a million pounds as I swing it up to my hip and point it at the truck.

Through a circle of darkness that steadily closes around my vision I see Rodney yelling at Skeeter and pointing at me. Skeeter hunches forward over the wheel and his shoulders jerk when he hits the gas.

The truck roars toward me, pulling toward the railing. The entire bridge shakes and my teeth clatter against each other.

I'm numb from the waist down and ice cold and the world keeps getting narrower.

They get closer and the world gets smaller and finally I jerk the trigger. The shotgun bucks in my hands and flies away but in my tiny sliver of vision I see the windshield of the truck crack and bust and Skeeter's shirt go red across the chest. He goes limp and loose around the wheel and the truck jerks left.

I'm blind when it goes through the hole, but I hear Rodney scream like a stuck pig and I feel the hot wind of their backdraft on my face and I have just enough time to think "I love you, darlin'" before it sucks me forward and I topple in behind them.

Snake Farm
Les Edgerton

It starts with trouble. You don't think it starts with peace, do you? William Goyen, in an interview with Reginald Gibbons

The guy in the cell next to mine confided in me once that his father abused him sexually. That isn't a news headline. What he told me later was, that his mother also assaulted him sexually. That's a story that goes above the fold. Either, by themselves goes on page eight if it goes at all. That both parents took him to bed is a headline. You know: *Man bites dog...*

His name was Jerome-something or other, I forget his last name, but I remember his prison number—#36693—since it told me right away how long he'd been there—before me at #49028. It's important to know how long your next-door neighbor has been inside—it tells you how you should probably conduct yourself around him. If he'd had a number newer than mine, that'd be different. That'd be someone I was over, you see?

He was a weight-lifter and a tall man. He took early parole by jumping off our third tier. The advantage in this kind of early parole is that you don't have to check in with a P.O. like a sixth-grader who's been grounded for not eating all of his supper.

The disadvantage is...It undoubtedly hurts when you stop, at least for a nanosecond.

The reason I mention James-something or other, Inmate #36693, is that he didn't make his swan dive because he was depressed over facing the rest of his life in prison. He didn't take an early out because he was being molested. Or because he'd been threatened.

He didn't even take it because he couldn't face one more meal of beans.

He took the flight to nowhere because of Thomas R. Melon.

Yeah. You read that right. Thomas R. Melon, the guy who writes those bestselling crime novels. Whose last novel was the sixth one of his twenty-two novels to be made into a movie, starring Mickey D'Angelo. Melon's the guy *People Magazine* does a feature on at least twice a year, the usual accompanying photo a shot of him staring soulfully out to sea, digging his toes into the sand, crinkly Photoshopped eyes. Who is regularly interviewed on PBS and MSNBC and even legitimate news organizations.

Ha! Got your attention now, don't I!

Thomas R. Melon who was known as a "franchise" to both the publishing and film worlds.

I'm sure you already have lots of questions at this point. "Story questions" as Thomas R. Melon referred to them in the few workshops he taught here at Pendleton Reformatory. One question answered, eh? Leading to even more questions. The biggest, of course, is how we came to partner up and create the justice system of human roach removal which you'll observe at the end of this.

I'll do my best to answer all of them. It's what Melon taught us in our workshops. To develop a tight plot, one that answers all the major story questions at the resolution. To avoid those "godawful amateur epilogues" (as he referred to them).

Let's begin...

I was Melon's star pupil in those classes back in the joint. His "discovery." Like he was Columbus and I was the New World of writers. A Grandma Moses of convict writers. A thing like that plays great in *People Magazine* and on *The View* and other mindless venues.

We met a couple of years ago. He'd pulled some strings and got permission to spend the night inside our walls for some "research" he was doing for a prison novel he was planning to write. He thought if he spent a night in a cell in Pendleton he'd soak up the atmosphere and would have an inkling about what it was like to do time.

Yeah...

I'll give you a minute to get your head around that...

Anyway, he spent the night in the cell next to mine and kept me up all night yakking, asking dumb-ass questions. Guess he figured everybody was like him. In the morning, he'd leave, stop at a diner and have him a cup of coffee and a big breakfast, go over his notes, get him a motel room to catch some sleep-eye. Me, I'd drag myself over to the chow hall, try to keep my eyes open while I stuffed down some cold powdered eggs and a liquid that didn't resemble coffee in any form that a Starbucks barista would recognize, and then hoof it over to my job, where I'd stand on my feet all day, cutting other inmate's hair.

About six months later, his fucking book came out, where his main character was the warden in this prison and some kind of amateur detective on the side. He got just about everything wrong with the prison scenes and the story was lousy to boot. It was worse than any James Patterson written-by-the-numbers crock-of-shit, if that tells you anything. I figured out who the bad guy was by page twenty-three and I don't think I'd ever encountered as many clichés in one single book as I had in that one. But, he mentioned me in the acknowledgments and I have to admit, that hit my ego bone. I mean, he was like a semi-big name and people on the bricks didn't know he was a complete phony, so it kind of made me a big deal for a while. I even got letters from those weirdos who like to write prisoners. I did what all of us do who get those letters—bled 'em for every blessed nickel I could, even tried to get one wasn't too awful fat to marry me so I could cop one of those conjugal visits. They all seemed to fall into one of two camps—either as big as a house and wearing a dress looked like a floral-patterned couch covering or a meth addict who was partial to tattoos and tooth decay. No bites on my proposals...Guess they were choosier than they looked.

As it happened, Melon got this idea he wanted to teach writing in the joint and got that arranged and that worked out well for me as he asked for me to be his assistant and that got me out of the barber shop once a month for all afternoon.

And that's where it began.

It got me out on early release and that's when the fun

started. With Melon's help and connections, I got me a book published. Picture of me on the back, looking hard like the suckers expected and wanted. Did some TV interviews, stuff like that.

Whole bunch of phony hooraw. All the book was just some shit I'd done in the past. Burglarizing bars, holding up liquor stores, fucking a bunch of women. Stuff like that. Stuff I went to outlawing for that lots of guys wished they had the balls to do, but hadn't. So, instead of doing what I'd done, they got some tattoos, hung out down at some strip club once a month, got a subscription to Netflix. Lived the *Reader's Digest* condensed version of the wild life. The sanitized, safe version.

Like that.

But, that was my audience. Them and the bad girls. The bad girls recognized me. I was the guy they'd known when they were young. The guy their husbands didn't know about. That was some funny shit, all right. I seen 'em when I walked off whatever TV interview I was doing. Or, in the bookstore when they had me signing books. I seemed to almost always end up in the parking lot getting my weenie waxed with one of them old gals in the back seats of their Suburbans. I found out one thing. Fans of writers were nice, but most weren't lookers. Whole different crowd than rock star or athlete's groupies.

The one good thing Melon did for me was getting me to read other writers. And, not just the usual suspects. Melon really knew what good writing was, even if he didn't do much of it himself. I found there were some fucking fantastic writers out there. Harry Crews, Ken Bruen, Ray Banks, Tony Black, Paul D. Brazill, Tom

Franklin, Larry Brown, Joe Lansdale, William Gay, Neil Smith, guys like that. Mostly Southern—although Banks, Bruen, Brazill and Black aren't Southern, but could be.
Even a blind hog can find acorns now and then.

Hi. It's me, your intrepid author, Thomas R. Melon. You can call me "Tom" or even "Tommy." All my friends do. I know I'm breaking all the rules by addressing my reader directly, but I do shit like that all the time—break the rules—and it hasn't seemed to hurt my sales much. Last time I checked—about two minutes before I sat down to write this, I had three books on different Amazon bestselling lists. Top ten for two of them and #19 for *Breaking Bad* on the Thriller/Heist/Novella/Noir/Experimental Fiction list. That ain't bad for a country boy! The meter just keeps goin' round and round!

All that crap about breaking rules is just that—crap. I use a million clichés, pretty much the same plot each time, and have a bunch of characters with names real parents never give their baby boys...and the readers eat it up. Hell, I'd even talk about my johnson like Elroy did and get away with it, except it maybe ain't that big. Ha-ha. Then, maybe it is...You'll never know...Unless you want to, that is. Only if you're a good-lookin' mama. Text me if you are and I'll sext you back...

Anyway, I've got this guy I'm teaching to write and got him hooked up with my agent and all, and Jim Twigs, our agent, told us he thinks a book we cowrote could be a big seller. So, here we are. My cowriter is a guy named Jake Mayes. I know you don't know his name yet, but you will. His first book is just out and I hear it's doing okay. It's not #1 or anything like that, but Twigs says it's holding its own and even got a mention in the *Times*. And, I don't want to brag, but I'm pretty sure he wouldn't have even written a book if it wasn't for me and for sure even if he had, it wouldn't have gotten published! So, there's that...

The book you're reading—which hasn't been written yet at this point in time—ha-ha—that's what I'm doing now—was laid out by our mutual agent (who I hooked Jake up with). There's two main characters—me and Jake—and it's kind of a memoir-kind of thing. Jim told us to just write our part of our time together—when and how we met, what happened in the last couple of years—stuff like that. Neither of us will see what the other is writing until Jim edits it and puts our two parts together. Which, since you're reading it, has been done. Obviously.

Anyway, that's how this thing came to be. I'm pretty sure Jake's going to be going on and on about how much I helped him and all that, but it might not show up in the final version you have in your mitts as I instructed Jim to tone down what I anticipate Jake is going to be saying. I want this book to help him, not me! I mean, like I need more publicity, right?!

Okay. Enough of the intro stuff. Let's get down to it.

I met Jake inside the walls of Pendleton Reformatory almost exactly two years ago. How that came about was I was planning my next novel—*Criminal Minds and Intents* was the original title, but if you bought it you know it as *Snake Farm*—it was #5 on the bestseller's list after all, so chances are pretty good you've read it, right? And, if you haven't, now would be a good time to glom onto a copy. Just sayin'...

Anyway, I'd written a bunch of really good crime novels, but I wanted to write one from the criminal's point of view. I know a whole bunch of criminals from over the years from down at the Dirty Vixen, but for this one I wanted to do some really deep—some "down and dirty"—research. I wanted the experience a criminal has. So, I called my dad. Dad is a big-time contractor (as you know if you've read my bio), and knows all kinds of people in the state and even region. Lots of folks owe him favors, if you get my drift.

"Dad," I said. "I want to spend the night in a prison. Can you make that happen?"

Turns out he could. He just happened to know the governor of Indiana and half an hour after we talked, he was back on the phone to me to tell me it was all arranged. I would be spending the next Thursday night inside the gray, concrete walls of one of Indiana's two maximum security prisons. Pendleton.

Just like that.

The day began when I took the superintendent, H.W. (Henry) Clinton, out to lunch. He gave me the real low-down on what to expect.

"I'm going to put you in a regular cell, Tommy. Just like the prisoners have. I have to warn you—it's small. But, you'll have it to yourself. No cellmate."

Doesn't bother me a bit. I've spent many a night in a small space. After all, I regularly travel to Europe and if you think a prison cell is small, you obviously haven't spent a night in an Italian hotel! Bring it on!

"And," he said. "You'll eat the evening meal in the chow hall. Don't expect sirloin steak! Ha-ha!" (Which was what we were both having at that moment.) Again, that didn't bother me in the least. If it was really bad, well, I just wouldn't eat it. I can afford to miss a meal now and again! Least that's what my girlfriend says. She's a hoot.

All in all, nothing he warned me about was concerning. Yes, I said, I understand that sometimes it's difficult to sleep with inmates yelling and cursing all night. Again, I'd spent more than one night in Rome!

When we arrived at the prison, Henry took me into his office where he had a pair of dungarees, a blue denim shirt with a number stenciled above the left pocket—#90666—tidy whitey underpants and T-shirt and white socks, and a pair of black brogans. After I changed, he handed me a large soup spoon.

"What's this for?" I said.

"It's your eating utensil," he said.

"Then I just pick up a knife and fork in the chow line?" I said.

"Uh, no. It's your only eating utensil. You keep it with you all the time."

Well, that sucked! I wasn't expecting sirloin, but even if it was a poorer cut, how was I supposed to cut it? I asked him that and he laughed.

"You won't need anything to cut beans," he said.

"Thursday is Bean Night?"

Again, he snorted. "Pretty much every night is bean night," he said. "There might be some pork fat in it but you won't have to cut it."

I *had* been packing on a few pounds lately. As good a time as any to do a bit of fasting...

I entered the inside of the prison at five in the afternoon. Just in time for chow. First, Henry turned me over to a guard—one of the "bulls"—and he escorted me through at least four different sets of steel doors and then we were...*inside*! A truly exciting moment. I confess my heart was beating at a furious rate. I'd been allowed to take with me a ballpoint pen and tablet, and I tried to walk and scribble furiously as we went on our way to Cellhouse J. We kept passing various inmates and each time I looked 'em squarely in the eye and smiled.

Kind of a surly bunch. Not a single one smiled back. In fact, some of the looks I got were downright scary. I faked it well, though. I put on my "jailhouse swagger" and strode right along with the bull, a guy named Edwin Jones. A black guy. He looked like he could handle himself if we got into a tough spot. I stuck as close to him as I could without it looking...you know...*gay.*

And...just as we reached the steps of J, a big burly inmate walked by us and from barely two feet away...blew me a kiss. I almost wet my pants but I acted as if I hadn't seen him.

The cell they'd assigned me was on the ground floor. Directly across from the desk of the officer on duty. I guessed that was so he could keep an eye on me in case trouble went down. I truly wanted the "real" experience, but was secretly glad they'd put me there. After all, if I wasn't going to be in that cell, a real convict would have been, so it wasn't that big of a deal, right?

Mr. Jones saw me into my cell, shook my hand, wished me luck—luck?—smiled, and exited. Almost

Les Edgerton

immediately, the door slid shut and locked with an evil
thunk!

Shit.

Before I'd entered the cell, I saw that the cell on the
left was unoccupied, but there was a guy in the cell on
the other side. I'd smiled at him and nodded before I
went into my cell, but he didn't return my greeting. Just
stared at me.

I looked around. Two racks that were hooked to the
wall by chains. A small shelf and a metal mirror, and a
small sink. That was it. The lower bunk was already
made up so I figured that's where I'd sleep. No chair or
anything to sit on, so I sat on the bunk.

Besides my spoon, the superintendent had also given
me a small cloth bag he called a "ditty bag." I meant to
ask him where that name came from, but had forgotten.
I opened it and dumped the contents out on my bunk. A
pair of headphones, a washcloth and small towel, a
toothbrush, toothpaste, a small bar of soap, and a small
white gauze bag and a packet of cigarette rolling papers.
A pack of matches. In the gauze bag was something
weird. It was full of tiny brown flakes. It smelled like
tobacco when I sniffed it, but it didn't look like any
tobacco I'd ever seen. It was stamped with the word
"Hoosier."

I knocked on the wall where the bunks were attached.
"Hey," I said. "My name's Thomas Melon. What's
yours?"

At first, there was just silence. Then: "Mayes. My
name's Mayes."

The bull who was sitting just across my cell at his
desk, shook his head at something that seemed to disgust

him, picked up a bunch of keys, and walked away down toward the other end of the cellblock.

I got up and moved down to the end of my bunk, close to the bars. "Mayes what? What's your last name?"

He must have been up toward the front of his cell too, as I heard him clearly. "That's my last name. Jake."

It took me a second to realize he was telling me his first name.

"Glad t'meetcha, Jake. What're you in for?"

"*Motherfucker!*" I jumped at the sudden vehemence in his voice.

"Hey—what's the—"

"Asshole, this your first time in the joint?"

My plan originally had been to act like I was an old con, but that story seemed to have collapsed. "Well, yeah. How'd you know?"

I could hear him sigh. "You never ask a guy what he's in for, punk-ass."

You don't? I didn't know that. Why on earth not? "Sorry," I said. "Why not?"

"You must be the writer," is what he said. Then: "Welcome to the snake farm."

"Yes," I answered. "Thomas Melon. You've probably read my books."

I heard a low chuckle. "Yeah, right. You seen the library in here?" He paused. "I guess not," he said. "They probably didn't give you the nickel tour, did they."

We continued talking and he gave me bits of advice. I asked him what the "Hoosier" was and learned it was free tobacco the state gave the inmates in case they couldn't afford store-bought, or, as he called them, "tightrolls."

"Cigarettes are money in here," he said. "Why the state gives you all the free tobacco you want. Fewer fights that way. It's crap, but at least it smokes."

I tried to roll one. Three times the paper burst apart from too much spit. The fourth time, I didn't use enough, and that didn't work either. Finally, on the fifth try, I got one together, although it didn't look that hot. I got about three draws out of it before it too, fell apart. Fuck it.

"What's that about a snake farm?" I said.

"Just my name for here," he said. "It's pretty much like that. Boring, except when someone gets bit. Then it livens up some. You'll see."

A whistle blew.

"What's that," I asked my new friend. "A riot going down?"

He laughed. And laughed and laughed. Finally: "Naw, man. It's the chow whistle. They'll be rollin' the doors soon."

Sure enough, almost as soon as he'd told me that, I could hear doors sliding open all over the place, on all three tiers. Except mine. It stayed closed.

Jake walked over to the front of my cell. "Uh-oh," he said.

Uh-oh?

"Looks like you've been tagged."

"Whaddya mean, *tagged*?"

"Somebody musta paid the hack. Why you're locked in. Bet while we're at chow, you get a visit. Somebody wants your brown eye."

My...Oh, fuck!

Then, he told me some other stuff. Something about a hammer...My blood sugar must have been low because I kind of blacked out for a minute. When I gathered my thoughts again, he was gone.

"Guard!" I yelled. Again. "*Guard!*" It was more of a scream than a yell, but I couldn't help it.

"What?" It was the guard I'd seen earlier at the desk. He looked perturbed.

"Have I been tagged?"

"What the fuck? What's 'tagged'?"

"I dunno. It's what he—" Jake was gone.

"Look, Mr. Melon, we can't let you go to chow. You probably wouldn't make it back. Somebody will bring your supper to you."

A long single file of convicts paraded past my cell, exiting at the cellhouse door which was visible from where I stood. More than one looked my way and more than one smacked their lips and winked at me.

I wasn't that hungry anyway.

That first meeting with Melon was funny. They brought him in just before chow and stuck him in the cell next to mine. At the time, I was over in J Block, kind of the honor cellhouse. Had a first floor cell, smack dead across from where the hack's desk was. Which was why they put him there, I figured. Keep a better eye on him in case.

Right from the start he was a jerkoff. Asked me what I was doing time for. I just about lost it at that and then realized he wasn't a real con and just didn't know any better. So, I decided to fuck with him a bit. When they blew the chow whistle, he asked if that meant there was a riot going down. See? Fruitcake, all the way.

Then, when they rolled the cells, they kept his locked. He freaked out at that and I got to have some fun. I told him it looked like somebody'd tagged him. I just made it up on the spot. Told him some queen musta seen him and paid the hack to keep him locked down when the rest of us went to chow. Told him some other stuff too. That when we left, whoever had the hots for him would come down and he'd know who it was because he'd be carrying a hammer.

"A hammer?" he said. "What's that for?"

"To bust out your front teeth," I said. "Lets you give better blow jobs."

I couldn't see him when I told him that, but there was a little noise from his cell, like he'd sat down hard. I guess I could understand that, I was him.

Then, we went out to chow and I had to dump half my supper in the garbage can as I'd been laughing too much to eat while I told my buddies what I'd done. That was okay. I still had two bags of Keebler's back in my cell and I always had my hotspot and a thing of hot chocolate powder. I wouldn't go hungry.

He appeared to be some kind of pissed off when we came back from chow. I stood outside his cell for the few minutes before we had to go back in for lockdown and tried to talk to him, but he pretty much ignored me. That was okay. I don't think he knew that in half an hour they'd be rolling the doors again. It was our night to have free time in the cellhouse. Half the cellhouses get to go out each night to the gym or the yard and the other ones got to have free roaming time in the cellhouse. We had a little black-and-white TV on the other side and some rows of benches. You could watch TV if you wanted, or just walk around, shoot the shit, play cards, checkers, shoot craps, play guitars, shit like that. All the cell doors stayed open and you could visit with your friends inside a cell. You could also get shanked, get raped, get your head busted open. All kinds of possibilities...

I figured I'd have some fun with him then...

Hooray! My new friend, Jake Mayes, talked the guard into letting me out of my cell during recreation period. Now I'll get the real low-down on what it's like being a real convict.

It turns out Mr. Mayes fancies himself a writer. That was a surprise—a pleasant surprise. It gives me an idea. Something I've mulled over at times. While he's giving me the cook's tour during rec hour, I'll pose it to him. My idea? To host a weekly writing class inside the walls! In fact, it's a done deal in my mind already. I'll make Jake my convict assistant. See if he does have any talent and if he does...who knows?

Ten minutes until they roll the doors!

Five minutes until we get out. I may have made a mistake. I talked the hack into letting Melon outside. He called up another hack so they could keep a better watch on him and Mr. Keyster (the hack) told me that if anything happened to the guy, it'd be my ass.

Just great...

Okay. They just cranked 'em open.

I met him on the walk.

"C'mon," I said. "Let's go 'round to the other side. They got a TV over there and it's where most of the guys go."

I had to chuckle at him. Out of his cell, walking down the range, every time I glanced around, his eyes were as big as soup bowls. You could feel the fear dripping from him.

We'd just turned the corner when a guy leaped down off the first tier in front of us.

A big-ass black dude.

Who I knew.

Jerome something. He was in for killing his Sunday school teacher or something. Plus his entire family. I thought he was over in safekeeping where they kept the really bad dudes.

Guess not.

He landed like a cat not five feet from us. Took a step toward us...something in his hand...

A bunch of papers.

His novel, turns out.

Turns out he found out Melon was here and he even knew who he was. Turns out he'd also been writing his life story and thought Melon would like it, get it published for him, get it on the bestseller list and make a pile of money. Turns out, he thought once all that happened, he'd be able to snag one of them pardons the governor gives out in honor of his cat's birthday once every ten years.

Turns out, all of that happened except: Melon didn't

like it, didn't get it published for him, which meant it never got on any bestseller or even any worstseller list, didn't make even a small pile of money, and for sure never snagged one of them elusive pardons.

Pretty much no parts of Jerome's dreams turned out the way he'd envisioned them.

Why he took the early parole...

Seems Melon decided he didn't want any more of the inmate experience and ended up canceling those writing classes after three or four of them. He did end up using the experience in a couple of his next books. He shoulda stayed a bit longer. He was still calling the hacks "bulls" in those books, which he woulda learned wasn't what we called 'em if he'd stuck around a bit longer. He still used words like "shiv" too. Our collaboration remained unpublished also. The only place it's appeared is in my cell. He left me his contribution and that's why I can let you see it here.

One thing he got out of it was the title to his next book. He called it *Snake Farm*. That came from me.

About a month after his last workshop, they moved me up to the third tier into the cell next to Jerome. You know, the guy who thought Melon was going to cream his jeans over his "novel" and make all kinds of exciting, magical things happen for him.

Melon didn't even read it. He told me that. He told Jerome he had but that it wasn't quite good enough and to keep at it. After that, Jerome sent him two-three rewrites and after the last one, he didn't even bother to send it back. Just ignored him. I passed on to Melon what Jerome said he was going to do to him next writer's workshop and that's when he canceled the gig. Jerome had tried to get into the class but Melon wouldn't approve him. I guess he saw the writing on the wall—Jerome, that is. A week after the last class was canceled, Jerome canceled himself.

And, that's where we're at right now. I'm on my way up to Melon's apartment. He thinks I'm going to turn in my contribution to our memoir. I kind of am, but not exactly. What I am going to turn into him is the last chapter. Which I'm writing right now. Which I'm going to end with a shank.

Schmuck like that shouldn't ought to be allowed to fuck with guys inside. Guy gets fucked by both his mom and his pop shouldn't get more grief from a lame like that. Melon shoulda at least read his book.

Just purely irritates me.

Truth or Consequences
(Waitin' Round to Die)
Christa Faust

Don't you fucking die on me, you son of a bitch. Not yet.

Seems like the sun is never gonna come up. It's cold as hell, but it's hard to tell if that's because it's actually cold here or because I'm gutshot and bleeding out slow. To be honest, I'm not even all that sure where "here" is. We're broke down on the side of some long straight road through nowhere. Utah, maybe. I just hope we made it out of fucking Wyoming.

I hated Wyoming like it was the other woman ever since you inherited that spread outside Meeteetse from your fuck-up brother back in '94. I get that things were rough for us around that time and we were coming off a couple of way-too-fucking-close-for-comfort brushes with the law. You took it real hard when we ended up having to kill that young girl in Quartzite and you were looking for a place to lay low and lick your wounds.

Thing is, I never signed on to be a rancher's wife.

When we first met, you were everything I ever wanted. The outlaw cowboy poet of my teenage dreams. It was 1966, and I was a sixteen-year-old runaway from the Bronx playing gypsy across the Great American Southwest. I had ridden a variety of forgettable men through San Angelo and Roswell and Las Cruces, but when I saw you smoking and squinting against the gritty wind outside a dive bar in Truth or Consequences, New Mexico, I knew you were the only one that would ever matter.

Less than five minutes later, you were fucking me against the rusted husk of a wheelless pickup truck out back.

Twenty minutes later, we were robbing the joint.

In the heady aftermath of that first time, everything felt so true, remember? So raw and real and like everything that had happened in our lives up until that moment was just some depressing show on black and white TV. Driving a stolen car across the Arizona border with the windows down and my hair whipping across my lips, I felt like somebody different and special. Not just the third of five unwanted daughters with a drunk loser dad and a faded ghost of a mom all packed into a cramped basement apartment on 231st street. I left that girl behind for good that night. That night, I became the woman in the songs you would later write about me. I was Truth, and you were Consequences.

It was true love, with a bullet.

Fuck, babe, that was so long ago. Before Wyoming. Before all the lies and drunken tears and other men. Before cancer. Before either one of us really understood the way things are.

Look, you knew I'd get bored in Wyoming. I got a restless spirit and an even more restless pussy. Up until then, you always gave me the action I needed, both in and out of the sack. You swore you'd rather die than settle down. Don't fence me in and all that cowboy bullshit. But watching you sit there on that rickety old porch every morning, looking out at the cold, indifferent mountains with a notebook balanced on one knee and that smelly mutt at your feet, I saw my hot-blooded partner in crime slowly fossilizing into an old man I didn't recognize. Maybe you were scared or tired of running or what fucking ever, but it drove me nuts that you didn't seem to need anything else anymore. Because I was always burning up inside with dark and ever-changing needs. Needs that could never really be satisfied, no matter how many men I fucked, robbed, or killed.

I probably should have left you for good years ago. Not like I didn't try, over and over again, but I kept on coming back. I'd take off for a few months, pull a quick score or a short con to pay for whatever plastic surgeries I needed to stay fuckable as long as possible. But I'd inevitably find myself in a ritzy hotel, coming down hard off a coke bender with some kid less than half my age passed out next to me, and I would suddenly need you so bad I could barely breathe.

When I would pull into your dusty driveway and get out of whatever bullshit luxury car I'd bought myself that week, I'd see you there sitting on the porch with your dog just like always. You'd stop playing that beat up old Washburn guitar, put out your cigarette and hold out your hand to me.

"Come on, then," you always said.

Then you'd take me to bed and it would be like it was 1966 all over again. Afterwards, I would fall asleep with my head on your chest, cheek resting against the scar from where I stabbed you that one time over that Mexican bitch in Bullhead City. I've fucked thousands of men in the past fifty years, but I could never sleep with anyone but you.

Of course, that all stopped when the doctors had to take your jaw off seven years ago. It didn't even work, because the damn cancer came back anyway. We had to have that Shoshone woman come in to take care of you, to clean your feeding tube and help you in the bathroom. She was good and strong, but I would have rather had somebody uglier. You liked her, though. Don't think I didn't notice you trying to look down the front of her scrubs while she was giving you a sponge bath. It's too bad I didn't come up with this blaze-of-glory plan until after they moved you to the nursing home. I would have liked to shoot that big titty bitch just for touching your dick.

Things got a little better between us when you were in the home. I was old enough by then that I couldn't get myself into too much man trouble. I spent most of my time by your bedside, pouring whiskey down your feeding tube when the nurses weren't looking, singing half-remembered songs and reliving all the wild stories of our bad old days. I kept thinking about how we swore they'd never take us alive, how we were gonna go down in a hail of bullets like Bonnie and Fucking Clyde. Live fast and die young, only that's not how it went at all and there we were on the other side of a mountain of hurt and disappointment and torn off calendar pages. You were dying, old and slow, and the surgeons just couldn't keep me pretty anymore. That was when I started to think maybe it's not too late for us to ride off into that lead sunset like we always wanted.

You couldn't speak but you could write, although you

didn't seem to have much to say. Over the years, you'd filled hundreds and hundreds of notebooks with tightly handwritten lines, mostly heavy shit I didn't really understand. The only part I could relate to was the stuff about how terrible I was.

How terrible and how wonderful.

But in the home, you mostly just wrote requests for more dope or to be changed or repositioned in bed. Sometimes, you would write that you loved me. You wrote it when I told you I was gonna bust you out of that place. Tapped the word LOVE with your pen three times like I might miss the point.

You're moving your fingers now, a feeble gesture that means you want to write something. There's blood and bile dribbling out of your feeding tube and what's left of your face has gone ashen and waxy. It takes a minute for me to find a pen and something to write on in the broke down stolen car. My hands are cold and not working so good, but I eventually find a cheap giveaway pen from an insurance company and a Walmart receipt. It takes you a long time to scratch out what you want to say and it's hard to read in the faint yellow glow from the cracked dome light, but I get it eventually and it makes me want to punch you.

GO HOME NOW.

You tap the word HOME like I might miss the point. I take the pen from you and throw it out the broken window.

You thought I was taking you home. Home to Meeteese and that shitty ranch. I killed seven people and three cops trying to give you the badass outlaw death you deserved, motherfucker, and all you really wanted was to go home? What are you Dorothy in the Wizard of Fucking Oz all of a sudden?

Okay, so maybe I fucked this up a little, since the hail of bullets that was supposed to take us home to glory only left us wounded and dying the hard way. What can I say? I've been killing cops for too long to not shoot back. But it's not like I didn't try. It's the thought that counts, right?

You're not listening anymore, are you? Your eyes have that cloudy, half-moon Frankenstein look now, the one I know way too well. It means you're as good as gone, and I might as well be talking to myself.

I can't help thinking of that young girl in Quartzite, remembering how her pretty brown eyes had gone Frankenstein like that after I'd cut her throat. I remember yelling at you to help me lift her into the motel bathtub so I could scrub your spunk out of her pussy. You were standing naked in the doorway, face sweaty and red from drink and you yelled at me.

"I never wanted this," you said "I just wanted you."

At the time, I figured you meant the admittedly ill-advised threesome thing. But now, watching you die years later, I have this cold, sickening feeling in my ruptured belly because I think I finally understand.

I thought I knew you all this time, but maybe I only ever knew the fantasy version of you that I created in my own head. Maybe the real you was that old man sitting on his porch with his dog, writing shit I didn't understand in a battered notebook. I thought I was giving you the outlaw death you really wanted, but you never wanted to be an outlaw in the first place, did you?

You only played outlaw for me because that's what I wanted.

I'd take you back home now if I could, babe. I would, I swear, but it's too late. You're already gone and I'm coming up fast behind you. All I can do now is sit here in the blood-slick driver's seat of a stranger's car and wait for the sun to come up.

Or death.

Whichever comes first.

ABOUT THE CONTRIBUTORS

J. L. ABRAMO was born in the seaside paradise of Brooklyn, NY on Raymond Chandler's fifty-ninth birthday. Abramo is the author of *Catching Water in a Net*, winner of the St. Martin's Press/Private Eye Writers of America prize for Best First Private Eye Novel; the subsequent Jake Diamond novels *Clutching at Straws, Counting to Infinity*, and *Circling the Runway; Chasing Charlie Chan*, a prequel to the Jake Diamond series; and the stand-alone thrillers *Gravesend* and *Brooklyn Justice*. www.facebook.com/jlabramo or www.jlabramo.com

TREY R. BARKER has published a bit of everything: crime to mystery, science fiction to nonfiction, plays to novels, and a short-story collection. He spent seventeen years, off and on, as a journalist before moving into law enforcement. Currently, he is a sergeant with the Bureau County sheriff's office, the crisis negotiator for the regional special-response team, a member of the Illinois State Attorney General's Internet Crimes Against Children Task Force, and an adjunct instructor at the University of Illinois (Champaign) Police Training Institute. He currently lives in northern Illinois, though he was born and bred in west Texas. Find him at www.treyrbarker.com and @treyrbarker.

ERIC BEETNER is the author of more than a dozen novels including *Rumrunners, The Devil Doesn't Want Me, Dig Two Graves, White Hot Pistol*, and *The Year I Died Seven Times*. He is co-author (with JB Kohl) of

One Too Many Blows To The Head, Borrowed Trouble and *Over Their Heads* and co-wrote *The Backlist* with author Frank Zafiro. He lives in Los Angeles where he co-hosts the Noir At The Bar reading series. For more visit ericbeetner.com.

LEVI BLACK is James R. Tuck and has several books out under both names. He is also a professional tattoo artist of twenty years, a former bouncer, and co-hosts the "Fanboy and Geek Girl Power Hour" podcast with his wife. https://leviblackbooks.wordpress.com

MICHAEL BUNKER is a *USA Today* Bestselling author, off-gridder, husband, and father of four children. He lives with his family in a "plain" community in Central Texas, where he reads and writes books...and occasionally tilts at windmills. In November of 2015, *Variety Magazine* announced that Michael had sold a film/TV option for his bestselling novel *Pennsylvania* to Jorgensen Pictures, whom is developing *Pennsylvania* for production into a feature film or television series. Michael is writing the first draft of the screenplay. Michael's latest (and best rated) novel is *Brother, Frankenstein* which was released in late April of 2015. Michael has been called the "father" of the Amish/Sci-fi genre but that isn't all that he writes. He is the author of several popular and acclaimed works of dystopian sci-fi, including the Amazon top 20 bestselling Amish Sci-fi thriller the *Pennsylvania Omnibus*, the groundbreaking dystopian vision Hugh Howey called "a brilliant tale of extra-planetary colonization." He also has written the epic post-apocalyptic WICK series, *The Silo Archipelago* (set in Hugh Howey's World of WOOL,) as well as many nonfiction works, including the non-fiction Amazon overall top 30 bestseller *Surviving Off Off-Grid*. Michael was commissioned by Amazon.com through their Kindle Worlds and Kindle Serials programs to write the first ever commissioned novel set in the world of Kurt Vonnegut's *Cat's Cradle*. That book is entitled *Osage Two Diamonds*, and it debuted on Dec. 17, 2013.

DELILAH S. DAWSON is the author of the Blud series, the Hit series, *Servants of the Storm*, *Star Wars: The Perfect Weapon*, a variety of shorts and comics, and *Wake of Vultures*, written as Lila Bowen. She teaches writing classes online at LitReactor.com and lives in the north Georgia mountains with her family. Find her online at whimsydark.com.

LES EDGERTON is a full-time writer with eighteen books in print. He teaches creative writing in an ongoing online class, and through private coaching of writers and writes in a variety of forms: novels, short stories, nonfiction books, screenplays. And the subjects he chooses to write about are just as varied, including sports, literary fiction, thrillers, black comedy, noir and the craft of writing. He has a checkered past, having spent two-plus years incarcerated at Pendleton Reformatory back in the sixties for burglary. He is all cleaned up now and you can invite him into your home and don't have to count the silverware when he leaves. His former life of crime is a plus in his opinion, as it helps inform his novels experientially and gives them a verisimilitude denied to many others. Graduated from

Indiana University with a B.A. in General Studies (Honors of Distinction) and earned an MFA in Writing from Vermont College. Work of his has been nominated for or been awarded: the Pushcart Prize, O. Henry Award, Edgar Allan Poe Award (short story category), the Texas Institute of Letters Jesse Jones Award, the Violet Crown Book Award, the Derringer Award, Spinetingler Magazine Best Thriller Award, literary grants, and others, had a short story included in the Best American Mystery Stories, 2001. His screenplays have been semifinalists in the Nicholl's Foundation Awards and finalists in both the Writer's Guild and Best of Austin competitions. http://lesedgerton.net.

CHRISTA FAUST is the author of over a dozen novels, including *Choke Hold, Money Shot* and *Hoodtown*. She worked in the Times Square peep booths, as a professional dominatrix, and in the adult film industry both behind and in front of the cameras. She lives and writes in Los Angeles. More info and social media links at www.christafaust.com.

Steeped in pulp magazines, old radio shows, and all things of that era's pop culture, **TOMMY HANCOCK** lives in Arkansas with his wonderful wife and three children and obviously not enough to do. He is Partner in and Editor in Chief for Pro Se Productions, is an organizer of the New Pulp Movement, works as an editor for Seven Realms, Dark Oak, and Moonstone. He is also a writer for various companies, including Airship 27, Mechanoid Press, Pulpwork Press, Dark Oak, and Moonstone. Tommy also works as Project Coordinator for Moonstone as well as produces and hosts two podcasts: "Pulped! The Official New Pulp Podcast" and "Pro Se Presents: The Podcast."

GRANT JERKINS is the critically acclaimed author of *A Very Simple Crime*, which *The New York Times* called "An extremely nasty study in abnormal psychology." The prize-winning debut has since been optioned for film. Jerkins is also author of the novels *At the End of the Road*, *The Ninth Step*, *Done in One*, and *Abnormal Man*. www.grantjerkins.com

KEN LIZZI lives in Oregon with his wife, daughter, books, home brewing gear, and antique weapons. And a cat. When he's not lawyering he writes fiction. All right, he writes more fiction. His novels *Reunion* and *Under Strange Suns* are available from Twilight Times Books. Follow him at http://www.kenlizzi.net.

RILEY MILLER's an English-teaching suspense writer. She lives in sunny South Carolina, but her stories stay dark. Check out a couple in *The Big Bad II* or *Voluted Tales* and visit Riley at www.rileymiller.net.

JAMES A. MOORE is the award winning author of over twenty novels, thrillers, dark fantasy and horror alike, including the critically acclaimed *Fireworks*, *Under The Overtree*, *Blood Red*, the *Serenity Falls* trilogy (featuring his recurring anti-hero, Jonathan Crowley) and his most recent novels, *The Blasted Lands* and *City of Wonders*. In addition to writing multiple short stories, he has also edited, with Christopher Golden and Tim

Lebbon, the *British Invasion* anthology for Cemetery Dance Publications. The author cut his teeth in the industry writing for Marvel Comics and authoring over twenty role-playing supplements for White Wolf Games, including *Berlin by Night, Land of 1,000,000 Dreams* and *The Get of Fenris* tribe book for *Vampire: The Masquerade* and *Werewolf: The Apocalypse,* among others. He also penned the White Wolf novels *Vampire: House of Secrets* and *Werewolf: Hellstorm.* Moore's first short story collection, *Slices,* sold out before ever seeing print. His most recent novels include *A Hell Within* (With Charles R. Rutledge) and the apocalyptic sci-fi thriller *Spores,* more information about the author can be found at his website: jamesamoorebooks.com.

BOBBY NASH's mama tried, she really did, but despite her best efforts he became an award-winning author anyway. Bobby writes novels, comic books, short stories, novellas, graphic novels, and the occasional screenplay for a number of publishers and production companies. He is a member in good standing of the International Association of Media Tie-in Writers and International Thriller Writers. Learn more at www.bobbynash.com.

MEL ODOM has written dozens of novels in several fields—action-adventure, computer strategy guides, fantasy, game-related fiction, horror, juvenile, movie novelizations, science fiction, and young adult—as well as comics. One of his best known fantasy novels is *The Rover* (2001), which in 2002 won the Alex Award, an American Library Association award given to novels written for adults that would also appeal to young readers. He lives in Moore, Oklahoma, with his wife and five children.

ERYK PRUITT is a screenwriter, author and filmmaker living in Durham, NC with his wife Lana and cat Busey. His short films *Liyana, On Command* and *Foodie* have won several awards at film festivals across the U.S. His fiction appears in *The Avalon Literary Review, Pulp Modern, Thuglit,* and *Zymbol,* to name a few. In 2015, he was a finalist for the Derringer Award. His novel *Dirtbags* was published in April 2014, and *Hashtag* was published in May, 2015. He is the host of the radio show "The Crime Scene with Eryk Pruitt." A full list of credits can be found at erykpruitt.com.

JAY REQUARD resides in North Carolina. When not writing and editing he enjoys fencing, boxing, cooking Indian food, and reading. He had a fluffy cat named Mona. You can find out more about Jay and his work at http://sitwritebleed.blogspot.com/.

CHARLES R. RUTLEDGE is the co-author, along with James A. Moore, of three novels in the Griffin and Price crime/horror series, *Blind Shadows, Congregations of the Dead,* and the forthcoming *A Hell Within.* His short stories have appeared in various anthologies including *Widowmakers, Strange Worlds,* and *Carnacki: The New Adventures.* He once wrote Chinese comic books for a living without being able to speak Chinese. Charles lives in the Atlanta area with far too many books and a cat named Bruce.

RYAN SAYLES is the Derringer Award-nominated author of *The Subtle Art of Brutality*, *Warpath* and *Goldfinches*. His short fiction has appeared in numerous Internet and print journals as well as anthologies and two collections. VitriolAndBarbies.WordPress.com

OTHER TITLES FROM DOWN AND OUT BOOKS

See www.DownAndOutBooks.com for complete list

By J.L. Abramo
Catching Water in a Net
Clutching at Straws
Counting to Infinity
Gravesend
Chasing Charlie Chan
Circling the Runway
Brooklyn Justice

By Trey R. Barker
2,000 Miles to Open Road
Road Gig: A Novella
Exit Blood
Death is Not Forever
No Harder Prison

By Richard Barre
The Innocents
Bearing Secrets
Christmas Stories
The Ghosts of Morning
Blackheart Highway
Burning Moon
Echo Bay
Lost

By Eric Beetner (editor)
Unloaded

By Eric Beetner and
JB Kohl
Over Their Heads

By Eric Beetner and
Frank Scalise
The Backlist
The Shortlist

By G.J. Brown
Falling

By Rob Brunet
Stinking Rich

By Mark Coggins
No Hard Feelings

By Tom Crowley
Vipers Tail
Murder in the Slaughterhouse

By Frank De Blase
Pine Box for a Pin-Up
Busted Valentines
and Other Dark Delights
A Cougar's Kiss

By Les Edgerton
The Genuine, Imitation,
Plastic Kidnapping

By A.C. Frieden
Tranquility Denied
The Serpent's Game
The Pyongyang Option (*)

By Jack Getze
Big Numbers
Big Money
Big Mojo
Big Shoes

By Richard Godwin
Wrong Crowd
Buffalo and Sour Mash (*)

(*)—Coming Soon

OTHER TITLES FROM DOWN AND OUT BOOKS

See www.DownAndOutBooks.com for complete list

By William Hastings (editor)
*Stray Dogs: Writing
from the Other America*

By Jeffery Hess
Beachhead

By Matt Hilton
*No Going Back
Rules of Honor
The Lawless Kind
The Devil's Anvil*

By David Housewright
*Finders Keepers
Full House*

By Jerry Kennealy
Screen Test

By Ross Klavan, Tim O'Mara and
Charles Salzberg
Triple Shot

By S.W. Lauden
Crosswise

By Terrence McCauley
The Devil Dogs of Belleau Wood

By Bill Moody
*Czechmate
The Man in Red Square
Solo Hand
The Death of a Tenor Man
The Sound of the Trumpet
Bird Lives!*

By Gary Phillips
*The Perpetrators
Scoundrels* (Editor)
*Treacherous
3 the Hard Way*

By Tom Pitts
Hustle

By Robert J. Randisi
*Upon My Soul
Souls of the Dead
Envy the Dead* (*)

By Ryan Sayles
*The Subtle Art of Brutality
Warpath*

By John Shepphird
*The Shill
Kill the Shill
Beware the Shill* (*)

By Ian Thurman
Grand Trunk and Shearer (*)

James R. Tuck (editor)
*Mama Tried vol. 1
Mama Tried vol. 2*

By Lono Waiwaiole
*Wiley's Lament
Wiley's Shuffle
Wiley's Refrain
Dark Paradise
Leon's Legacy* (*)

(*)—Coming Soon